*The new Zebra Rege_____
cover is a photograph of an actual regency_____
The fashionable regency lady often wore a tuzzy-muzzy tied
with a satin or velvet riband around her wrist to carry a fra-
grant nosegay. Usually made of gold or silver, tuzzy-muzzies
varied in design from the elegantly simple to the exquisitely
ornate. The Zebra Regency Romance tuzzy-muzzy is made of
alabaster with a silver filigree edging.*

A MOST TEMPESTUOUS MATCH

"You presume a great deal, madam," Justin said as
he drained his glass and set it down with a thump. "Be
careful or I will not answer for the consequences."

"No, you never do, do you? I think it is high time
you did, my lord, and—"

"If I didn't think of the consequences, madam, I
would not have married you."

"And whose fault is that?" Melissa cried.

"I warn you, this is a dangerous subject," he said
very quietly. "I do not wish to discuss the circumstances of our marriage."

"But you've been well paid for it, have you not?"

"That tears it." He advanced upon her, and finally
realizing she had gone too far, Melissa began to back
up. But before she could escape, he caught her up in
his arms and swung her over his shoulder.

"Put me down!" She pummeled his back with her
fists as he carried her up the grand staircase to her
bedroom. . . .

THE BEST OF REGENCY ROMANCES

AN IMPROPER COMPANION (2691, $3.95)
by Karla Hocker
At the closing of Miss Venable's Seminary for Young Ladies school, mistress Kate Elliott welcomed the invitation to be Liza Ashcroft's chaperone for the Season at Bath. Little did she know that Miss Ashcroft's father, the handsome widower Damien Ashcroft would also enter her life. And not as a passive bystander or dutiful dad.

WAGER ON LOVE (2693, $2.95)
by Prudence Martin
Only a rogue like Nicholas Ruxart would choose a bride on the basis of a careless wager. And only a rakehell like Nicholas would then fall in love with his betrothed's grey-eyed sister! The cynical viscount had always thought one blushing miss would suit as well as another, but the unattainable Jane Sommers soon proved him wrong.

LOVE AND FOLLY (2715, $3.95)
by Sheila Simonson
To the dismay of her more sensible twin Margaret, Lady Jean proceeded to fall hopelessly in love with the silver-tongued, seditious poet, Owen Davies—and catapult her entire family into social ruin . . . Margaret was used to gentlemen falling in love with vivacious Jean rather than with her—even the handsome Johnny Dyott whom she secretly adored. And when Jean's foolishness led her into the arms of the notorious Owen Davies, Margaret knew she could count on Dyott to avert scandal. What she didn't know, however was that her sweet sensibility was exerting a charm all its own.

A Gentleman's Desire

MARY KINGSLEY

ZEBRA BOOKS
KENSINGTON PUBLISHING CORP.

My thanks to my sister-in-law, Christine Kruger, for the beautiful bookmarks she designed,
[and]
To my parents, Bill and Madelyn Kruger, for their help and support.

ZEBRA BOOKS

are published by

Kensington Publishing Corp.
475 Park Avenue South
New York, NY 10016

Copyright © 1991 by Mary Kruger

First printing: March, 1991

Printed in the United States of America

Chapter One

"Ye'll be safe here, miss," Bennett said, his portly figure waddling just a bit as he crossed the room to close the shutters. " 'Tis only an attic, I fear, but 'tis the best I can offer you," he went on. "If I knew you were coming I'd have saved a room, but with the mill nearby—"

"Don't trouble yourself, Bennett." The girl who had followed him into the room took off her black silk bonnet, running fingers through curls the color of autumn leaves as she surveyed the room. It was very plain and very small, furnished simply with bed, dresser, and washstand. The ceiling sloped nearly to the floor and the window was tiny, but to her it was a haven. "This will do admirably, and I shall only require it for the one night."

"Yes, miss," Bennett said, placing her portmanteau on the floor and frowning. "But if I may say so, miss, ye could do worse than to stay here. Lunnin's a powerful wicked place, all I hear."

The girl permitted herself a small smile. "Quite possibly it is, but I am sure I shall manage, Bennett. There must be plenty of positions available for a girl willing to work."

"Aye." The innkeeper eyed her doubtfully. Such a little thing as she was, and so pretty, there was little doubt in his mind what kind of position she would end up in. Couldn't tell her that, though. Miss, young though she was, had a mind of her own. Came of having carroty hair, Bennett supposed. "But if things don't work out, Miss Melissa—"

"Hush, don't use my name!" The girl looked around as if they were in the inn's crowded, noisy taproom, surrounded by the carousing gentlemen who had traveled from all over England to see the prizefight held near Taunton that day.

Bennett smiled. "Now don't ye worry about a thing, miss," he said, laying a comforting hand on her shoulder. "Old Bennett'll see to it ye're taken care of."

"Thank you, Bennett," Melissa said, giving him the smile that had always made his heart turn over. "I know I can rely on you."

Bennett straightened, his fatuous expression the only clue to his thoughts. Be a shame if she came to harm in London, and so he would do what he could to look after her. Owed that much to Master Richard's child. "That ye can, miss. Be ye needing anything else?"

"No, thank you, but please, remember. No one must know I am here."

"Don't ye worry about a thing, miss. There's not a one here who'd wish any harm to ye."

"Thank you, Bennett." She smiled again. "And good night."

The innkeeper bowed himself out of the room, and Melissa was at last alone, at the end of what had been the longest, most nightmarish day of her life. By the light of the single taper the room looked cozy and inviting, spotlessly clean, as was the rest of the Hart and

Hind. At this point, however, it would not have mattered if it had been a pigsty. Here she was safe from *him*. The inn was sanctuary, now that the only home she had ever known was lost to her.

Swinging the portmanteau onto the bed, Melissa began to undress, exchanging her black bombazine for a prim, high-necked nightgown of white lawn. She was yawning by the time she had splashed water onto her face and run a comb through her curls, and the feather tick looked so inviting that she was certain she'd fall asleep instantly, in spite of the din coming from downstairs. Extinguishing the taper, she climbed into bed. Thank heavens Bennett still had this room, she thought, sleepily, and snuggled into the mattress.

She was not insensitive, and the events of the day had upset her greatly, but she was young and healthy and very tired. In spite of the noise, in spite of her worries and her grief, Miss Melissa Selby, daughter of the late Sir Richard Selby and his lady, was soon fast asleep.

The corridors of the old inn were dim when Justin, Lord Chatleigh, at last stumbled up the stairs to find his bed. It had been a pleasant few days, he thought, agreeably befuddled by the claret he had consumed in vast quantities in the inn's taproom. Tolerable food here, and a capital mill this afternoon, with Cribbs, the champion, in rare form. Tomorrow it would be back to Surrey for him, and the Hall. The thought made him frown.

Damn, now which one was his room? Justin swayed as he stood, considering this problem. Bad enough he'd been relegated to an attic, but even worse if he couldn't find his room. Wouldn't do to stumble in on some stranger, he told himself, while the corners of his mouth turned up idiotically at the thought. No, wouldn't do at all.

Second door, third door? Justin peered owlishly at both of them, and then, nodding, made up his mind. Second door. With great determination he put his hand on the knob. It wouldn't turn.

"Damn," he muttered, and applied himself to it again. It resisted, but he was a strong man. Of a sudden the latch gave, and, not expecting it, Justin tumbled into the room.

"Damn!" Regaining his feet, he scowled back at the door. Surely he wasn't so castaway as that, in spite of all that claret? Damned tolerable vintage too, for a country inn. Now, where was the damned candle? Maybe he should have brought his man along with him, if only to have the room prepared.

A few minutes' further stumbling exploration brought him to the dresser, where at last he found what he sought, the taper that the good innkeeper had left for him. Striking a lucifer, he put the flame to the wick; finally enabling himself to see his surroundings, the plain plaster walls, the oak dresser, the ceiling sloping nearly to the floor. An attic, yes, but it would do. He'd had worse billets in Spain. Not surprising, either, considering all who had come to see the mill, and he supposed he shouldn't complain, when even such a toplofty gent as the Marquess of Edgewater was forced to take a room just the other side of the corridor. Justin grinned at the thought. *Good for him. Take him down a peg or two.*

Yawning hugely, he began to strip off his clothes, letting them fall where they would: the coat of bottle green superfine, a product of Weston's skilled tailoring, tossed carelessly upon a chair; his neckcloth atop it. He pulled his shirt over his head to reveal a broad, muscled chest. Justin stretched, turned, and then

8

stopped, standing very still, not sure he believed his eyes. He shook his head, but the vision remained. Damn, there was a girl in his bed!

Bemused, he lowered his arms and let the shirt fall to the floor. Well, and what was this? He hadn't thought such an insignificant country inn would provide such — service. He was grinning at the thought as he crept, surprisingly quietly for so large a man, closer to the bed to observe this unexpected bounty.

As if unaware of his presence, the girl slept on. Justin's eyes strayed to where the coverlet rose and fell with her breathing, and then returned to her face. She looked absurdly young and innocent to be plying her trade, but Justin had learned long ago how deceptive appearances could be. He would accept this offering without protest, because, no doubt about it, the girl was a beauty. Luxuriant coppery curls framed the perfect oval of her face and contrasted with the porcelain whiteness of her skin, marred just a bit by the sprinkling of freckles across her small, straight nose. In sleep her full lips were relaxed, and her eyelashes made dark, spiky crescents upon her cheeks. Aye, a beauty, no question about that. A sleeping beauty. A princess.

His impatient fingers fumbled with the buttons of his pantaloons, and at last he was free of all encumbrances, free to accept his prize. The feather mattress sagged under his weight, the ropes supporting it whining in protest, and the girl stirred. Justin smiled down at her, still a bit bemused by his good fortune, then bent his head. "Wake up, princess," he whispered, his lips descending, and at that moment the girl suddenly reared up into his arms.

Melissa's sleep had been deep and dreamless, en-

9

hanced by the knowledge that, for the first time in years, she was safe. It was only by gradual degrees that something other than the usual bustle of the inn began to impinge on her consciousness, an awareness that something was wrong. Still half-asleep, Melissa considered the problem. Had there been some sound to awaken her? If so, there was nothing now, except, perhaps, the sound of breathing. . . . Melissa's muscles tightened. Someone was in the room with her.

No, it was a dream. She'd had this dream before, so vivid that she could actually feel it happening; could hear the footsteps quietly crossing the floor, feel the comforter being pulled back, the bed shift as the intruder climbed in. A dream, and in a moment she would wake up, heart pounding, to discover that all was well, and she was safe. Wake up, she told herself, and opened an eye just enough to realize that, this time, it was no dream. A man was bending over her, not *him,* as she'd feared, but a stranger, handsome and smiling and utterly terrifying.

"Wake up, princess," the man whispered, and at his words the paralyzing fear that had gripped her suddenly let go. As his head bent to hers, she suddenly reared up, seeking escape—and found herself trapped against a broad, masculine chest.

Ah, so the wench is willing! Justin's arms tightened about the girl. Willing, and quite a spirited armful, too, he decided, though some part of his drink-clouded mind found it strange that a doxy would be garbed in a pristine nightgown buttoned snugly to her neck. And her lips, those full lips he had admired, were as soft and sweet under his as he had imagined. What a little wildcat she was, moving eagerly against him, her hands on his chest. "Shh, princess," he mur-

10

mured, releasing her mouth to trail kisses along her cheek, her eyes, her brow; and the girl twisted her head away.

"No . . ."

"No," Melissa moaned, unable to do more, though every fiber of her being was outraged by this attack. He was too big, too heavy lying atop her, and she could scarcely breathe, let alone make the kind of protest she desired. Even her hands, pushing against his chest, were ineffectual. "Oh, no. . . ."

"Shh, princess." Justin tenderly laid a hand across her parted lips. The girl's eyes flew to his, and for a moment their gazes held. Then, to Justin's immense surprise, she sank her teeth into his thumb.

"Ow!" Justin yelled, snatching his hand back and rolling a little off her, and Melissa drew in her breath.

"Help!" she shouted. "Help, oh help me. . . ."

"Be quiet, little fool!" Justin caught hold of her flailing wrists and pulled them above her head, holding her down, and again their eyes met, hers darkened by panic, his lit with an odd gleam.

"Oh, please . . ." she gasped.

"Damn. We both know why you're here," he snarled, and again brought his mouth down on hers. This time it was no slow, tender kiss; this time it was hard and punishing, his tongue forcing her mouth open, his teeth cutting into the soft flesh of her inner lip. This was worse than any nightmare from the past.

"Please," she begged again, when he at last came up for air, and he looked down at her.

"Please?" he said, shifting his embrace so that he held her wrists in one hand. "Please what?"

11

"Please—"

"Please this?" And with that, his free hand came down upon her breast. Melissa gasped, and he took advantage of her parted lips to kiss her again, persuasively this time, his tongue slipping easily into her mouth to caress hers. The touch of his big hand was amazingly light as he cupped her breast, his thumb moving caressingly across her nipple. To Melissa's horror, strange feelings began to spread outwards from his fingers, warmth and languor and, unbelievably, pleasure. The thought made her struggle even harder.

"Ah, princess, don't fight me when we both want it," he murmured into her hair.

"I don't—"

"You do. You do."

She did, she did. It was getting harder to push against him, harder to struggle against the strange weakness that was pervading her limbs, impossible to think of anything but the feelings he evoked in her, so easily, as his thumb rasped across the hardened tip of her breast, again and again. When the touch stopped she almost cried out in protest, and when he leaned on his elbows, freeing her arms, she blinked up at him, uncomprehendingly.

"Ah, your breasts are so beautiful, m'dear, like two ripe, firm apples," he murmured.

Dumbly she followed the direction of his gaze to see that, somehow, he had managed to unbutton her nightgown, exposing her to his hungry eyes. The cool draft on her skin at last awoke her. Before Justin could guess what she was about, she twisted from beneath him and stumbled across the floor. Snatching up the pitcher from the washstand, she held it threateningly over her head.

"Get out of my room!" she cried, and it penetrated

dimly through Justin's confusion that her accents were not those of a common drab, but were a young lady's.

"Now, wait . . ." he said, holding his hand out to her, and at that moment someone pounded on the door.

Chapter Two

For a split second they stayed in tableau, staring at each other, and then the doorknob rattled. "Miss?" Bennett called anxiously. "Miss Melissa?"

Justin swore, an oath Melissa had never heard before, and pulled the quilt around himself just as the door burst open. Bennett stood in the doorway, blinking at them. "Miss Melissa?" he said, unbelievingly. "And—my lord?"

"My lord?" Melissa glanced towards the man still sitting on the bed, his hair disordered and his eyes, filled with a dawning horror, staring back at her. Slowly, she lowered the pitcher. "Bennett—"

"Miss Melissa?" Justin broke in. "Miss who, innkeeper?"

"Why, Miss Selby, of course, my lord."

"Miss Selby. Holy God." Justin thrust his hand into his hair. *God, she is of the quality.* He was in a fix now.

"Ye're all right, miss?" Bennett looked towards Melissa. "I mean . . ."

"What?" Color flooded Melissa's cheeks as she glanced down and saw that her nightgown was still unfastened. Hastily she pulled it closed, scooping up an article of clothing from the floor to hold before herself. "Yes, Bennett, I . . . I think this gentleman mistook

14

his room, and—"

Justin raised his head at that. "My room. Paid for it."

"No, my lord," Bennett said. "Yer room is the next one down."

Justin stared at him, and Melissa caught at Bennett's sleeve. "Bennett, it was a mistake; I know it was. There was no harm done and no one need know—"

"But that's just it, miss. Everyone heard ye. Everyone does know."

"Oh, God," Justin groaned.

"You're no help," Melissa snapped. "Bennett, if you tell everyone I simply had a nightmare and bid them all to go along, then when it's quiet this gentleman can go back to his room."

Justin looked up. If only he hadn't drunk so much. If only he could think straight. Though her suggestion had merit, he had got himself into an intolerable situation, and in honor there was only one way out. "I'll have to marry you," he said.

"What!" Melissa exclaimed, turning towards him, and at that moment the door, still ajar, opened.

"So, this is where you've got to, Chatleigh." The elegant gentleman who lounged in the doorway looked around, in one comprehensive glance taking in the room's occupants. Though it was late evening, the shine of his boots could not be surpassed, and his neckcloth was meticulously knotted. A smile faintly touched his lips. "Got yourself in another scrape, old chap?"

Justin dropped his head into his hands for a moment. Oh, God, it needed only this! "No scrape, Edgewater," he said, looking up. "Present you to my wife. Understand if I don't rise."

"Your wife?" Edgewater raised his quizzing glass and carefully studied the disheveled girl. "I see.

15

Hadn't heard of your nuptials, old chap."

"I'm not—there weren't . . ." Melissa spluttered.

"Whirlwind courtship, and all that," Justin said, staring at Edgewater without liking. "Excuse us now. M'wife suffers from nightmares."

That faint smile briefly appeared on Edgewater's lips again. "I can't imagine why. I will leave you to your rest, then. Remind me to congratulate you in the morning."

With a gentle click he closed the door behind him, and the others were left momentarily speechless. It was Bennett who broke the silence. "I'm that sorry, miss. That there lock hasn't been working right, but with all the excitement, the mill and all, I clean forgot."

Melissa waved her hand. "It's not your fault. Look, sir, whoever you are, I am not your wife and I have no intention of becoming your wife."

Justin shook his head, an action he immediately regretted. "Can't see any other choice." He rose, and for the first time Melissa realized just how big he was, so tall that his head almost brushed the rafters. The quilt he clutched about him did nothing to hide the broad expanse of his chest, or the muscles of his arms.

She took a hasty step back. "Can you not have the decency to go away and put on some clothes?" she snapped.

"Would, but you're holding my shirt."

"What? Oh!" Melissa looked down at the cambric garment she had snatched up from the floor and tossed it from her. "Here. Now, please leave, and we'll forget this ever happened."

"Can't do that, miss." Bennett's voice sounded unusually grave. "Afraid Lord Chatleigh's in the right of it."

"What?" Melissa stared at him. "But I can't marry

16

him!"

"Don't see ye got much choice, miss. And might be it's the best thing for ye." Melissa stared at the older man, and he nodded. "Leave ye two to talk it out," he muttered, then went out, closing the door firmly behind him.

What a night, what a night, and how he was going to explain this to his wife, he didn't know, Bennett thought, as he worked his way downstairs, reassuring the other guests as he went. Powerful fond of Master Richard's children, he and his spouse both were, and he would never forgive himself that harm had come to Miss Melissa in his inn. But that young Lord Chatleigh was a gentleman. Prepared to do the decent thing, at least.

"I tell you, I know she's here!" a voice drifted up the staircase, and Bennett paused on the landing. If he'd been a swearing man, he would have let out much the same oath as Justin had, but Mrs. Bennett was a strict Methodist and did not approve such speech. Bennett's thoughts were dark as he continued down the stairs to greet his latest, unwelcome guest.

". . . and you will tell me where she is before I lose my patience!" The man who stood in the hallway was tall and thin and was dressed in funereal black. At the moment his hand was cruelly gripping the arm of the inn's errand boy.

Bennett's mouth tightened. "Sir Stephen?" he said, bustling forward. "What do ye here this time of night?"

Sir Stephen whirled around, and the boy scampered off to safety. "Is she here?" he demanded.

"Don't know what ye mean, sir." Bennett pushed past him. "Excuse me, sir, very busy, the prize fight,

17

ye know."

"Hang the prize fight!" Sir Stephen grasped Bennett's shoulder, holding him back. "Don't try to cozen me, Bennett. Where else would she run to?"

Bennett didn't answer immediately. Instead, he looked hard at Sir Stephen's hand, still resting on his shoulder, and, after a moment, Sir Stephen drew it away. Bennett was not a young man, but his breadth and barrel chest were not due to fat. "Who, sir?"

"Miss Selby, damn you, who else? If I hear you have been harboring her, Bennett, I'll—"

"Ye'll what?" Bennett glared at the other man. Sir Stephen might in his own way be powerful, but he had never scared Tom Bennett, no sir. "There's not a one in this neighborhood who will support ye."

Sir Stephen's eyes narrowed. "No? Well, we shall see about that, won't we, Bennett? Since I am in the right. Now, where is she?"

"She's not here."

Sir Stephen's eyes narrowed further.

"Look, sir, best ye go home. She's likely there right now—"

"I tell you, she isn't! Let me by, I wish to find her."

"No." Bennett stood in front of the staircase, squarely blocking it. "Won't have ye disturbing my guests. Gentlemen from Lunnin, come to see the mill." A crafty look appeared in his eyes. "Been drinking all night. Spoiling for a fight, they are."

As if to prove his point, at that moment several young men stumbled out from the taproom, two of them with their arms around each other and singing loudly, if not melodiously, the third berating them in increasingly annoyed tones. Not one gave Sir Stephen more than a glance as they pushed past him to reach the stairs, still arguing.

"Go home," Bennett said, more quietly. "If Miss

Melissa is still missing in the morning, then I'll help ye look. The good Lord knows I don't want any harm to come to her."

Sir Stephen stared at him through narrowed eyes, then turned on his heel. "Very well. But if I learn you have been deceiving me, Bennett, it will go ill for you." He paused at the door of the inn. "Very ill."

Bennett stared at the closed door for a moment, muttered some words his wife most definitely would not have approved, and then turned and scurried back up the stairs.

"He's right, you know," Justin said, when the door had closed behind the innkeeper. "Nothing else for it."

"There must be!" Melissa, her cheeks still red, rooted in her portmanteau for her dressing gown. "You don't wish to marry me any more than I wish to marry you, Lord . . . ?"

"Chatleigh." Justin rubbed at his eyes. "No, but nothing else for it, ma'am. Especially not with Edgewater."

"Edgewater?"

"Damned dandy who looked in at us just now."

Melissa knotted the sash of her dressing gown around her waist. "Is he a friend of yours?"

"Edgewater? Hardly. No, he'll be delighted to spread the word of this."

"But you didn't have to tell him we were married!"

"Couldn't think what else to say."

Melissa stared at him. *Men!* "Not that he believed it."

"No, but by the time he tells anyone who matters, we will be." His eyes, sober now, met hers. "Afraid there's no help for it."

"But you could just let me go. No one knows who I

19

am, no one cares, and I could just go on as I planned—"

"And have it said I seduce young ladies of quality?" His smile was mocking. "Haven't sunk that low yet."

"Oh, haven't you!"

"Thought this was my room!"

"Well, it isn't!" They glared at each other. "For heaven's sake, would you please put on some clothes?"

"Certainly." He stood up, his bulk seeming to fill the room, and Melissa was again reminded how very large he was. "Might want to turn your back. Unless you'd like to watch?"

"Ooh!" Melissa spun around. Justin, pulling on shirt and pantaloons, stared at her thoughtfully. Younger than he'd realized, and not a doxy, which would have made matters easier. He could cheerfully have paid her off, then, but one couldn't offer coin to a lady of quality. What was she doing in an inn alone, without even a maid to lend her countenance? Something havey-cavey here.

Justin was just pulling on his boots when Bennett rushed in. "Miss, Sir Stephen is belowstairs!"

"What!" Melissa whirled around. "Oh, Bennett, you didn't tell him I was here!"

"No, miss, he's gone. But he'll be back. Powerful upset, he was."

"Sir Stephen?" Justin asked, and Bennett glanced at him. Might be here was someone who could help Miss Melissa.

"Yes, my lord. Sir Stephen Barton."

Justin looked quizzically from Bennett to Melissa. "My stepfather," she said.

"Stepfather?" Justin looked thoughtful. "Might be another way out of this."

"Excuse me?"

"If I could talk to the man. Maybe between us we

20

could settle something—"

"No!" Melissa grabbed Bennett's arm. "Oh, Bennett, please don't make me go with him! Please!"

"Now, miss, don't ye fret." Bennett patted her hand. "Sir Stephen is gone, and Lord Chatleigh said he'd stand by ye." He looked over at Justin. "And I'll see to it he does, or my name's not Tom Bennett."

"I see." Justin slowly lowered himself to the bed, staring at them both through narrowed eyes. "I see what it is."

"My lord?"

"And suppose I decide not to marry this—young person?"

Bennett frowned, puzzled by Justin's tone. "I can't force ye, my lord, but—"

"But for a certain fee, you'll keep quiet about this. I see."

"No!" Bennett shook off Melissa's hand and stood four-square, his large hands bunched into fists. "By God, sir, no one insults Tom Bennett like that."

"Bennett." Melissa caught at his arm again. "What on earth—"

"He thinks, miss, that this was a trap." Bennett glared at the other man. "He thinks we set a trap, working together."

"Didn't you?" Justin almost looked bored. "Won't be the first time it's been tried."

"I don't understand." Melissa ignored his contemptuous gaze. "Why would we do something like that?"

"For the money, of course. Either force me into marriage—or make me pay to insure your silence."

"What!"

"Oh, yes. A good plan, and you picked your partner well. An innkeeper, to claim that this isn't my room—"

"But it isn't!"

"—while you play the whore."

21

"By God, sir, I'll not stand here and listen to such insults," Bennett roared, and Melissa caught his arm again.

"Oh, Bennett, never mind, it's not worth it! The man must have windmills in his head if he thinks Mrs. Bennett would allow such goings-on in her house!" Bennett blinked at her and slowly lowered his arm. "Let it go, Bennett. I don't want to marry him."

Justin rose and reached for his coat. "Well, Bennett? If you would show me where you put my things, perhaps I could get some sleep tonight."

Bennett's hands balled into fists. "Oh, no, my lord, not until I have yer word—"

"Bennett. Never mind, it doesn't matter," Melissa said.

"It does matter, miss, he's dishonored you."

Justin let out a bark of laughter. "Should have thought of that before you set this up! It's your scandal now."

"Oh, no, my lord!" Melissa quickly stepped in front of Bennett and stared up at Justin, so annoyed by his implication that his towering height did not intimidate her. "You were the one who announced our marriage to the world!" Justin's eyes narrowed. "Handy for us that Edgewater came along at that moment, wasn't it?"

"By God, madam—"

"So now who's trapped, my lord?"

Justin let out that oath again.

"My lord!" Bennett exclaimed.

"Damn!" Justin glared at them. They were right. Damn, if it had been anyone else but Edgewater he would be tempted to walk away from the mess, but now he was in for it. Once the news reached London, as Edgewater would surely see it would, it would be his scandal. "Damn. Why didn't I just keep quiet?"

He looked so harassed, his hair on end where he

22

had raked it with his fingers, that in spite of herself Melissa felt a stab of pity. "You thought you were doing the right thing—"

"The right thing?" Justin turned, and the expression on his face was so savage that she took a step backwards. "Oh, yes, Miss Selby, you banked on that, didn't you? Damn." His hands clenched into fists, and for a moment he stared at them. "All right," he said, finally. "All right. I'll marry you."

The inn was quiet at last. The young bucks who had caroused in the taproom had long since sought their beds, or fallen into drunken stupors where they sat. In the innyard the waning moon shone coldly on the damp cobblestones, and in the stables the only sound was the occasional snuffle or nicker of a horse. The very world seemed to be asleep but, long after everyone else in the inn was at rest, Melissa lay in the bed that had earlier been so inviting, staring at the shadowy ceiling and trying to figure out what had happened to her life.

Too much had happened to her lately, there had been too many changes, and this latest was the most bewildering of them all. She had no wish to marry! The thought of it made her feel hot and then cold. Marriage had not been a part of her plans for a very long time. Of course, Chatleigh had felt honor-bound to offer for her, but he obviously was no happier about it than she was, and that did not bode well for the future. She had no idea what kind of man he was. He might be a rake, a gambler; he might beat her, or he might . . .

Melissa tossed onto her side, her knees drawn up to her chest. No, she had to be honest with herself on that score. He might try to force her, but, heavens, he

23

wouldn't have to use much force! She had learned that to her own chagrin that very night, and even now she could feel the warmth his touch evoked, the little frissons of pleasure and excitement that had run through her as his fingers touched her breast, and the need, aching, deep.

Melissa moaned and curled up tighter, turning her head into the pillow, her eyes squeezed shut as waves of shame washed over her. No, he wouldn't have had to use much force at all. Another moment or two and she would likely have given in to him. He was unknown to her; yet his touch had awakened feelings she had never before known. No proper young lady feels that way, she thought sitting up in bed with her arms wrapped around her knees. It only confirmed something she had suspected about herself for some time. There was something wrong in her.

So, now what could she do? Undoubtedly there were advantages to the match; it would, at the least, save her from an intolerable situation. Under other circumstances, she might even have been interested in Chatleigh. He was certainly handsome enough, with his tousled brown hair, his regular features and strong, even, white teeth; he had behaved like a gentleman, once he had realized she was not a doxy; and he had the indefinable bearing of a military man, which Papa would have approved. He was also an earl, and though that didn't really matter to her, at least he appeared to be an honorable man. But she didn't love him, and she could not conceive of a marriage with a worse beginning, mutual mistrust and, on his part, dislike. It would be better if they had never met. It would be best if she could just run away and hide.

The thought made her raise her head from her knees. If she didn't marry Chatleigh she would be ruined, but then, if she stayed with her original plan and

24

went on to London, no one would know who she was. *Yes!* She flung back the quilts and jumped out of bed. She would go on as she'd planned. She'd gotten herself into this mess; she was the only one who could get herself out.

Dragging her portmanteau towards her, she packed her few belongings and then lay down again. Dawn was near so she must not sleep, she told herself. But, though she meant to close her eyes only for a moment, when she opened them again the room was bright with the first rays of the sun.

Melissa sat bolt upright, banging her head on the sloping wall and scrambling from the bed. Oh, no, she hadn't meant to sleep! Hastily splashing water onto her face, she pulled on her clothes. Though she could hear movement and voices outside, within all was quiet. It was still early. Doubtless Chatleigh was sleeping; it was well known that the *ton* never rose before noon, and besides, he was likely to have quite a head this morning, after imbibing so much the past night. She certainly needn't fear that he'd block her escape. Most likely he'd be glad to be rid of her.

Down one flight of stairs, then another. Near the bottom a stair creaked so sharply that she stopped, her breath caught, until she was certain no one would come to investigate the noise. From there she could see most of the hall and the door to one of the private parlors, standing open. There was no one in sight. She could leave without being remarked.

On tiptoe she ran down the remaining stairs and crossed the hall, glancing into the private parlor as she did so. It was then that all her carefully laid plans fell apart. For there, sitting at the table and staring at her, his fork poised halfway to his mouth, was the Earl.

Chapter Three

"Oh!" Melissa dropped her portmanteau. Justin gave her a long look and then calmly resumed eating his breakfast, taking a pull on his ale before speaking.

"Good morning." He touched his napkin to his lips and then leaned back. "Care to join me?" he said, gesturing carelessly towards the repast that covered the table.

"I—no. I—I didn't think you'd be up!" Melissa glanced down the hallway, but there was no one to rescue her from this.

"One thing you'll soon find, m'dear. I have a very hard head. Come." He crossed the room to her. "Must insist you join me."

"No, I can't. That is, I'm not hungry."

"Nevertheless." He grasped her arm in a grip that, though gentle, was firm, and she knew it would be fruitless to struggle. "Ready to go so soon?" Justin scooped up her portmanteau in his other hand and kicked the door shut behind them. "Must say, didn't think you'd be this eager."

"I'm not! Oh, it's not proper for us to be alone here."

"Proper?" Justin's eyes mocked her as he seated her and then resumed his place. "Rather think we've gone beyond 'proper' already."

26

Melissa's hands flew to her flaming cheeks. "You are no gentleman, sir, to remind me of that!" Justin shrugged and tucked into his eggs again, and Melissa watched him resentfully. How could he be so calm? Sitting there, eating breakfast as if this were any ordinary morning, and looking as if he'd just come from the hands of his valet. Though he wore a Belcher kerchief knotted around his throat rather than a neckcloth, his shirt was crisp and white, and the coat that sat so well upon his broad shoulders was unwrinkled. That gave him an unfair advantage, especially since her gown, the same one she'd worn yesterday, was sadly crumpled.

"Perhaps it's just as well you're here," she said, gathering her courage. "I believe we need to talk."

"Talk?" Justin glanced at her and then went to tug on the bellpull. "About what?"

"You know quite well!" Melissa stared at him as he sat down again. "About this mad start, this marriage—"

"Yes, my lord, is there something you need?" a maid asked from the door.

"Yes. Breakfast for the young lady, and quickly. We leave within the hour."

"But I'm not hungry," Melissa protested, and Justin shrugged again.

"Best eat." He cut into his beefsteak. "Long ride ahead of us. Hope to make Wells by this afternoon."

"I'm not going." Even to her own ears Melissa sounded sullen and sulky, but she couldn't seem to help it.

"Don't blame you. None too fond of Wells, myself."

"That wasn't what I meant!" Not for the world would she tell him that Wells sounded impossibly distant to her, or that she had never been farther afield than Taunton. "I will not marry—"

27

"Excuse me, my lord, miss." The maid was back, carrying a heavily laden tray containing bacon and eggs and ham, hot toast and muffins, and a pot of tea. Melissa flung herself back in her chair, her arms crossed upon her chest, and glowered at him.

"Best eat," Justin said again. "Pour you out some tea?"

"Thank you, I'll do that myself," she snapped, and reached for a piece of toast. She might as well eat. She would need to keep up her strength to deal with this infuriating man.

Over the rim of his tankard Justin watched her. Prettier than he'd remembered. Innocent-looking, too — no wonder he'd been so taken-in — but a spoiled little wench. Well, he'd soon break her of that. Couldn't say he blamed her for trying to decamp. In fact, he'd expected it, and though he'd arisen at an ungodly hour to stop her, he was in perfect sympathy with her feelings. If his sense of honor didn't demand that he do the right thing, might be he'd run, too.

"How old are you?" he asked.

Melissa looked up, her eyes wary. "Eighteen, my lord."

Justin briefly shut his eyes. Eighteen. God, barely out of the schoolroom, and already, like the rest of her sex, up to such tricks. What would she be like when she gained some experience? "And do you always wear black?"

"No. I am in mourning." Justin said nothing, but merely looked at her. After a few moments she put down her toast. "My mother died this week past, of an ague."

"Your mother died just last week and you're setting traps already?"

Melissa's head shot up at that. "I did not trap you, my lord," she said, her voice tight, "and I miss my mother very much."

"My condolences," Justin said, after a moment. "And your father?"

"Dead these past four years."

"Excuse me, meant Sir Stephen."

"He is not my father!" she flared, and then under Justin's steady regard subsided, though she wasn't sure why.

"Stepfather, then. If he exists."

"Oh, he exists. Unfortunately." Melissa pushed back her curls from her forehead. "Poor Harry. I should never have left him there."

"Harry?"

"My brother."

Justin leaned back. "Am I to expect a visit from an outraged brother, then?"

"Harry? Hardly." Melissa smiled, and for the first time he noticed her eyes, not green or gray or hazel, but an odd, beguiling combination of the three. "No, he'll be returning to Eton soon, and in any event, he doesn't believe in fighting."

"Coward, is he?" Justin drawled, expecting her to flare up, but, to his surprise, she smiled again.

"Hardly. Harry has many reasons for not believing in fighting, but cowardice isn't one of them. You'll see when you meet him."

"Madam, I have no intention of allowing you to foist your impecunious relatives upon me."

"Impecunious! I see." The corners of her mouth turned up. "My, you do know how to talk when you want to."

"Beg your pardon?"

"Never mind."

Justin shot her a look, but her face was expressionless. "Any other people in this mythical family of yours?"

"No. My mother was an only child, and I've never met Papa's relatives. You see, when he married my mother—"

"Spare me." Justin held up his hand. "Don't want to know the details."

"I should think you'd want to know more about me, my lord, since I am to be your wife."

Justin's gaze on her was calm. "Oh, I know enough about you, m'dear. None of it to your credit, I'm afraid."

Melissa glared at him, and Justin returned to his tankard. Rather odd that her stepfather hadn't yet arrived either to claim his daughter or to demand payment for her ruin. He must know by now that she and Bennett had caught a live one, a genuine earl. Well, they were in for a surprise, Justin thought, smiling grimly. They'd soon find that this particular earl didn't have a feather to fly with.

There was a quiet knock on the door and then Bennett bustled in. "Good morning, my lord, Miss Melissa." He beamed at Justin, and Melissa threw him a sour look. The traitor! "The chaise is ready, sir, when ye want it."

"Thank you, Bennett," Justin said.

"The chaise?" Melissa rose, scraping her chair back. "But I tell you, I am not going."

"Now, miss." Bennett turned to face her. "Thought we settled this last night."

"No, Bennett, we weren't thinking clearly—"

"Thinking clearly enough this morning," Justin said. "Thank you, Bennett. Be done here in a minute."

"Yes, my lord." Bowing, Bennett closed the door behind him. Melissa stared at it a moment, her fists clenched, and then whirled to face Justin.

"I don't want to marry you!" she cried. Justin shrugged and picked up his tankard again. "Oh, how can you sit there so calmly, when—"

"Does no good to get upset. Sit and finish your tea."
Melissa glared at him. "Come on. Sit."

Much to her surprise, Melissa found herself sitting
at the table again. How had he made her do that,
without even raising his voice? "Please, my lord, if you
will only listen—"

"Leave soon as you're done. Wells is a long ride."

"Oh, what is in Wells that is so important?"

"A bishop."

Melissa's look was blank.

"Have to have a special license to get married so
soon, you know."

"Oh!" Melissa's cup clattered onto its saucer as her
hands flew to her cheeks, so pale that for a moment
Justin felt a reluctant stab of sympathy. "Oh, please,
must we?"

"Come, now, not so bad a prospect, is it?" he said,
giving her his most charming smile.

"Oh, but could you not just let me go? I promise I
won't tell anyone what happened. I know you're only
trying to protect my good name—"

"Not your good name. Mine." Justin rose abruptly
and looked down at her, his eyes hard. "We will be
married, or I will return you to your stepfather immediately."

Melissa's eyes widened. Had he but known it, he
had hit upon the only way to convince her. He had
trapped her, as neatly as he thought he himself had
been trapped. But she would not submit tamely. My
lord earl would soon learn that he had not obtained a
comfortable, conformable wife. "Very well, then, my
lord," she said crisply, rising to her feet. "But you will
live to regret it."

"Don't doubt that," Justin said to her back as she
swept out of the room before him. Her shoulders stiff-

31

ened, but other than that she gave no sign she'd heard him. Stubborn and spoiled, he thought. God help him.

Outside the inn the post chaise stood waiting, the job horses stamping and blowing in the cold. Bennett and his wife, waiting to see them off, gathered Melissa into their arms before allowing her to enter the chaise.

"Well now, to think I'd ever see the day, my little girl marrying an earl!" Mrs. Bennett said, her eyes suspiciously moist.

Melissa disentangled herself from the clinging embrace and stepped back. "You'll see to Harry, won't you? He'll be so alone. And tell him to write to me? I'll send you my direction." She glanced over her shoulder. Justin, talking to the coachman, appeared not to be attending. "Wherever I am."

Bennett's eyes followed her gaze. "Now, miss, don't ye be thinking of running away. He's a good man."

"And how do you know that?" she demanded.

"Doing the right thing by ye, ain't he? Many another man wouldn't."

"How lucky for me, to find an honorable man." She made a face at her betrothed's back, and at that moment, he turned.

"Ready to go, m'dear?" he said, and if he'd seen her grimace, he gave no sign.

Melissa put her chin up, glaring at him, and then nodded. "Yes, my lord," she said, allowing him to help her into the chaise. She would not cry. She would not let him see her cry.

"My lord." Bennett plucked at Justin's sleeve as he prepared to climb in, and Justin turned. "Take care of her. She's very dear to us."

Justin looked at him for a moment before speaking. "Should have thought of that before you set your trap."

"Oh, my lord, it wasn't any such thing!" Mrs. Ben-

32

nett protested, and Bennett shook his head.

"Sorry ye feel that way, my lord," he said. "She's a good girl. Treat her well and she'll be the best wife—"

"Thank you, I don't need your advice." Justin shook off Bennett's hand and climbed into the chaise. His face was hard as the door closed behind him, and under the force of that look, Bennett quailed. Might be it wasn't such a good idea to let Miss Melissa go with him, after all.

Melissa glanced at Justin as he sat next to her, and then turned away. The postilions mounted and set the horses into motion. As the chaise jolted off Melissa took one last, long look at the Hart and Hind and the two people who were so dear to her. Then the chaise swept through the gate and onto the road, and was gone.

This was the crucial moment.

The Marquess of Edgewater, having already attempted, and discarded, six freshly-laundered and starched neckcloths, was now on the seventh, his valet standing by with yet another one draped over his arm, should this effort fail. The valet held his breath as the Marquess finished tying the cloth, and then stepped back to survey himself critically in the tiny mirror. Then, ever so carefully, the Marquess lowered his chin. The neckcloth creased in exactly the right place, and the valet let out his breath.

"Perfect, my lord," he said.

"Of course." The Marquess gave himself another thorough scrutiny and was satisfied with what he saw, the fawn-colored pantaloons, the white ruffled shirt, the brocaded waistcoat, and the hessians, with the shine that many gentlemen envied. Some said that George Brummel, the Beau, used champagne in his bootblack; Edgewater had his own formula, and he shared the secret with nobody. "My coat," he said, snapping his fingers, and the valet scurried forward with the coat of deep blue Bath cloth, its brass buttons nearly as big as saucers. By dint of much struggling Edgewater was at last fully attired, and the valet set himself to smoothing any wrinkles that dared mar the fit of the coat. A final brushing of the hair, styled *à la Brutus*, and Edgewater was done, stepping back to admire the results. Very nice, indeed. Too nice for the country, of course, but one must always maintain one's standards.

The valet turned away to finish packing, and Edgewater completed his ensemble with the addition of various fobs and seals and, of course, his quizzing glass, without which he would have felt naked. Dreary place, the country; dreary places, country inns. One never knew who one would have to associate with, though last night's fracas with Chatleigh had been tolerably amusing. Not surprising that Chatleigh, clumsy oaf that he was, had managed to get into some kind of trouble. It would be interesting to see how he got himself out.

A chambermaid was already at work in the room across the corridor when the Marquess at last sauntered out. Ah, so Chatleigh had left already, had he? Edgewater wondered who the girl was. Foolish of Chatleigh to claim her as his wife, when all the world could see the sort she was. Ah, well, it would be a bit of gossip to enliven the rounds, once he returned to London. One must find some way to amuse oneself.

The Marquess was very much looking forward to returning to town as he walked down the inn's stairs, heading for the private parlor he had engaged for his breakfast. Bad *ton* to mingle with the hoi polloi, or the local people. Take, for example, the man who was standing in the hall, talking urgently and angrily to the innkeeper. Edgewater shuddered as he passed them, appalled at the cut of the man's coat. Really, provincial tailors were quite incompetent. True, the man was in mourning, but that was no excuse for a coat that rode up on the shoulders and wrinkled across the back. Edgewater nodded at the innkeeper and went on into the private parlor. It was only as he was closing the door that the conversation caught his interest.

"I tell you, Sir Stephen, Miss Melissa is not here." Bennett's voice sounded weary. "If she was —"

"Do I think you would tell me? Oh, no, Bennett," Sir Stephen said. "I know she is here. Someone saw her come in here last night — yes, you didn't know I knew that, did you? And her name was not on the waybill for the stage this morning. I demand you tell me where she is!"

"I don't know, Sir Stephen, and that's the truth." Bennett spread his hands. "I'll ask around about her, and if ye want to look over the inn —"

"I certainly do," Sir Stephen said, and pushed past him to reach the stairs. Bennett watched him for a moment, muttered something under his breath, and then went after him; and, at last, Edgewater closed the door.

Interesting, he thought, crossing the room to tug on the bellpull. Wasn't Melissa the name of the girl who had been in Chatleigh's room last evening? So what had Sir Stephen Barton's daughter — for Edgewater had recognized the man, having met him once in the dim past at a gaming hell — been doing with Chatleigh? Interesting, indeed. This was something that would bear watching.

* * *

35

The post chaise, somewhat spattered and dusty after three days of hard traveling, rode across the North Downs, nearing the end of its journey. Ahead Justin rode on horseback, and though this was what he preferred, that was not what had driven him to it. He simply could not abide his bride's company, and not for any reason that made sense to him. She was just too damned attractive.

Justin shifted a bit in the saddle. His wife. Damn. Last thing in the world he wanted was to be married. Oh, he'd always known he'd have to marry eventually, if only to secure the succession, but there had seemed enough time, even with his heir, his brother Philip, still in the thick of the fighting on the Peninsula. The death of his father had been a surprise; Justin had confidently expected that the old reprobate would live forever, in spite of his tendency towards apoplexy. Now the eighth earl, Justin had reluctantly sold out of the army, to return home to a mountain of bills. Once the debts had been discharged there was little left over for the crumbling, decrepit, neglected estate that was Chatleigh Hall, and so Justin had added another requirement to those he would need in a bride. She must be an heiress. Instead, he found himself saddled with an insignificant country miss, gently bred or not.

And too damned pretty. He had to stop himself from glancing into the chaise. Even now, when he knew she was not the innocent she appeared, she somehow contrived to look demure and sweet. Her bonnet, though of black silk, managed on her to look as fetching as the airiest confection from the best milliner. Curls the color of new-minted pennies clustered about her face, and her features had the delicate perfection of a cameo. Her cloak, also of black, was all-encompassing against November's chill winds, but Justin had a very clear picture of what was underneath. Too clear a picture.

Which, he told himself, wrenching his mind away from a memory that was much too enticing, was precisely why he was in this situation. Getting an heir on her might not be so distasteful, but he would have to be wary of her wiles, else he would find himself in deeper trouble. She would have no power over him. Marriage was not going to change his life.

Inside the chaise, Melissa glanced up from the book she had brought along to enliven the trip, and caught a glimpse of her husband, riding ahead. Having never traveled before, she had been just a little excited about this journey, in spite of the circumstances, and she had hoped to spend the time becoming acquainted with her new husband. Instead, he had barely come near her. After three days of marriage he was still a stranger to her, but that was all of a piece with what had gone before.

Melissa leaned back. Her wedding, so different from what she had always dreamed, already was shrouded with an aura of unreality. There had been no flowers, no music, she'd worn black rather than white, a bonnet instead of a floating tulle veil crowned with blossoms. The little church where they had been married by a bewildered clergyman had been empty, save for the cleric's wife and his deacon, standing as witnesses. Most importantly, the man who had stood beside her, repeating the vows, was a stranger. When he had slipped his signet ring on her finger in lieu of a wedding band, she had looked up into his eyes, to find them chill and remote, and she had shivered. He was her husband, and she was no longer Miss Selby.

Melissa closed her eyes tightly, her fingers, icy cold inside the black kid gloves, twisting together. God help her, it was true. She was really married, and because it was too overwhelming to deal with just then and she was very tired, she drifted into a light doze.

She was in the tiny attic room at the Hart and Hind again, and this time, candles were lit all around, filling it with a soft radiance. She was in bed, and she was wearing — well, she wasn't certain what it was, but it was so diaphanous, so shining that she felt naked. There was a man in the room with her, and though she felt the familiar thrill of fear, it quickly left. He was Justin, her husband, and this was right, it was natural. She smiled and held out her arms to him, and he came onto the bed with her and took her into his embrace. She felt blissfully warm, safe and secure and cherished, as his lips came down on hers, not in hard, punishing kisses but in a lovely, persuasive one. This time she could respond, her arms tightening about him, and when his hand slid down to her breast, she moaned. . . .

The chaise jolted to a stop. *Oh, heavens!* Melissa thought, coming abruptly awake. Color stained her cheeks as Justin wrenched the door open and thrust his head inside. "What is it?" she asked, breathlessly. "Why are we stopped?"

"The Hall's ahead," he said. "Going to ride on to warn the servants."

"Oh. Very well." Melissa sat back as the door closed and the chaise started off again. Chatleigh Hall, at last. It would be good to be done with traveling. Perhaps here, in her new home, she would shake the feeling of unreality that bedeviled her. Perhaps matters would not be so bad as she feared.

The chaise jounced as it made a sharp turn, and she caught a glimpse of pillars on either side, the one on the left missing stones from the top. She grabbed the strap to steady herself against the swaying of the chaise as it continued down the rutted drive. The Hall should be coming into sight at any moment, she thought, craning her head to look out the window and catching a glimpse, as she did so, of her husband riding far ahead. Instantly color flooded her cheeks again, and the memory of her dream intruded forcefully upon her, as real and vivid as if it had actually happened.

But it hadn't, she reminded herself, sternly directing her mind away from those disturbing images. And she was glad of it. She was! After all, he was a stranger, and she had no wish to be so intimate with him. She was surprised, however, that he had not sought her bed at any of the inns they had frequented during their journey. Perhaps he simply wished his marriage to be consummated at his home?

Her stomach clenched at the thought, and, at that moment, the chaise rounded a bend. There, still some distance ahead, was Chatleigh Hall.

Instantly Melissa forgot her apprehension and leaned forward to see her new home. Oh, it was majestic! Enormous, as befitted the home of an earl, and very old. At least, the central portion was; she guessed it had once been a simple manor house, until wings had been added, stretching to infinity on either side. Oddly enough, the mixture of architectural styles, Tudor and Jacobean and Palladian, was pleasant, and didn't distract at all from the impressiveness of the house that surveyed its grounds from a slight rise.

It was only as the chaise drew closer that Melissa began to notice the signs of neglect, her trained eye picking them out unerringly. Surely the stones in the west wing needed repointing, and was that actually grass growing up between the gravel of the drive? And the windows were filthy. Something has to be done about this house, she decided as the chaise swung around and came to a stop in front of a broad, shallow set of stairs that swept up to a heavy, carved door. It was a good thing the Earl would be in residence, to see to such things; it was a good thing she had experience in running a house. It was a challenge, but her heart leapt at the opportunity. She was mistress of this house. Here she would become a wife, she thought, and shivered again, whether in anticipation or fear, she didn't know.

The postilion came to open the door for her. As she clambered down, stiff from too many hours of traveling, the door to the house opened and Justin came out, slapping his gloves against his palm and followed by another man, just pulling on his coat. Travel-weary though she was, Melissa couldn't help but appreciate the picture that Justin made, quite the lord of the manor in his buckskins and boots.

"Come, m'dear." Justin took her arm. "Must introduce you to the staff."

"Yes." She sounded breathless as she lengthened her steps to match his. It wasn't fair that he was so tall, and she, so tiny.

"Jenkins, the butler," he tossed, over his shoulder as she stumbled up the steps through the arched doorway, and she glanced back at the man, gaining in her very brief look only the impression that he looked like a weasel. "Mrs. Jenkins, the housekeeper."

"Oh!" Melissa stopped dead just past the doorway, for the moment not even seeing the woman who curtsied to her, in her wonder at the first sight of her new home. The hall, probably once the Great Hall, reached up several stories to a skylight designed in a glorious mosaic of color. The fireplace looked large enough to roast an oxen, and a long refectory table stood in the middle of the floor. It was a magnificent space, or, rather, it would be if it were cared for, but here, as well as outside, the signs of neglect were all too clear. The floor of black and white marble tile was dull and in need of a good washing, the brass balusters of the grand staircase that curled up to a landing and then separated, in their flight to the next story, were dark from lack of polishing, and the lustres of the enormous chandelier overhead had obviously not seen a dust rag in many a day. There was certainly more than enough here to keep her busy. She must meet with the housekeeper at the first opportunity.

So thinking, she turned to greet the woman Justin had just introduced. Mrs. Jenkins was small, her hair iron gray, and the apron she wore over her dress of black serge was soiled. Melissa was startled by this mark of disrespect, but more disturbing was the way the housekeeper was looking at her, coolly and calculatingly. "Mrs. Jenkins," Melissa murmured, and the woman bobbed another curtsy.

"My lady," she said. "Forgive the way the house looks, my lady, but we had no warning you was coming."

"I quite understand. This is the rest of the staff?"

"Yes, my lady. Hard it is to keep staff here, buried in the country."

"I see." Melissa walked down the line of people waiting for her, receiving their bows and curtsies with a nod. Besides Mrs. Jenkins and her husband, whose sharp features still looked weasel-like after a second, longer glance, there were one footman, one scullery maid, and two parlormaids. So few to run a house of this size! Melissa's heart sank at the enormity of the task that stretched ahead of her. "I take it there's outside staff, as well? And a cook?"

"No, my lady. That is, there's outside staff, but no cook." Melissa turned to stare at her. "His lordship's rarely here, you see, but now . . ."

"I see," Melissa murmured again. "Then who does the cooking?"

"I do, my lady, as well as the housekeeping."

"Well, then, I must rely upon you, Mrs. Jenkins. I

41

can see we've much to do."

"I do what I can, my lady! There's the cleaning, and the ordering, and what with these here lazy girls as maids—"

"Of course, Mrs. Jenkins. I'm sure you've done your best," Melissa said soothingly. The last thing she needed was to make an enemy of this woman. Getting this house in shape again would require a great deal of help, but it could be done. This was her home. Her future.

For the first time since her adventure had started, she felt some excitement at what lay ahead, and some hope. Her eyes shone as she turned to Justin to share her vision with him, only to see him pulling on his gloves. "Are you going out again, my lord?" she said, forgetting for the moment that the servants still stood nearby and were interested spectators to this scene.

Justin barely glanced at her. "Going to London, m'dear."

"What!" Melissa ran after him as he set off towards the door. "But you can't just go and—"

"Got business to see to."

"But Chatleigh, you just can't leave me here!"

"Easy, m'dear, the servants." Gently but firmly, he disengaged her clinging hand from his arm. "Got what you wanted, ma'am. You're a countess." His glance took in the hall, and his smile was cold. "Wish you joy of it," he said, and swept out the door, leaving her standing alone and bereft in the cavernous, echoing, unwelcoming hall.

Chapter Four

The door closed with a solid thud with which there was no arguing. A few moments later the jingle of harness and the clop of hoofbeats confirmed Melissa's fears. She had been brought to this singularly dismal house, and abandoned.

A frown creasing her forehead, she turned back, in time to see Mr. and Mrs. Jenkins smirk at each other. She stiffened. That would never do. "Well," she said, dusting her hands together as if to dismiss what had happened. "I would like to be shown to my room, Mrs. Jenkins."

"Ain't ready yet, my lady." Mrs. Jenkins returned Melissa's stare. "We had no warning you was coming."

"I see." Melissa drew off her glove, one finger at a time, her eyes never leaving the housekeeper's face. "But I am here now, and I wish to wash the dirt of the road off me."

"But my lady—"

"And I will take tea in the drawing room while I am waiting."

"Yes, my lady, but—"

"Yes?" Melissa raised her chin and gave the woman a distinctly steely look. She had dealt with more than one impertinent servant in her time. "Is there some

43

problem with your housekeeping, Mrs. Jenkins?"

The maids, clustered together, giggled, and Mrs. Jenkins glared. Her eyes however, were the first to drop. "No, my lady. Liza, Charity!" she barked, and the maids immediately stiffened, their faces assuming the blank, wary look they'd worn before. "See to her ladyship's room! At once! And I will see to your tea myself, my lady."

"Thank you, Mrs. Jenkins. I knew I could rely on you." Melissa smiled, but the other woman merely dropped a curtsy and turned away.

"The drawing room is just upstairs, my lady," Jenkins said, coming forward after throwing his wife a look. "If you would follow me?"

"Thank you, Jenkins." Melissa lifted her skirts and ascended the broad marble staircase, as dull and grimy as the entrance-hall floor. She had her work cut out for her, and now it would be even harder. She'd managed to make an enemy of the housekeeper, the last thing in the world she'd meant to do. It was Chatleigh's fault, she thought, as she reached the top of the stairs and turned to the right, down a corridor with paneled walls darkened by the smoke of long-dead candles. If he hadn't humiliated her in front of the servants, perhaps she would not have felt such a need to assert her authority.

"The drawing room, my lady." Jenkins threw a door open, and Melissa stepped in.

"Oh," she said, and stopped short. Jenkins scurried in before her to pluck the holland covers off the furniture, while Melissa watched in dismay, tugging at the fingers of her other glove. Handsomely proportioned, the drawing room had the potential to be splendid, but, again, the signs of neglect were obvious, in the chipping plaster and the dusty moldings and fireplace. The moldering, nile green draperies were so old that they looked about to fall of their own weight. But the coffered ceiling was fine, she noted, and the parquet floor needed only a good polishing to bring back its luster. Even the furniture, though in need of re-upholstering, was acceptable.

"Jenkins, why is everything like this?" she asked, as she sat on a gold brocade sofa.

Jenkins, taking a swipe at the dust that lay thick on a nearby table with a holland cover, looked up, and his eyes were wary. "Like what, my lady?"

"So, well, dusty and neglected and—"

"We done our best, my lady, but with them there lazy girls—"

"Oh, I'm sure you have!" she said, hastily. "I realize you haven't the staff to maintain this house, and if the family's not here—"

"That's just it, m'lady. Family's never here. Haven't been for years. Not much money, neither." And with that, he gave her a wink, which astonished her more than anything else in this unusual day had, and whisked himself out the door.

Melissa stared after him. "Really!" she murmured, and then, still tired and stiff from the long journey, rose to explore the room. Yes, as she'd suspected, the mantel was definitely Adam, and particularly fine, too. So were the plaster moldings upon the walls, which she thought might once have been painted a bright, sunny yellow. They could be repainted and re-paired, but the painting over the mantel would have to go. Melissa's nose wrinkled as she looked up at it. It was a depiction of a stag, brought low by a hunter's arrow, being savaged by dogs. "Really!" she said again, and at that moment, the door opened.

Melissa tensed, but to her relief it was only the foot-man. He was a young man, and Melissa had liked his open countenance when she'd first looked upon it. She liked it even more now, after the veiled hostility of the Jenkinses. "Your tea, my lady," he said, placing the tray on the table Jenkins had so inadequately dusted, and Melissa came forward.

"Thank you . . . I'm sorry, I'm afraid I didn't catch your name downstairs?" She smiled at him as she sat on the sofa again, and he stopped, arrested by that smile.

"Phelps, my lady."

"Phelps. Tell me, Phelps, why is there only one of you?" she said, pouring herself a cup.

"Excuse me, my lady?"

"One footman, I mean." Phelps's face suddenly developed that wary look she'd seen too often this day, and she sighed. "I'm not the enemy, Phelps. All I wish to do is run this house as it should be run."

"Yes, my lady." Phelps cast a look back towards the door and then came forward. "If they let you."

" 'They'? Who are you talking about?"

"The Jenkinses, my lady." Phelps looked towards the door again. "Used to having their own way, they are."

Melissa stared at him over the rim of her cup. "But surely they realize that, now the Earl's married, things must change."

"Oh, yes, my lady. They realize that."

"And all I wish to do is help. Why is there so small a staff?"

"That's the Jenkinses. They're hard on servants."

"Hard?"

"Find fault when there's none to be found. Hard to keep people, with that."

"I see." Melissa nibbled at a piece of bread. "Why have you stayed?"

"I have family hereabouts." Phelps leaned forward. "If I was you, my lady, I'd watch out for the Jenkinses—"

"Phelps, why are you still here?" Jenkins said sharply from the doorway, and both Phelps and Melissa looked at him with startled, guilty eyes. "Get to your other duties."

"Yes, sir." Phelps bowed. "If I may be excused, my lady?"

"Of course," Melissa said, rising. "Thank you, Phelps. And, Jenkins, there's no need—"

"Your room is ready, my lady, when you are done with your tea."

Melissa looked at him for a moment, and then nodded. "Thank you, Jenkins." Best not to antagonize him anymore. "I am ready now."

The day was drawing in, and the corridors of the old house were dim as she followed Jenkins up another staircase and down a bewildering maze of hallways, until he stopped and threw a door open. "The Countess's rooms, my lady."

"Thank you," Melissa said. This time she hid her dismay at the condition of the room, dark and dusty and dank with the chill of long disuse. Someone had certainly liked nile green, she thought, looking at the brocade bed hangings and drapes. It wasn't her favorite color, and she wasn't pleased with the furniture, which was heavy, carved mahogany, so dark it was almost black. Most likely she'd suffer from nightmares in this room, she thought, wrinkling her nose at the musty smell. She would have liked to open a window, but a drizzling, damp mist had materalized. She hoped Chatleigh, wherever he was, had bogged down in the mud.

"Thank you, Jenkins," she said, dismissively. "Please send one of the girls up with hot water."

"Yes, my lady." Jenkins bowed and left the room and Melissa, at last alone, sank down onto the chaise longue, rubbing her aching temples with her fingers.

It was not how she had imagined her homecoming, but that wasn't surprising. Nothing that had happened in the past few days had been as she'd imagined, not the hurried wedding or the long journey, or being left alone on what should have been her wedding night. She didn't understand herself. She was glad that she didn't have to deal with her husband and what he would demand of her. She was glad, too, that she was still untouched, and yet some part of her was disappointed, almost hurt, that he had left her. She couldn't imagine why. She hadn't really liked the way his touch had made her feel, the odd sensations caused by his hand on her breast, the warmth, the languor, the desire to wrap herself around him and—

"Excuse me, my lady. Your hot water. Shall I put it in the dressing room?"

"What? Oh!" Melissa sat up suddenly as the maid came into the room, lugging two cans of water. "Yes, thank you—Liza, is it?"

"Yes, my lady. Will you need anything else?"

"No, thank you, Liza. I think I will just wash and go to bed. Mind I'm not disturbed."

"Yes, my lady." Liza bobbed a curtsy and left the room, and Melissa was again alone, bereft and bewildered. Mama was gone, Harry was far away, but most lowering of all was the knowledge that her husband had abandoned her. Melissa stared at her empty bed, her spirits sinking to their lowest ebb. Never in her life had she felt so lonely, so discarded and used, and, as she climbed into bed and stared up at the shadows flickering on the canopy from the candle, she wished, for the first time, that she had never left home.

London was thin of company these days, and the traffic was lessened, Justin noticed as he strode along towards his aunt's Grosvenor Square home on this fine morning. Most of the fashionable world had repaired to their estates for the upcoming holidays, until Parliament opened again in January, and he was glad of it. After the events of the past week, it was good finally to be back at his rooms in the Albany, where Alfred, his batman, reigned supreme, jealously guarding him from the outside world. He would, perhaps, have to open up the London house eventually, but for now his manner of living suited him down to the ground. It was, at least, decidedly less expensive.

Justin frowned and reached down absently to rub his left thigh, where a musket ball had got him at Talavera. Money was going to be a problem, particularly since his plan to marry an heiress was no longer possible. And what Aunt Augusta would say to that, he didn't want to imagine.

The door knocker of Lady Helmsley's house had been removed. Justin frowned as he took the stairs two at a time and knocked on the door with the knob of his walking stick. Not like Aunt Augusta to leave town. She hated the country, and would rather be where she could keep her finger on what was happening.

The door was opened by an elderly gentleman. "My lord!" he exclaimed. "We didn't expect you."

"Morning, Fitch." Justin sauntered past the butler into the entry hall, his stick tucked under his arm. "M'aunt not at home?"

"No, my lord. Of course, she didn't expect you."

"Of course not. Where is she?"

"Bath, my lord."

"Bath!"

"Yes, my lord. Gone to take the waters."

"You're not serious." Justin stared at him. "She ill?"

"No, my lord. Well," he hesitated, "her rheumatism's

49

been acting up, but don't let on I told you."

"Of course not. Well. Have to see her when she returns."

"Yes, my lord. And, my lord?" Justin turned from the door. "May I wish you happy?"

"What?"

"On your nuptials, my lord."

"Devil blast it!" Justin exclaimed, and Fitch blinked. "You've heard of that, then?"

"Yes, my lord, we—"

"Damn, must be all over town, then. Damn Edgewater."

"My lord?"

"Nothing, Fitch. Does m'aunt know?"

"No, my lord, not that I know. But in Bath—"

"Yes, I know, everyone gossips. Damn." Justin stood a moment, thinking. He could go to Bath himself, but he very much feared that the gossip would reach there before him. The damage was already done. "Thank you, Fitch," he said, and went out the door, running down the steps to the street.

So that was that, he thought, swinging his walking stick as he strode along. Sooner or later he would have to face the old dragon, but, for now, he'd been reprieved. And there was enough for him to do here. There was boxing at Gentleman Jackson's saloon, and going to Tattersall's to select horses for his sadly depleted stables, and any number of things. The next few days promised to be quite pleasant.

"Justin?" a feminine voice called from behind him. "My goodness, it is you!"

Justin turned, to look at the carriage drawn up before his aunt's house and the girl who had just emerged from it. Her blond ringlets danced as she came towards him, and her blue eyes were wide. "Eleanor!" he exclaimed, his heart sinking. Eleanor, of all people.

One of the loveliest girls he had ever laid eyes on, and the last person he wished to see. Miss Eleanor Keane, the woman he had once thought he would marry.

Jenkins clattered down the backstairs and came into the kitchen, where his wife, her mouth set in a thin line, was shoving dishes onto a tray. "Ladyship's luncheon ready yet?" he asked, and Mrs. Jenkins gave him a murderous look. "What is it?"

"That woman!" she exclaimed. "Really, Mr. Jenkins, who does she think she is?"

"The new countess," he said, mildly, and lifted the silver tray spotted with tarnish that gave evidence to its long disuse. "Here, Phelps. Take this upstairs to her ladyship."

"Ladyship, indeed." Mrs. Jenkins's eyes smoldered as the footman rose from the long deal table, at which he had been eating his own luncheon, and took the tray. "Looks at me like I'm dirt, she does."

"Now, Mother, don't get yourself into a pelter." Jenkins glanced at the table, where the scullery maid, her cheek clearly bearing the imprint of a hand, was chopping onions, and his voice lowered. "Things won't change."

"Oh, won't they? I took her on a tour of the house this morning." His wife's lips tightened still further as she remembered the Countess's comments on the state of the house. "She's talking of hiring more staff."

Jenkins turned. "You, girl." The scullery maid, her eyes red, looked up at him. "Can't you do that someplace else?"

"But sir, Mrs. Jenkins said—"

"You heard Mr. Jenkins," Mrs. Jenkins snapped. "Now go into the pantry, Rose, and wash them dishes!"

"Yes, mum," Rose murmured, and went out, throwing them a resentful look.

Jenkins went to sit by the table. "So she'll hire more staff," he said. "We'll just let them go again."

"Not this time. She'll hire more. And she'll talk with the shopkeepers, Mr. Jenkins. She's already asked why the butcher sends us inferior cuts."

Jenkins shifted in his chair. "What did you tell her?"

"That he didn't realize she was in residence and thought the meats were for servants. But it's worse than that, Mr. Jenkins. She's asked to see the account books."

"So? Let her."

"What!"

Jenkins leaned back on two legs of the chair, his arms crossed on his chest. "Said, let her. Probably won't notice anything, even if she can do sums."

"And if she does? What then, Mr. Jenkins?" Her hands were knotted into fists on her hips.

"What can she actually do?"

"Do? She can call the law down on us. She can—"

"But without the Earl's support?" Mr. Jenkins grinned as his wife's mouth suddenly shaped itself into an O. "Without him to back her up, what can she do?"

"Nothing," Mrs. Jenkins said slowly, and smiled. "Why, nothing, Mr. Jenkins."

"Told you there was nothing to worry about." He got up from his chair and crossed to her, laying a hand on her shoulder. "Don't you worry, Mother. We'll sort her proper."

Mrs. Jenkins regarded him for a moment and then turned away, her head bobbing in a sharp, satisfied nod. Mr. Jenkins was right. They'd handle that slip of a girl who thought herself a countess, or her name wasn't Martha Jenkins.

"Eleanor!" Justin walked towards her, his feeling of well-being rapidly dissipating. Good God, he'd forgotten about Eleanor. Now what the devil would he do? "Didn't know you were in town."

Eleanor laughed, a high, tinkling sound. In a pelisse of powder blue velvet that exactly matched her eyes, she looked striking. "But, Justin, don't you know Daddy likes to spend Christmas in town? So much more civilized, he says." She laughed again, but her clear blue eyes were hard and accusing. "But, come, what are *you* doing in town? I thought you'd be in the country with your little bride."

Justin's collar suddenly felt tight. "Yes, well, had business in town. Didn't know you'd heard about it, Eleanor."

"But it is the talk of the town! Such a delicious *on-dit*, you know, so many people were happy to tell me about it."

"Eleanor, I'm sorry—"

"You met her at an inn, I hear?"

That was so uncomfortably close to the truth that he stiffened. "No. Knew her before."

"Oh? And what does your aunt have to say?"

"She's away from town."

"Oh, is she? Pity, I wished to speak to her. Well, no matter." She started to turn, and then stopped. "And when will we have the pleasure of meeting your lovely bride? I am planning an intimate dinner Tuesday next, just twenty people or so, you must bring her—"

"She's at Chatleigh," he said, before she could go on.

"Chatleigh! Didn't she wish to come to town with you?"

"No, it's not that, it's . . . well, she's not well."

"Oh." Eleanor took a step backwards, and her eyes grew opaque. "Oh, I see. Well. I mustn't keep the horses standing."

Justin stepped forward. "Here, let me help you."

"I can manage." She shook off his arm, accepting the help of a groom to climb into her carriage, and Justin stood back as the equipage drove away.

Damn! he thought, walking along again. Damn, he hadn't expected this, though he should have. Couldn't blame Eleanor for being upset, since their eventual betrothal had been an accepted fact. Not that he loved her; hardly. The engagement had been his aunt's idea, and he had fallen in with it. Eleanor was pretty enough, and her father was rich enough. She was also, at twenty-three, more intelligent and sophisticated than girls just out of the schoolroom, and so at least she didn't bore him. Now everything had changed, and there was no way to get free.

Or was there? Perhaps matters weren't so serious as they appeared. The marriage was unconsummated, and though he had stayed away from his wife only to save his sanity, now he saw that it might serve another purpose. He might be able to obtain an annulment.

The thought made him grin, and, tipping his hat forward, he set off again, swinging his cane freely. Suddenly, life looked a lot brighter.

Life had never before looked so gloomy, not even when Melissa had realized what Mama's death would mean. Outside rain poured down, and the cold gloom pervaded everything in the house. Melissa wrapped her shawl around her more tightly and leaned forward to stir the drawing-room fire with a poker, coughing when a backdraft sent a plume of smoke into the room. Most of the chimneys smoked. Another thing to see to.

The trouble was, there was so much to do that it

was daunting. No one had taken proper care of this house for years, and everywhere she saw neglect and waste: paintings so dark with dirt that their subject matter was indistinguishable; linens, folded carefully away, infested with mildew; stained and peeling wallpaper in the music room, where the damp had gotten in. Oh, she could fix everything, but no one would thank her. It would not make her husband return to her.

Melissa poked at the fire again and then leaned back, frowning as she drained her tea. Best not to think of Chatleigh; best to think of other things. Her staff, for instance. She didn't know quite what to do about them, though she had been running a house for years. It wasn't that the Jenkinses were overtly disobedient or insolent. On the contrary, they accepted all her orders with every sign of acquiescence. Somehow, though, nothing ever got done. When Melissa had spoken with Mrs. Jenkins about the necessity of hiring more staff, the woman had agreed, but so far, no one new had been hired. Melissa had talked about giving the house a thorough cleaning and then starting on redecorating, but dust still lay thick on most of the furniture. Mrs. Jenkins had agreed that, yes, milady should see the household account books, but Melissa had yet to lay eyes on them.

The thought of that made her frown deepen, and she crossed to the bellpull. Several minutes later, she tugged on it again. When a third tug still brought no results, Melissa strode out of the room, her brow knotted. Really, this was going to have to stop! She realized the house was inadequately staffed, but that didn't excuse letting a summons from its mistress go unanswered. Something would have to be done. She was not a wife, nor did she feel like a countess, but this was something she could do. It was high time she took over the running of this house.

"Phelps," she said, leaning over the balustrade half-way to the ground floor, and the footman looked up. "Where is Jenkins?"

"Don't know, my lady."

"Don't know?" Melissa continued down the stairs. "Does he do this often? Disappear like this?"

"I imagine he's busy somewhere in the house, ma'am."

"I would believe that if I saw any evidence of things being done!" she snapped, and Phelps straightened, his face going stiff. Oh dear, she hoped she hadn't made another enemy. "Might he be in the butler's pantry, do you think?"

Phelps unbent just a trifle. Couldn't blame milady for getting upset; the Jenkinses were enough to try a saint's patience, and milady, with that red hair, likely possessed little of that virtue. "Might be, my lady. Shall I go and see?" he asked, and, just then, someone knocked on the door.

"See who that is, first," Melissa said, and she was relieved when Phelps smiled. Her own smile faded when Phelps opened the door and the caller announced himself.

"One moment, sir, I shall see if her ladyship is receiving," the footman said, and Melissa stepped forward, resigned to her fate.

"Come in, Sir Stephen," she said.

Chapter Five

The morning post, lying on a silver salver, brought with it a thick envelope addressed in an unfamiliar hand. Justin, eating his breakfast as he read his mail, cut a piece of ham, took a pull of ale, and then finally gave in to his curiosity. Reaching for the mysterious envelope, he slit it open with with the letter opener and shook the communication out. A frown gathered on his forehead, and he abruptly turned it over, to read the signature.

"Devil take the woman!" he exclaimed, and Alfred stuck his head in from the pantry.

"Did you say something, sir?"

"Damned woman."

Alfred came into the room, wiping his hands on the towel tucked at his waist. "The Countess, sir?" he said. In the last week he had heard a great deal about the Earl's marriage, and he was greatly in sympathy with his employer.

"Yes, damn it, the Countess." With one quick motion Justin tore the letter across. "Asking for money. Rather, having her man of affairs ask for her."

"Not good, sir."

"No, not good. Damned if I'm going to bankrupt myself so she can buy fripperies!"

"No, sir."

"Bring me paper, Alfred. Deal with this at once."

"Yes, sir. And, uh, sir?"

"What is it?" Justin said, snapping his fingers for the paper and pen.

"The letter from the Marchioness."

"What?" Justin scrabbled through the remainder of the mail until he came to a square of creamy vellum addressed with a bold, almost vertical handwriting. "Oh, good God," he muttered. Here it was, then, the summons he had been dreading. His aunt had returned to town.

"Well, Alfred," he pushed his plate away and rose, "seems I won't be going to Gentleman Jackson's after all."

The look Alfred gave him was sympathetic. "No, sir. Shall I lay out your new coat, sir?"

"Yes, Alfred. But, paper and pen first." He sat down again. Best to deal with the upstart countess first.

"So here you are, daughter." Sir Stephen strolled into the hall. "Very unnatural of you, child, not to tell me where you were going."

"What are you doing here?" Melissa asked, not moving.

"Why, I've come to see you, of course. You may go," he said, turning to Phelps.

"No." Melissa's hands clenched. "Phelps, please stay. Sir Stephen will not be staying."

Sir Stephen shook his head, clucking his teeth. "How unnatural of you, daughter. Can you not even offer your father some refreshment on such a day? A brandy would not come amiss. . . ."

"You're not my father. And how did you know I was here?"

" 'Twas easy enough to learn, daughter, once I found you were at the inn, and who you went off with." His eyes traveled around the hall, and the covetous look Melissa knew well came into them. "Done well for yourself, haven't you? An earl, no less. And where is his lordship?"

"Not here at the moment."

"Pity, I wanted to meet the man who was so impetuous as to carry you off. But, come, surely there is some place where we can be private?" He slanted a look towards Phelps. "We shouldn't discuss our affairs in front of the servants."

"We have no affairs," Melissa snapped, and went pale as Sir Stephen's eyes, cold, polished obsidian, came back to her.

"No. Pity, that," he said, and though his voice was soft, something about it made Melissa's skin crawl. "You are all I have left. I was hoping for better relations with you, daughter."

"I am married, sir. My loyalty must remain with my husband."

"Of course. But I am sure you won't deny your own father the pleasure of a visit. You, there." He snapped his fingers at Phelps. "I have baggage outside. Bring it in."

"No!" Melissa cried, coming forward and then stopping suddenly when Sir Stephen's eyes came back to her. Of all the things she disliked about this man, she hated his eyes the most. "I am sorry, sir, but you cannot stay. We haven't the staff to deal with guests."

"But what is a little inconvenience, compared to the pleasure of being with you? And it will be a pleasure. You!" He rounded on Phelps, who had not moved. "Why do you stand there? Get my bags, I say!"

"My lady?" Phelps said, looking from one to the other, and Melissa shook her head.

"No. My stepfather will not be staying. Would you kindly escort him out, Phelps?"

Phelps took a step away from the wall and then, as Sir Stephen turned his eyes on him, halted for just a moment before squaring his shoulders and coming forward. "Yes, my lady."

He was a large, strong-looking young man. Sir Stephen stood his ground for a moment, but then pulled back. "Do not touch me! Very well, I will go." He clapped his hat on his head. "I can see I am not wanted. But I won't forget you," he said, looking up at Phelps before turning towards Melissa. Pitching his voice so that only she could hear, he added, "And you had best remember, daughter. You are mine."

When Melissa went white and took an involuntary step back, Phelps judged it time to intervene. "Good day, sir," he said, holding the door. Sir Stephen gave them one last malevolent look and went out, his head held high. Melissa, her knees suddenly too weak to support her, sank down on the bottom stair, her face in her hands.

"My lady?" Phelps said after a few moments. "Do you need assistance?"

She looked up. "No, Phelps, thank you. But I do not want that man in this house. If he comes again he is to be shown the door."

"Yes, my lady."

"Furthermore — Where have you been?" she said, staring beyond Phelps at Jenkins, who had just come into the hall.

"In the kitchen, my lady," Jenkins said, "polishing silver. Is that acceptable to my lady?"

Melissa stiffened at the veiled insolence in his voice. "I expect someone to answer when I ring, Jenkins."

"Oh, did you ring, my lady? Seems like that bell in the drawing room just don't work right."

"I see." Melissa stared at him, hard, but his countenance was bland. "Then we must have it repaired. And where is Mrs. Jenkins?"

"In her room, my lady. Working on the household accounts."

"I see. That will no longer be necessary."

"My lady?"

"I will be taking care of the accounts myself. You may bring the books to me in the drawing room."

"But, my lady—"

"Now, Jenkins!" Melissa whirled, her skirts swirling around her. "Do you have some problem with that?"

"No, my lady. It's just that Mrs. Jenkins has always seen to the accounts."

"And I will be taking them over." When Jenkins hesitated, Melissa rose to her full five feet. "I grow tired of this, Jenkins, tired of having all my commands disobeyed and my summons ignored. You will bring me those account books now."

Jenkins glanced at Phelps, standing impassive against the wall, and then bowed. "Yes, my lady," he said in a colorless voice, and left the room.

Melissa put a hand to her forehead for a moment, then straightened. "Well," she said, and Phelps cleared his throat. "Yes, Phelps, what is it?"

"May I say something, my lady?"

"Yes, Phelps, what?"

"I'd be careful of them there Jenkinses. Don't want to get on their bad side."

"It is they who should be worried about getting on my bad side!" she exclaimed, and then smiled. "And am I on your bad side as well, Phelps?"

"Oh, no, my lady!"

"I am glad to hear it, Phelps," she declared and went back up to the drawing room.

* * *

61

The sound of a cane thumping on the polished parquet floor of the hall alerted Justin to the fact that he was no longer alone. He was not looking forward to this interview. Lady Helmsley had long been one of society's leaders, and a stickler for proper behavior. Fortunately, his clothing was well tailored. His buckskins were faultless, the bottle-green superfine coat fit across his broad shoulders like a second skin, and his boots had quite a respectable shine. With his neckcloth tied neatly, if conservatively, into the Oriental, he felt he looked presentable. Not a damned dandy, but acceptable. Even Aunt Augusta would not be able to find fault with his appearance.

"So. What is this I hear?" Lady Augusta Helmsley sailed into the morning room of her Grosvenor Square home, her bosom preceding her like the prow of some magnificent ship. "Got yourself leg-shackled and didn't tell me?"

"Hello, Aunt," Justin murmured, bending to kiss her cheek. She stared up at him, her dark eyes cold and beady, and Justin suddenly wished he had not tied his neckcloth so tightly. "Trust you're feeling better?"

"Don't think to play off any of your tricks on me, my boy. I'm wise to your game. Oh, sit, sit, never could tolerate you towering over me." She stomped over to her favorite sofa, a crimson and gilt, and Justin perched uneasily on the edge of his chair, which seemed much too fragile to bear his weight. "Offer you some refreshment?"

At the moment, Justin would have liked nothing more than a stiff whiskey, but he was aware of Augusta's strict regard for the proprieties. "Tea, I suppose."

"Tea!" She stared at him. "What do you want to go maudling your insides with that stuff for? I begin to despair of you, boy. Tea, indeed. Fitch!" she roared.

The butler appeared at the door. "Yes, madam?"

"Bring us some Madeira, Fitch. And then don't disturb us."

"Yes, madam."

"Aunt, must tell you —" Justin began, but Augusta held up her hand.

"Hold your tongue, boy, until Fitch comes back. Enough of a scandal now, without gossiping in front of the servants."

"Yes, Aunt," he muttered, and leaned back in the gilt chair, which creaked ominously. Arms crossed on his chest, he managed to gossip on the latest *on-dits* until Fitch had served the wine and then retired.

"So, boy?" Augusta said, as she sipped at her wine. "What is this mad start of yours, and why was I forced to hear of it from Clarissa Lovelace?"

A smile briefly touched Justin's lips; Aunt Augusta and Mrs. Lovelace were old rivals. "Enjoy Bath, Aunt? Hear the waters are effective."

"Don't give me any of your sauce, boy." She glared at him. "What I want to know is what you are about! You may be sure this marriage of yours is all the talk in Bath, yes, and here as well! I want to know why you felt it necessary to make me such a laughing-stock!"

Justin moved uneasily in his seat, his feet shuffling together. "Didn't mean to, Aunt."

"No, of course not, you never do." Her voice was biting. "Clumsiest boy I ever did see. And now what's to become of you? You will take your seat in Parliament this January, Justin, but God knows what good it will do now. Certainly won't help the Chatleigh name, as I had hoped." She glared at him. "Good God, boy, even your father at his worst did nothing so bad."

Justin squirmed. Had Augusta been born a boy she

would have assumed the title, and he suspected she would have been a better earl than his father had been. Better, for that matter, than he himself was. "Could always do something else," he said, mildly.

"Such as? Turn farmer? And how, pray tell, do you plan to restore your estate, since you made such a foolish marriage? I'll wager she's making demands of you already." Justin's face reddened. "Tell me, boy, how did you come to marry some unknown?"

"Well." Justin shuffled his feet again.

"Stop that!" she snapped. "Well, boy? I am waiting."

Justin resisted the impulse to run a finger under his collar. There was nothing for it, but at the moment he would rather be facing all of Napoléon's armies.

Augusta heard him out in silence, as he told of finding a girl in his bed and the natural conclusion he had reached. By the time he reached the end of his tale, she was staring at him incredulously. "Do you mean to tell me," she said, "that you were trapped by a country bumpkin of an innkeeper?" She boomed out at the last words, and Justin winced.

"Afraid so, ma'am," he said, draining his Madeira. This was worse than he'd feared. He'd received dressing-downs in his time from superior officers, but Aunt Augusta had them all beat.

"My God, even from you I wouldn't have expected it, boy." It was a measure of her agitation that she rose and began to pace the room, her cane thumping in counterpoint to her words. "Got yourself into a pretty mess. And what do you do? Leave her at Chatleigh and come haring up to town."

"What else could I do?" Justin retorted, stung. "Girl's not fit to be in company."

"Why? She breeding?"

"Good God, no!" This time he gave in to the impulse, raking his fingers through his hair.

64

"Thank God for that," Augusta muttered, sitting again. Since that was one of the rumors, it had been her fear that Justin was indeed trapped, but now perhaps something could be done. "Well, boy? And what do you intend to do?"

"Don't know, Aunt." Justin leaned back, legs stretched out and arms crossed on his chest.

"What's the girl's family like?"

"Not much of it left," he said, wishing for the first time that he had listened when Melissa had tried to tell him of her background. "Mother's dead, so is her father. Got a younger brother and a stepfather, Sir Stephen Barton."

"What!" Augusta sat bolt upright, and two spots of color appeared on her cheeks. "Good God, boy, you have botched it."

"Why?" Justin leaned forward, his hands clasped between his knees. So there really was a stepfather. "You know of him, ma'am?"

"Yes. Too well. A rum sort. Last I'd heard he'd married some widow and gone through her money." The look she gave her nephew was exceedingly cold. "Which means, boy, it will be very expensive to get you out of this."

"There's a way out, then?"

"Yes, but it's going to cost. Me, not you." She eyed him coldly. "I will get you out, but it won't be easy. If you can assure me you haven't touched the girl—"

"I haven't."

"Then perhaps we can arrange an annulment. But we'll pay dearly for it, boy. I with money, you with your reputation."

"God," Justin muttered, crossing his arms again. He had married in the hope of saving his name; now it seemed it would be smeared, no matter what. "Very well, ma'am, if you will tell me what you plan, I will

65

go back to Chatleigh—"

"You? You most certainly will not. Made a mess of things already, boy. No. I will pull your chestnuts out of the fire."

"Thank you, Aunt." Justin rose.

"Don't thank me. You're putting me to a great deal of trouble, boy." The look she gave him was distinctly unfriendly. "I hope you will be worth it."

The nightmare, about *him*, came again that night. When her hands stopped shaking Melissa fumbled for the flint on the table, lit the tallow candle, and then sat, hunched up in the middle of the massive bed, her arms wrapped around her legs and her head resting on her knees. Would she never be free? Here she was, a married woman, haunted by memories and wanting nothing more than to be comforted. A pair of strong arms about her, a broad chest under her cheek, warm brown eyes smiling down at her, and lips that—

"Don't be more foolish than you can help!" Melissa exclaimed. She must be in bad case indeed if she were thinking about her absent husband at a time like this. She could do without him. She could survive without anyone, if she had to.

Still, getting back to sleep would be difficult. The room was not conducive to rest, and she felt lost in the enormous bed. Finally, she swung her legs over the side, thrusting her feet into slippers and pulling on her dressing gown. If she could not sleep, she could at least work. She had yet to finish reviewing all the account books, and there was something about them that bothered her.

Some time later Melissa, sitting at the escritoire in her sitting room, lifted her head and stared unseeingly ahead. The account books were spread out before her, several scraps of paper, covered with her neat writing, pushed to the side. It couldn't be, could it? Her fingers traced down the column of figures again. But maybe it was. Certainly something was wrong here, with this column, and if here, elsewhere as well? And if she was right, that meant . . .

Melissa shoved the account books aside. If she was right, then she had a serious problem, and she didn't have the slightest idea what to do about it. If only her husband were here . . . But no, she wouldn't think of that.

Morning brought her little counsel. After breakfast Melissa took the account books to the drawing room, which was starting to show signs of improvement. The fireplace was swept daily, the tables shone with polishing, and, though the upholstery and the curtains were still shabby, Melissa had hopes of transforming this room, as well as the rest of the house. If she had cooperation, that is, but that was beginning to seem less and less likely. After what she had discovered, she doubted she'd get any help at all.

For a moment, dazed from all the figuring, she rubbed her eyes with the heels of her hands. Melissa had handled servants for years, but they had been old Selby family retainers, indulgent to a growing girl and competent at their jobs. The Jenkinses were a different story, surly and disobedient. They were, however, more than just insolent. They were also thieves.

Melissa had realized it when she had come across a bill for a new uniform for Rose, the scullery maid. She might have have let that pass, had she not seen Rose's much-patched and darned clothing with her own eyes. From there, once she knew what she was looking for, it was easy to see that the Jenkinses had conspired with everyone, shopkeepers and tradesmen alike, to cheat the estate. No wonder the butcher sent inferior cuts of meat, the greengrocer poor vegetables. With the Earl absent it had been easy for the Jenkinses to pay inflated bills for poor goods, undoubtedly sharing the difference with the tradesmen. Someone would have to put a stop to it. Melissa only hoped she could.

For a wonder, Jenkins came promptly when she rang, and though his eyes flickered towards the account books, he made no argument when told to fetch his wife. That lady sailed in a few moments later, wiping flour-dusted hands on her apron. "What is it, my lady?" she asked, without preamble. "I was just in the middle of baking."

"This is more important," Melissa said, looking up at the other woman. "I have been reviewing the accounts and I have found some irregularities."

"Irregularities my lady? But I can't imagine what. Of course, Mr. Jenkins and me, we haven't had none of your fancy schooling and we can't do sums so good—"

"I think you can do figures well enough to steal."

Mrs. Jenkins stiffened. "We ain't no thieves!"

"No? Then how do you explain this?" Melissa asked, and detailed the discrepancies she had found.

Mrs. Jenkins's face remained stony. "Times are hard, my lady, and things are expensive. Course, you wouldn't know that," she said, her voice savage. "Wouldn't know what life is like for us poor people—"

"Oh, cut line! I know very well what things cost, I have been running a house for years!" Melissa glared at her. "I don't want to have to take action, Mrs. Jenkins, but if you and Mr. Jenkins will not cooperate, I may have to."

"And what will you do? What can you do? Oh, no, my fine lady, you won't get far talking like that!"

"What do you mean?"

"I mean that it's the Earl pays the bills around here, and everyone knows he's up and left you!"

Melissa stood up so fast her chair fell back. "Why, you insolent—"

"Careful, my lady. We can make life very unpleasant for you." Mrs. Jenkins's grin was evil. "And there ain't nothing you can do about it."

"Wait, I haven't dismissed you," Melissa cried, but the Jenkinses, already near the door of the drawing room, only laughed. A moment later the door slammed behind them, and Melissa was left staring at it.

Chapter Six

"Really!" Melissa's hands clenched into fists. She had tried to treat the Jenkinses fairly, but this was too much. When the time came to fight, one had to do it. That she had learned. She was not Major Sir Richard Selby's daughter for nothing.

She ran down the stairs and was relieved to see only Phelps in the hall. She spoke to him rapidly for a few moments. At first he looked incredulous, then angry, and finally determined. "Yes, my lady," he said, when she had finished. "I'll do what I can."

"Good! You are with me on this, then?" She looked anxiously up at him, and not for the first time Phelps, gazing into her eyes, thought that the Earl was a fool.

"Yes, my lady. I'm with you."

"Good. Now go! We must act quickly." She turned, her hands suddenly cold and clammy. If only Chatleigh were here, she could face anything — *Oh, nonsense!* she thought, and headed towards the kitchen.

As in most great houses, the kitchen wing was a distance from the main block. By the time she reached it, Melissa was out of breath, and she took a moment to look around the room, composing herself. A good working area, she thought, long and wide with an enormous fireplace, but sadly old-fashioned. When matters had been settled she would see to modernizing it, at least installing a Rumford stove, since Cook at home liked hers so much. At the moment, however, that was the least of her problems.

The Jenkinses were at the other end of the room, standing by the table and apparently arguing. "Mr. and Mrs. Jenkins," Melissa said, her voice clear and carrying, and they looked up, startled, aware of her for the first time.

Jenkins recovered first. "What does her ladyship want?" he sneered. "Best get upstairs where you belong and not bother us."

Melissa took a deep breath. The time for nervousness was past. "I've come to give you another chance. Will you cooperate with me, or won't you?"

Jenkins looked at his wife, and they both grinned. "And if we don't, what'll you do, eh, my lady? Write to the Earl about it? If he'll even answer your letters."

That was so close to the truth that Melissa had to bite back a retort. "The Earl left me in charge here—"

"Ha!"

"—in his absence, and I must do as I see fit. If you won't cooperate then I'll have no choice but to dismiss you."

"And what if we don't go? Eh?" Jenkins advanced upon her, one stubby finger pointing for emphasis, and Melissa stepped back. "What will you do then, my fine lady? Eh?"

"You'll go," Melissa said quietly, wondering about the wisdom of confronting these people alone. The polite facade had fallen from Jenkins's face and he looked menacing, his eyes cold and hard, his mouth twisted into a sneer. "The Earl will be behind me on this."

"Oh, will he?" Jenkins grinned. "Don't think so. No, my lady." He took another step, and Melissa suddenly

71

came up against the wall. "We're staying, and there's not a thing you can do about it."

Oh, where was Phelps? Melissa thought desperately. "Then I shall have to call the law down upon you," she said, somehow keeping her voice calm. Jenkins was very close, and there was no escape.

His laugh was low and triumphant. "You won't," he said, and Melissa recoiled, from the smell of onions on his breath and the menace in his voice. "Got no proof."

Melissa raised her chin. "I have the account books."

"Not anymore, you don't. Mother!"

Mrs. Jenkins came forward. "Yes, Mr. Jenkins?"

"Best go get the account books, while my lady and I have a talk."

"I don't think so," a voice said, and Phelps stepped into the room, blocking the doorway. "Stand away from her ladyship."

Jenkins barely glanced at him. "This don't concern you."

Phelps reached out a big hand and pushed Jenkins away. "You're wrong," he said. His voice was quiet, but there was something so solid and determined-looking about him that Jenkins pulled back. "It is my concern."

"And mine." The groom stepped in from the passageway leading from outside.

"Mine, too." The gardener followed him; his assistant behind him. "Sorry we took so long, milady," he added. He carried a spade; the groom, a pitchfork. For the first time the Jenkinses looked uncertain.

"Are they bothering you, my lady?" the footman asked.

"Yes, Phelps," Melissa replied. Her knees sagged as she slipped past Jenkins. "Did you get it?"

"Yes, my lady. Got their strongbox right here."

"What!" Mrs. Jenkins surged forward. "But that's our money! You got no right—"

"I have every right! It is the Earl's money, is it not? Estate money? Small price to pay for all you've taken over the years."

"Shall I show them out, my lady?" Phelps asked, coming swiftly to stand before Melissa as Jenkins surged forward.

"Yes, please, Phelps. Now."

"You'll make us go, just like that?" Mrs. Jenkins's voice rose. "After all the years we've worked and slaved, to let us go without a character?"

"Be glad I don't turn you over to the authorities!" Melissa snapped.

"All right! We'll go." Jenkins stared hard at Melissa. "But you'll regret this, my fine lady."

"I doubt it. Phelps, if you would?"

"With pleasure, ma'am!" Grinning, Phelps sketched an ironic bow to his erstwhile superiors. Their heads held high, the Jenkinses sailed past him, and Melissa drew her first easy breath since the confrontation had started.

"My lady," Liza peeked out from the scullery, "is it true? Are they really going?"

Melissa turned. "Yes, Liza. They're gone."

Liza came into the kitchen, followed by Rose. "What now, my lady?"

"Well." Melissa gestured them closer. "Now we start work. Yes, Liza, I know there are few of us, but I plan to hire more staff."

"For me, too?" the gardener said.

Melissa smiled. "Yes. For you, too. I want this house to shine! We have a lot of chores ahead of us, but as long as we work together, we can do it. Have I your support?"

The two girls looked at each other. "All I know is

you got rid o' those Jenkinses," Rose said, greatly daring.

"Good." Melissa smiled again. "Go about your work now. And . . . thank you." She smiled at them as they filed out, the gardener and his assistant pulling at their forelocks, the girls curtsying. It was over and she had won. The thought of what she had done made her feel so giddy that she sank down onto a chair, her head in her hands. "I did it," she muttered. "I did it."

"My lady?" She looked up to see Phelps. "Are you all right?"

"Yes, Phelps. Are they away?"

"Yes, my lady, and they didn't take anything more, I didn't give them the chance. Jeffrey will drive them to the Crown. They'll find their way from there."

"Very good. And you gave them the money."

"Yes, ma'am." He frowned. "But, my lady, do you think that was wise, giving it to them?"

"They did earn some wages, Phelps, and this way they can't complain of being cheated."

"They won't thank you for it, ma'am."

"No matter. They're gone, thank God. Phelps . . ."

"My lady?"

"How long have you been a footman?"

"Five years, my lady."

"Excellent. Do you think you could handle being butler?"

Phelps drew in his breath. He'd been certain that that position would be filled by some lofty individual from London. "Oh, yes, my lady! I'll do my best."

"I'm sure you will. If the Earl approves, of course." Under her breath she added, "And if he ever answers my letters."

"My lady?"

"Never mind." She rose and shook out her skirts. "I think I deserve a cup of tea. Will you bring it to me in

74

the drawing room?"

"Yes, my lady, of course."

"Thank you." She smiled at him and turned, and an idiotic grin spread over his face. Butler! he thought, and jumped into the air, clicking his heels.

The late afternoon sun shone into the hall through the casement windows, in it dancing, gilded motes. Melissa, balanced precariously on a ladder, removed another lustre from the crystal chandelier, lowered this for cleaning, and then wiped her forehead with her sleeve. Hard work, this, since the chandelier had not been cleaned in an age, but her efforts were already bearing fruit. The lustres that had already been dipped in soapy water, rinsed, and then carefully buffed, caught the sun in their facets, sparkling refracted rainbow colors on the dark oak paneling.

Melissa stretched tired muscles. It was just one day since the Jenkinses had left, and already the atmosphere in the house was lighter. For the first time, she truly felt that she was the mistress, and that she could restore the place as she wished. Just why that was so important to her, she didn't know, since, with so few servants, she would have to do much of the work herself. Sometimes the prospect of renovation loomed so large, and promised to be so expensive, that it was daunting.

Carriage wheels crunched on the gravel outside just as Melissa replaced the luster. "Oh, dear!" She wiped her hands on her skirts and started to climb down. "Phelps?" she called, though she knew he was most likely in the butler's pantry, taking up his new duties. Oh, dear, someone would have to open the door to the visitor, and she, with a mobcap pulled over her curls and her skirts kilted up, was not the best choice. She pulled her skirts down just as the door knocker crashed down, echoing through the hall. Dear, dear, Melissa thought, and she hurried to respond, praying it would not be any of the neighbors she had met at St. Mary's the previous Sunday.

It was not. Instead a postilion, his livery dusty from the road but his wig still firmly affixed to his head, stood before her, and behind him stomped a very old lady, her cane thudding with each step. Melissa watched the woman, fascinated. She was short and exceedingly plump, with a bosom that jutted out so that she appeared in imminent danger of toppling over. Her gown of purple satin dated from another century, full-skirted with cascades of lace at the sleeves, but the black velvet cloak and the multicolored brocade turban looked new. Two bright spots of rouge dotted the raddled cheeks, and the eyes that came up to survey Melissa were bright with malice. "Well, gel?" she barked. "Why do you stand there? Let me by."

"But . . ." Melissa protested, falling back before this apparition.

"Don't just stand there like a ninny gel. Announce me to your mistress! New here, ain't you?" She gave Melissa a thorough scrutiny. "Hmph! Things were much better done in my day! Now run, gel, and tell your mistress Lady Helmsley wants a word with her."

Melissa opened her mouth again, and at that moment Phelps, struggling into the new black coat of which he was very proud, hurried into the hall. "My lady!" he exclaimed, looking at Melissa, and Lady Helmsley turned towards him.

"Who're you? Where is Jenkins?"

"Gone, my lady."

"Gone? Well, no matter, we'll soon get to the bottom of this!" She continued her progress across the hall, the thumps of her cane echoing, her expression disapproving in spite of the improvements in the large room. "Well? What are you waiting for? Show me to the drawing room and announce me to your mistress! Since this maid here seems to be too stupid to do it."

"But she is—"

"Now, if you please!"

Phelps glanced helplessly past Lady Helmsley for guidance. Melissa, her hand to her mouth, quickly shook her head and gestured towards the stairs. "Very well, my lady. If you'll just come this way?"

"About time," Lady Helmsley muttered, and followed Phelps slowly up the stairs.

Phelps ran into Melissa a few moments later on the first-floor landing. "Oh, my lady," he began.

"Shh!" Melissa glanced past him towards the drawing room. "Who in the world is she, Phelps?" she whispered.

"His lordship's aunt."

"What!" Again she looked quickly towards the drawing room, but there was no sign the old lady had heard. "Oh, dear! Bring her tea, then, and tell her I shall be with her presently. And send Liza to me," she called over her shoulder as she scurried off to her room.

Some time later Melissa slipped quietly into the drawing room, having washed and changed into a simple round gown of black sarcenet, with a pleated white ruff at the neck and starched white cuffs. Liza had brushed her curls until they shone, and though she no longer appeared a scruffy maidservant, she looked much too young to be the lady of the house.

Melissa paused for a moment, watching her guest, who remained unaware of her, frown at the portrait that hung over the mantel in place of the hunting scene. Oh, dear, Chatleigh's aunt. She had known she would someday have to meet her husband's family.

She just hadn't realized they would be so redoubtable.

Taking a deep breath, she stepped forward, the thin silk of her gown rustling. "Good afternoon, Lady Helmsley," she said in a clear voice. The other woman started and turned towards her.

"Good God, gel, weren't you ever taught not to sneak up on people?" she snarled, and then her eyes widened slightly. "But you are—"

"Forgive me for not being on hand to greet you, or rather," she smiled, "for not greeting you when I was on hand. Please, sit down." Melissa motioned towards the sofa that faced the fireplace. Formidable the woman might be, but she was also old, and the hand clutching the cane was white at the knuckles. "That fire draws well since the chimney has been cleaned. You must forgive my appearance downstairs. I am afraid we are short on staff."

"Yes," Augusta murmured, for once in her life at a loss for words. "So you masquerade as a common servant. About what I expected, from what my nephew said."

"Oh, dear." Melissa reached over to feel the teapot and then went to the bellpull. "I can imagine just what he did say."

"You needn't look amused, gel. It was bad enough."

"I'm sure it was. Phelps, please bring us some fresh tea. And, Lady Helmsley, I'm sure you must be sharp-set after your journey?"

"Don't bother about me, gel." She glared from Melissa to Phelps. "And who is he?"

"The butler. You might just ask Mrs. Barnes if she would make us some watercress sandwiches, Phelps."

"Yes, my lady," Phelps said, and left the room.

"Mrs. Barnes!" Augusta stared at her, arrested in the act of biting into a piece of bread and butter. "Not the Mrs. Barnes who was nanny here?"

"Yes, I found her in a cottage on the estate, and I've asked her to come back as housekeeper."

Augusta regarded her through narrowed eyes. "Getting above yourself, ain't you, gel? Hiring staff without consulting anyone?"

"I've consulted Chatleigh. That he may not choose to read my letters is his problem."

Augusta leaned back in the corner of the sofa. "Can't say I blame him, gel, knowing you as he does. Out for the money, ain't you?"

Melissa gestured about the drawing room. "What money?" she asked, her eyes innocent.

"Don't think to cozen me, gel!" the older woman retorted, thumping her cane. "I know what you want. Well, you won't get it. Don't think I will countenance your presence in this family."

"Thank you, Phelps." Melissa waited while Phelps set the tray down, then reached for the silver pot. "And so, why are you here?" she asked in a quiet voice that would have warned anyone who knew her.

"To get my nephew out of this mess."

"I see." Melissa slowly sipped her tea. "In other words, to buy me off."

"If necessary."

"And if I refuse?"

Augusta's eyes flashed. "Oh, you won't refuse, not if you know what's good for you. I can make life very uncomfortable for you gel. You'll regret the day you ever joined this family—"

"Oh, really!" Melissa set her cup down hard and jumped to her feet, striding across the room. "I already do regret it! What have I gotten since my marriage but insults, loneliness, and hard work?' I tell you, madam, I rue the day I met your nephew, and if there were any way out of this mess, I'd take it! But I am stuck, and so are you. And I wonder," she went on,

79

her voice bitter, "if you'd be so eager to dissolve this marriage if you knew that your precious, stupid nephew has had the good fortune to marry an heiress?"

"Good God," Augusta said softly, staring up at her. "Oh, come off down your high ropes, gel, and sit. Come on. Sit." She patted the sofa. Melissa glared at her for a moment and then sat down, indignation roiling within her. "Do you expect me to believe that?"

"Believe what you want, ma'am."

"Then what in God's name were you doing in his room like a common whore?"

Melissa drew herself up. "I am not a whore, madam," she said quietly, but her eyes flashed. "I am the daughter of Major Sir Richard Selby, and by God, I am not a whore!"

"Major Sir—!" Augusta stared at her. "Good God, you're not Townsend's granddaughter!"

"Yes, ma'am."

"Good God! I think, gel, that you had better tell me your side of the story."

Augusta's tone may have moderated, but there was no disobeying it. Melissa folded her hands in her lap, took a deep breath, and began. For the most part her story was met by silence, until she described how Justin had reacted when the innkeeper had come into the room. At that, Augusta made a noise that sounded suspiciously like a snort. Looking up, Melissa was startled to see the older woman's eyes sparkling with malicious amusement. For the first time, the humorous aspects of the situation struck her, too, and by the time she was finished she was nearly choking with laughter.

"Men are such fools. Not to see at once that you are quality, gel," Augusta said, conveniently forgetting that she had not seen it immediately either.

"Of course, the circumstances, ma'am," Melissa murmured, but her eyes were bright.

"Nonsense! Nevertheless," her brow furrowed, "what were you doing in that inn? Best tell me the truth," she added sharply, as Melissa hesitated. "Can't help you if you don't."

Melissa's eyes rose at that, but in spite of what Augusta had just said her face was not encouraging. "I was running away, ma'am, as you may have guessed. I planned to obtain a position in London, where no one would know me."

"Why?"

Melissa hesitated again. "You know of my stepfather? Sir Stephen Barton?"

"Yes. Nasty sort."

"Yes. So you understand. He made my life, and my brother's, a living hell." Melissa turned her head, but if Augusta, studying her, learned more from her expression, she didn't let on.

"He is a problem, if we are to launch you successfully," she said, briskly. "So is your mother."

"My mother was the sweetest, kindest—"

"Doubtless. She was also connected with trade. The daughter of a merchant!"

"But that is why I am an heiress, ma'am," Melissa said demurely, and Augusta shot her a look.

"Regardless. It is a problem, gel. You may be sure that many people remember your father, and that Townsend disinherited his heir for making such a disastrous marriage."

"Papa wouldn't have wished to be a viscount, anyway. He was happy in the army."

"Doubtless," Augusta said dryly. "At least your lineage on your father's side is good, and you are presentable, gel. Or you will be." She cocked her head. "Redheads ain't quite the style, but if we can get you

81

into some proper gowns, I think you'll do."

"Thank you," Melissa said, her tone ironic.

Augusta shot her a look. "You'll need help, of course, but plenty of time for that before the season starts."

"Do you mean . . . are you saying I should go to London?"

"And why not? You are Countess of Chatleigh, are you not?" The older woman rose, a trifle unsteadily, and Melissa's hand shot out to catch her arm. "I would go to my room now."

"Yes, of course. But are you sure about London?"

"Do you wish to go?"

"Oh, yes, very much, but what of Chatleigh?"

"You let me see to him." Augusta turned in the doorway. "I'll handle him."

"Oh, I don't doubt that, ma'am," Melissa said, and the two women smiled, in perfect charity with each other.

Early morning. Though the sun was beginning to rise and the day showed promise of being clear and bright, still the mists rose from the valley. Inside the inn all was quiet, except for the bustle of the servants. The Crown had been known for its hospitality for years; why, hadn't it once played host to King Edward IV? But such a venerable, well-run inn was apt to be expensive, as Sir Stephen Barton had found last evening when he'd called for an accounting of his bill. Much too expensive for a man whose pockets were continually to let. It was his daughter's fault, of course, ungrateful child that she was. A child should see that her father was taken care of in his old age.

His bag packed, Sir Stephen crossed the room in stockinged feet and unlatched a window. It creaked ominously as he swung it open, but no one seemed to notice. Good. As convenient as the Crown was to Chatleigh Hall, it had one problem common to all inns. It expected guests to pay their shot, and this, Sir Stephen was not prepared to do.

There, the ground wasn't far away, and luckily a sturdy vine of ivy grew nearby. Sir Stephen looked around, but there was no one to be seen. Out first went his portmanteau, falling solidly to the ground. Following that went his boots and his greatcoat, and, at last, Sir Stephen himself. For once in his life he was grateful for his lack of stature as, clinging to the ivy, he began to climb.

He was about halfway to the ground when a noise made him look down. "Hey!" he cried, but softly. A man with a sharpfeatured face was bending over the scattered belongings. At Sir Stephen's cry, he snatched up the greatcoat and took off at a shambling run. For Sir Stephen, this was the final indignity. Anger gave him speed and the courage he usually lacked. He scrambled down the remaining ivy and set off at a run himself, heedless of the rough stones under his stockinged feet. No one stole anything from Sir Stephen Barton!

In spite of the man's lead, Sir Stephen gained on him. He brought the thief down with a tackle that drove the air from the man's lungs, pinning him down before he could escape. "Give me back my coat, you—" he gasped, when suddenly something hit him from behind.

"You leave my husband alone!" a woman shrieked, raining blows down upon Sir Stephen's defenseless back.

Sir Stephen twisted around. "Madam, cease at once!" he yelled, jumping to his feet and holding up his arms to shield his face.

"Don't you touch my husband, you you—"

"Mother, stop!" the man called. "Guess we showed him."

"But he attacked you, Mr. Jenkins!"

"No matter, Mother." Jenkins rose to his feet, a picture of wounded dignity as he shot his cuffs and straightened his rusty black coat.

Sir Stephen glared at them. "You're nothing but a pair of common thieves," he said.

"And what are you, guv'nor?" Jenkins said. "Leaving the inn without paying?"

"That is not your affair. My coat, please."

Jenkins hesitated.

"Now!" Sir Stephen stretched out an imperious hand, and Jenkins, too accustomed to obeying the commands of the quality, handed it to him. "I've a mind to turn you over to the authorities."

"Oh, please, guv'nor, don't do that!" Jenkins stared at him in alarm. "Got hard enough times as it is."

"You should have thought of that before undertaking to steal." Sir Stephen pulled on his greatcoat, looking now the complete man of fashion, except for the hole in his stocking through which his toe showed.

"The quality don't understand hard times," Mrs. Jenkins said. "Like her, up to the Hall."

"Lady Chatleigh?" Sir Stephen was suddenly alert. "What about her?"

"Well, turned us off, didn't she? Without even a character, and us with all the years we worked there."

"Turned you off, did she?" Sir Stephen, his hands plunged into the pockets of his greatcoat, stared at them, as likely a pair of thieves as he'd ever met, and a smile slowly spread across his face. "I see. I think perhaps we could be of service to each other."

* * *

"My lord!" Phelps stammered as he opened the door to a loud and persistent knock. "But we didn't expect you!"

"Who the devil are you?" Justin paused inside the doorway, drawing off his gloves and slapping them against his palm. "Ah yes. The footman. Where is Jenkins?"

Phelps moved forward to help Justin out of his greatcoat. "Gone, my lord."

"Gone?" Justin turned his head. "Where?"

"He and Mrs. Jenkins were sacked, my lord." In Phelps's voice was a trace of the pleasure that still gave him, nearly a week later.

"The devil they were!" Justin stared at him. "What the devil else has been taking place here in my absence?" he asked, and as his eyes went around the hall he could see that for the first time in years it was clean. "Good God. Never mind that. Who are you, anyway?"

"Phelps, my lord. The new butler."

"Phelps. I will be in the drawing room. Tell the Countess to wait on me there."

"Yes, my lord. But I believe her ladyship has gone for a walk on the estate."

"Then find her," Justin snapped, and climbed the stairs.

In the drawing room, more surprises awaited him. Though the furniture had yet to be reupholstered, the plasterers and painters had been in. The chipped and peeling moldings had been repaired, the walls were again a sunny yellow, and new drapes, this time of light blue brocade, hung at the windows. Wrinkling his nose at the smell of new paint, Justin walked farther in. The drawing room looked almost as it had when he was a child, even to the portrait of his mother, rehung in its place of honor over the mantel.

Justin gave it a long look, and then turned on his heel. He wouldn't wait tamely for his wife to come to him. He would find her, instead.

The house was, at last, beginning to shape up. The hall had been thoroughly cleaned; the marble tiles shone, the brass balusters sparkled, and the paneling glowed with the patina of age and beeswax. The drawing room was improving as well, and at last Melissa was turning her thoughts to her own suite of rooms. Clad in a rough woolen gown, her cloak pulled around her and sturdy brogues on her feet, she strode through the Home Woods on this crisp autumn afternoon, her mind filled with plans. Light colors, cream and teal and gold, and crisp chintz bedhangings, and perhaps the massive dark furniture wouldn't loom so, not anymore . . .

A howl split the afternoon peace, the cry of an animal in pain, and the little noises that filled the woods, the rustling of small animals and whatever birds remained, suddenly ceased. Melissa stopped dead, and the cry came again, so mournful, so frightened and frightening that it raised the hackles on the back of her neck. For it wasn't just any animal. There were words in that cry.

"Where are you?" she called, and the cry came again, from everywhere, from nowhere. "Where are you?"

This time there was no answer. Melissa stood irresolute on the path, glancing back in the direction of the Hall. If someone were hurt, perhaps she should run for help? But then the cry came again, and this time she thought she knew its direction. Onward, ahead of her.

Without thought, she broke into a run. "I'm coming!" she gasped. "I'm coming, hold on," and with that, she burst into a little clearing. There, on the forest floor, his leg caught in a trap, was a small boy.

"Oh, no!" Melissa dropped to her knees as she recognized him, the son of one of the estate's tenants. "Georgie?"

"Oh, milady, I'm that sorry," the boy gasped.

"Never mind, Georgie, how did this happen? Never mind, I'll get you out. Oh, dear!" she exclaimed, for the teeth of the trap, cruel, strong iron, refused to budge, no matter how hard she tried. "Oh, no I'll have to get help, Georgie."

"Oh, milady, don't leave me."

"Just for a moment. Here." Pulling off her cloak, she draped it over him. "I'll be right back. I promise." She set off at a run again, past trees whose huge trunks looked menacing, down a path that had previously seemed short and pleasant but was now interminable. She had to make the Hall and summon help before Georgie lost more blood; he'd already lost a prodigious amount, it stained her dress. The trees opened ahead of her. There was a stitch in her side, but if she could just make it . . .

From somewhere Melissa summoned strength. Putting on a burst of speed, she dashed out from the last of the trees, onto the smooth lawn — and into the arms of the Earl.

Chapter Seven

The air went out of Justin's lungs with an "Oomph!"

"My lord," Melissa gasped, pulling back, and his hands grasped her arms.

"What the devil—what are you doing?" he demanded.

Her breath came almost in sobs. "My lord, a boy, caught in a trap . . ."

His grip suddenly tightened. "Where?"

"In the woods. Back there."

"Get help." Justin abruptly released her and set off into the Home Woods, his long legs making nothing of the distance. Melissa, dazed, watched him for a moment, and then turned, breaking again into a run. Her part was not yet done.

At the stables she gasped out her tale. Jeffrey, the groom, ran out, followed by a man who, though unknown to her, looked at her with narrowed eyes. Winded, Melissa leaned against the wall to catch her breath, her hand pressed against her side. She had done her part, but in her mind she could see Georgie's eyes, huge and dark with fright and pain. He was only a boy, even if, as she suspected, he was poaching at his father's behest, and he would be surrounded by strangers. She couldn't let him face that alone.

Once again she set off into the woods, running as fast as she could, in spite of her burning lungs and aching legs. Finally, panting, she reached the clearing, where Justin already knelt by the trap. The other man was kneeling at the boy's head, holding down his shoulders.

Justin glanced up, looking briefly surprised. "No place for you here," he said. "Jeffrey, see if there's a stick we can use to wedge it open. Go on back to the Hall."

This last was addressed to Melissa, who dropped down onto her knees by Georgie's head. "Hallo, Georgie. Holding on?"

"Yes, milady. But it hurts," he whimpered.

"I know it does. I'm staying." She raised her head and stared defiantly at Justin, and he frowned.

"Then stand back out of the way," he said gruffly.

"Oh, milady," Georgie whimpered again, and Melissa took his blood-stained hand in hers.

"Don't you worry, Georgie, I won't leave you." Brushing back Georgie's sweat-darkened hair from his forehead, she looked up.

Justin's eyes were opaque. "Very well. Can't help you if you faint," he said, and went to work, as Jeffrey came back with a stout stick. He had already discarded his coat, and the muscles in his arms, corded and strong, stood out against his shirt as he strained with the stick, thrusting it between the teeth of the trap to pry it apart. For a moment Melissa was transfixed, as an image came to her mind: Justin standing in the tiny attic room in the Hart and Hind, filling it with his presence, his naked chest blatantly masculine. There were strength and power in those broad shoulders, and gentleness in his hands.

The stick slipped. Georgie moaned through gritted teeth, and Justin swore. Confused by her feelings,

Melissa dropped her eyes. Heavens, such things to be thinking of, at a time like this!

"Hold on to him," Justin said. "About ready to go."

"Now, just you hold on, lad," the man who held Georgie's shoulders said. "His lordship will have you out in a trice."

"Milady," the boy whimpered.

"Yes, Georgie, I'm here. You must soldier on, my Papa would always say."

"Your father was a soldier?" Georgie looked up at her, interested in something beyond his pain for the first time.

"Indeed he was. Met his end at Talavera, I'm afraid. Major Selby."

The man kneeling across from her lifted his head sharply, but at that moment the trap let go and there was no time for speech. "Damn!" Justin exclaimed, ripping frantically at his neckcloth as blood spurted from the wound. "Damn thing must have hit an artery."

"Need a tourniquet, sir," the man said, pulling off his own cravat. Justin took the neckcloth without comment, knotting it swiftly about the boy's leg. The stick he had used to pry open the trap did double duty as he thrust it through the knot, turning it to tighten the pressure and thus stem the flow of blood. Dimly he was aware that his wife had jumped up when the trap had let go, and his lips twitched in annoyance. Just what he needed at this time, a female having the vapors.

"Here." A pile of cloths was thrust at him, and he looked up to see Melissa. "You'll need these for bandages."

"Thank you," he said, briefly. Melissa dropped down beside him, reaching for Georgie's wrist. The boy had fainted, from the pain and loss of blood, but to her

90

relief his pulse, though weak, was steady.

"There's a pulse." Again she reached out to smooth Georgie's hair, and then brushed her own curls back, leaving a streak of blood on her cheek. "Will he lose his leg?"

"Might, my lady," the strange man said. "Seen things like this on the Peninsula."

"We'll do what we can, Alfred," Justin declared, loosening the tourniquet just a bit. The blood spurted again but then, to his relief, the flow eased. "He'll need a leech."

"There's a new doctor in the village, a young man. He's said to be quite good," Melissa said, and Justin glanced over at her.

"You don't faint at the sight of blood."

"No. Do you?"

In spite of himself, Justin grinned. "Hardly. Thing to do now is get him inside." He looked up at Alfred. "Best get back to the Hall and get something to carry him. And take her ladyship with you."

"Yes, sir," Alfred replied, and at the same time Melissa shook her head.

"No. I promised him I'd stay with him, and I shall."

"Don't be ridiculous." Justin spoke briskly as he began bandaging the wound, using the strips of cloth Melissa had handed him. The bits of lace trimming on them puzzled him, until he realized what they meant. She must have torn her petticoat to provide bandages. His eyebrows rose briefly in surprise. "Nothing more you can do here."

"He wanted me to stay, my lord." Melissa's chin was outthrust. "So I shall stay."

"He doesn't even know you are here."

"Nevertheless. Do you even know who he is?"

"Dickie Turner's son, isn't he?" Justin knotted the last bandage and knelt back, wiping his forehead with

91

his sleeve. "Like to know what he was doing here. And who, I wonder, has been setting traps in my woods?"

"Your agent, I believe, to catch poachers. Poor lad."

Justin stared at her. "Before you become sentimental, you might like to know that Turner is a known poacher."

"And would he deserve this?" she retorted. "Georgie certainly didn't."

Justin's face softened briefly. "No, he didn't, poor lad. But I must have a word with his father."

"I understand Turner only takes rabbits, and other small game."

Justin's sharpened gaze focused on her. "Yes, so?"

"So he only poaches because his family is hungry."

"None of my tenants are hungry," Justin retorted.

Melissa shrugged. "You are never here, my lord. How would you know?"

Justin glared at her, but she was spared his response by the return of the other men, carrying a litter piled high with blankets. Melissa stepped out of the way and watched as Justin lifted Georgie, unconscious still, and placed him upon it. She had been right. There was gentleness in her husband's hands.

"Take him to the Hall now, no time to lose," Justin said. "Doctor been sent for?"

"Yes, sir," Alfred said. He glanced past Justin, and frowned.

"Go, then." Justin watched them off and then turned to see what had caused that look on Alfred's face, seeing only his wife, leaning against a tree. "Well, madam?"

Melissa looked up. She was suddenly so tired that every movement was an effort. "Yes?"

"Do you intend to stay there all day?"

"No, of course not." She let out her breath and took a step away from the tree. Then she swayed, and her face paled.

Justin crossed the clearing in two quick strides and caught her about the waist. "Thought you didn't faint," he said, his voice gruff.

"I don't." Melissa closed her eyes, briefly giving in to the temptation to lean against his broad shoulders, to be enfolded in his sheltering arms. But this was the man who had once called her "whore," she reminded herself, and stiffened. "I am quite recovered, my lord."

"Are you?" Justin peered down at her. "Doubt that. Long walk back to the Hall."

"I can make it. I'm not such a poor honey."

"No, you aren't, are you?" He crossed to pick up his discarded coat and, to Melissa's surprise, draped it over her shoulders. "Must be cold."

"A little," she admitted, grateful for the coat's warmth as they set off together. "But what of you?"

Justin shrugged. "Faced worse than this in Spain."

"I wish you would tell me about that sometime," she said, startling both of them.

Justin glanced down at her, his eyes opaque. "Best save your breath, madam. Long walk back to the Hall."

Melissa looked up at him and bit back her retort. He was looking very grim. That odd moment of closeness had been an aberration, something that was not likely to happen again. She wasn't sure why that depressed her so.

They stopped at the stables to check that Georgie, installed in a room in the servants' quarters, had been properly cared for, and then went on to the house, Melissa's steps dragging. All she wanted to do is sleep, she thought as the massive door opened.

Phelps stood back from the door. "My lady!" he exclaimed. "Are you hurt?"

Melissa tried to smile. "No, Phelps, not me," she

was saying, when Mrs. Barnes came bustling in from the back of the hall.

"There, lamb, I heard what happened," the kindly woman said, coming forward and putting an arm around Melissa.

"Nanny?" Justin stared at her. "Is it really you?"

"And who else would it be, Master Justin?" Once Mrs. Barnes had been nursemaid to Justin and his brother. Both were tall, strong men now, but one thing hadn't changed: she could still cut them down to size. "What were you about, Master Justin, to let your lady walk home in such a state?"

"Well, uh." Justin shuffled his feet. "She didn't want—"

Melissa interrupted. "I'm all right, Mrs. Barnes, only rather tired and dirty, so if you'll send Liza to me, I'll go change—"

"One moment, madam," Justin said, his voice crisp, and Melissa turned from the stairs. Nothing was as he'd remembered. The old servants were gone, new ones had been installed, and his wife seemed to have won the respect that should have been his. "I require a word with you."

"For shame, Master Justin," Mrs. Barnes scolded. "Can't you see her ladyship's burnt to the socket?"

"No, it's all right, Mrs. Barnes." Melissa slipped Justin's coat from her shoulders and held it out to him. "If you will give me a chance to change and remove all of this dirt I shall wait upon you in the drawing room."

"Very well," Justin said, and, turning on his heel, he walked out.

"Now, lamb, don't let him worry you."

"I'm not." Melissa was smiling. Mrs. Barnes meant well, but this issue was not one open to advice. Whatever lay between her and her husband could not be settled by anyone else. She wasn't afraid of Justin. What frightened her were her reactions to him.

Sometime later, having bathed and changed into her black sarcenet gown, Melissa walked into the drawing room. Justin, his hands in his coat pockets, was standing at a window, staring out onto the drive, but at the sound of her footsteps he turned. He, too, had changed, exchanging his soiled buckskins for pantaloons of a pale fawn color that complemented the forest green of his coat. His hair, still damp from washing, had been carefully brushed, and his entire appearance had almost a military precision.

Melissa took a deep breath. "Good afternoon, my lord."

"Good afternoon, madam," he said, formally. His eyes flickered up to his mother's portrait as he walked over to her and then away.

"Have you heard anything of the boy?" she asked, sitting on the sofa nearest to the fire. The afternoon sun was golden and mellow, and the room was growing perceptibly cooler.

"Yes. Won't lose his leg, so I've been told." He sat beside her, and she suddenly jumped up, crossing the room to tug on the bellpull.

"Thank heavens for that, though I imagine he'll be lame? What will happen to him?"

"We'll find him something on the estate."

"Oh, good. I understand he loves horses and he's very good with them." She chattered. "Would you like tea, my lord? I could do with some." Justin's face had grown dark. "Especially if you're going to scold me."

"Scolding is hardly the word, madam," he began, when Phelps came in. Justin waited impatiently as Melissa told the butler what they required, tea for herself and burgundy for his lordship, and some of Mrs. Barnes's rock cakes, if she had made any. Justin's face grew darker throughout this, and when Melissa came back to the sofa, it was his turn to rise. "And what is Nanny Barnes doing in the kitchen?"

"Cooking. Somebody has to. Of course, it will only be until we can hire somebody new, but there's hardly been time for it, and—"

"Madam, enough!" Melissa stopped at seeing the look on his face. Until this moment, she had not realized that he had a temper. "I would like to know why you saw fit to change the staff without consulting me."

Melissa's chin went up. "I did consult you, my lord! I wrote to you—"

"Asking for things."

"Asking for permission! I never asked you for a penny. Not once."

Justin looked skeptical. "Regardless. You had no right."

"No right! But I am mistress here!"

"I don't believe I gave you that authority."

"Oh, yes, you did, when you married me."

Justin was about to retort to that, but at that moment there was a soft knock on the door. He abruptly wheeled around, crossing back to the window, while Phelps brought in the tea tray, and only when he and Melissa were again alone did he turn back. "Why didn't you tell me about your family?" he asked. One of the more uncomfortable moments of his life had come when Augusta had tartly informed him of his wife's background, something he should already have known. The worst part was that he had known, and respected, her father.

Melissa, pouring out a cup of tea, looked up at him, standing near the fireplace, his foot upon the fender. Her earlier anger had simmered down; Papa had always warned her to put a guard on her temper, no matter the provocation. And this time, the provocation was great, indeed. "As I recall, my lord, I tried."

"Well, it made me feel like a fool."

"I don't imagine that would be too difficult," she muttered.

"I beg your pardon?"

"I am so sorry, my lord, but I would rather feel foolish than have my entire life disrupted!" She set down the teapot with a thump.

"Don't expect me to pity you," he retorted. "You've done well enough for yourself, got yourself a title."

Two spots of color appeared on Melissa's cheeks. "Really! For all the good it's done me." Her voice was bitter. "All this marriage has brought me is loneliness and scandal."

"Ha! You got what you wanted. The granddaughter of a man in trade marrying an earl?"

"Oh, so we're back to that again, are we, how I trapped you? Well, my lord, if you hadn't been so willing to step into the trap we wouldn't be here today!"

"No, but you've made the most of it, haven't you?" His gaze went around the room, avoiding and then finally settling on the portrait of his mother. "I want that painting removed immediately."

"Why?" Melissa asked in surprise. To her, the portrait was much more suited to this room than the hunting scene that had hung in it before. Painted by Gainsborough, it depicted a beauty dressed in the style of the last century, in a gown of pale blue brocade. Clouds of dark hair, unpowdered, were piled upon her head, and around her throat was a magnificent diamond necklace. But her eyes were what compelled one's attention. The painter had caught a variety of expressions in her gaze, sensuality, curiosity, and more than a hint of mischievousness. They were her husband's eyes, she realized with a jolt. "I think it's a charming picture."

"Regardless. I want it taken down. And in future, madam, you will consult me about any changes."

"But you're never here! How can you tell what is needed? The house is practically falling down, and as for the farms, if you look at the books you'll see that the Jenkinses . . ."

"Enough." His voice was quiet, but there was steel in it. To her own surprise, Melissa subsided. "I will not argue with you on this. The estate is not your responsibility."

"Then whose is it? No one's overseen anything here in years, and everything is falling apart."

"I have an agent."

"But he doesn't seem to do anything! I think he would, if he had the money and the direction, but he's been held back all this time. Somebody's got to take the reins."

"Not you, madam."

"Who, then? You? And what do you know about it?" she said, her voice sarcastic. "Who are you but just another member of the *ton?* Oh, I've heard about people like you; my father told me. Living only for your own enjoyment, bleeding your estate dry and never accomplishing anything."

"Madam, enough!" Justin roared, and Melissa blinked in surprise. *My God, I sound like my father,* he thought. It was the last thing in the world he wanted. Still, she had to be told. This was his estate, his responsibility, not hers. "You'll not deal with estate matters."

Melissa sat down with a thump. "So what am I do do?" she said, bitterly. "I thought I could at least run this house. I don't feel like a countess, and God knows I'm not a wife."

Justin raised his head. "Ah, now we come to it," he

said, softly. "And is that what you want, madam?"

Their eyes met, and Melissa's were the first to drop. "I . . . don't know. I hardly know you." She looked up at him, unaware of how appealing she looked, her brow slightly furrowed in a frown, her eyes confused. "But I don't want to go on like this, not knowing who I am, where I belong."

Justin made a motion with his hand. "God knows I'm not happy about this, either." He looked down into the fire and then turned to face her. "It appears, madam, that we have no choice."

Melissa licked lips gone suddenly dry. "What does that mean?" she whispered.

"Oh, for God's sake, don't look at me that way," Justin snapped. "If the prospect of being my wife is so distasteful to you, then I won't touch you."

Relief surged through Melissa, mingled with another emotion that felt oddly like disappointment. "Thank you, my lord."

"Call me Chatleigh, at least. And don't thank me." His eyes bored into hers. "I shall want heirs someday."

Melissa shivered, but she forced herself not to look away. "Yes, of course. I too, would like children."

Justin returned the look, and let out a bark of laughter. "We'll see," he said, cryptically, and moved away from the mantel. "My apologies, madam. Got things to do. Still keep country hours for dinner?"

"Yes, of course," Melissa said, and watched him go, frowning. For the past few weeks she had had the Hall very much to herself, and she had grown accustomed to being in command. Now her husband had returned, and intended to take up the reins. It galled her that he hadn't said one word of praise, that he'd shown no gratitude for all the work she had done. After all, hadn't she done it for him?

Melissa went very still. Oh, Lord, she thought,

sinking down onto the sofa, her hands to her cheeks. If that was true, what would she do now?

The great house was quiet and all was in darkness, save for one room. That had been his father's study and now, Justin supposed, it was his. He sat in a tattered leather armchair, his long legs stretched towards the fireplace. An occasional flame from the dying fire lit his face, tense with strain, and glinted off the bottle of burgundy that stood on the table near his elbow. The low level of wine that remained testified to the fact that Justin had been sitting there for a very long time.

A log in the fireplace suddenly cracked in two and fell with a pop, sending sparks up the chimney. As if awakened by the sound, Justin stirred. Stretching, he reached for the bottle and poured the dregs into his goblet. Time for bed, he thought, and the corners of his lips twitched. Aye, time to go to an empty bed. He pictured his wife's sweetly rounded, soft body lying in the next room. He had remembered that she was a shrew, a schemer, but he had conveniently forgotten her beauty, her large, expressive eyes, her sweet smile, her very feminine form. Now he could not forget any of it. How he would sleep that night, he didn't know.

Outside, the wind, presaging the storms of winter, howled around the house; inside, Melissa instinctively huddled deeper in her bed, the comforter tucked around her. It had been an odd evening. Dinner had passed in silence, and afterward she had withdrawn, leaving her husband to his port and cigars. She hadn't seen him since, and surely she wasn't disappointed. Attractive though he was, tall and strong and far more handsome than she'd remembered, he had not proven to be the best of company. She would do very well without his presence.

And so she had gone to bed, alone, telling herself she was glad of it, cold though her bed was on this blustery night. Her sleep was dreamless and undisturbed. Until, that is, her door suddenly crashed open.

Melissa sat up with a start, her hand going to her heart, which was pounding alarmingly. The room was dark, except for the glow of a candle in the doorway, and, disoriented as she was, it took her a few moments to realize that the door led to the Earl's suite, adjoining her own. A figure moved through the opening and into her room. Her heart stopped, and then started again, pounding even louder. It was her husband. In spite of his assurances to her, he had come to claim his rights.

Chapter Eight

For a moment Justin stood in the doorway, unable to see beyond the glow of his candle, but knowing that his wife was awake and aware of him. With careful steps he walked farther into the room, and at last his eyes fell on Melissa, sitting up in bed, her eyes wide and dark, a mobcap set askew on her tumbled curls. He did not stop until he had reached the side of the bed.

So this was it, Melissa thought, staring up at him. His eyes glinted in the candlelight, so she was unable to assess his mood; but she suspected that he would deal with any opposition she might make easily and ruthlessly. His shirt was open at the neck to disclose the dark mat of his chest, and his hair was disordered. Most telling of all, however, was the scent of wine. Her husband had been drinking. Did he want her only when he was foxed?

"My lord?" she said, when the silence had gone on for too long. Justin started, like a sleepwalker awakened from a dream, and slowly reached out his hand. Melissa did not flinch, but watched it as it came close, expecting at any moment to feel its touch upon her cheek. She felt oddly suspended and expectant, and not at all afraid. If it were going to happen, then it would happen. "Justin."

Justin's hand suddenly jerked back. He stared down at her for a moment and then, abruptly, turned on his heel and walked away. A moment later the door closed behind him, and Melissa was again alone in the darkness, startled and bewildered.

"Has his lordship risen yet?" Melissa asked as she sat down at the table for her breakfast.

"Yes, my lady. He breakfasted some time ago," Phelps said, placing a cup of coffee before her.

"Really!" Melissa stared ahead for a moment, not seeing the rather dingy paint of the breakfast room's walls. She had forgotten that Chatleigh was not an idle aristocrat. After last night, she would have thought he'd sleep in, but he apparently had a very hard head. "Is he still in the house, do you know?"

"No, ma'am. Said he was going to check on the boy and then ride over the estate."

Melissa's head came up at that. "Really! Well. I must check on Georgie myself, poor child." She took a sip of coffee. "Thank you, Phelps, that will be all. Oh, and would you please let me know when the Earl does return?"

"Yes, my lady," Phelps said, and withdrew, leaving Melissa alone with her thoughts. She felt restless and unsettled this morning, and annoyed with her husband. Because he had come to her room, she told herself hastily, not because he had left.

It was midmorning when Justin, by way of Phelps, requested to see her. "Oh, bother!" she exclaimed, climbing down from the ladder upon which she had perched to dust the picture frames in the morning room. "And just look at me—tell him I'll be there presently, Phelps." Grumbling to herself, she dashed up to her room, pulling off the mobcap and running her fingers through her short curls. He couldn't have caught her at a worse time. She would have to change.

No. She paused in the act of unbuttoning her dress. Better that he see how hard she had been working. Hastily washing her face and dragging a comb through her hair, she turned away with a defiant sniff. Let him think what he would.

If Justin thought anything of her attire when she entered his study, he didn't show it, except, perhaps, for the slight quirk of his mouth. "Well?" Melissa said, and Justin's mouth quirked again. She looked like a child expecting to be punished yet determined not to show any fear. "You wished to see me?"

"Sit down." Justin gestured to a chair near the desk, and she sank into it, her head erect and her hands folded in her lap. Defiance and pride were so written into every line of her body that Justin found himself smothering a smile. He was feeling more kindly disposed towards her today, though he had a confused memory of going into her room last evening. He was quite certain that nothing had happened, however, and that was just as well. Better to avoid any entanglements with her, even if she was not quite what he had expected. Yesterday she had shown amazing fortitude and kindness, for a woman, in dealing with young Georgie Turner, and last evening she had looked quite alluring, in spite of her prim nightrail and cap. . . .

Which was something he would not think about, he told himself firmly, setting his mind on other topics. He was much more at ease this morning, well rested and well fed, and Mrs. Barnes had fussed over him as she should, making him feel welcome, at last, in his own house. For there was no question that the place did feel like a home again. The level of service was such as it had not been since his mother's time, and everything was clean. If the furniture were shabby and scarred, still not a speck of dust was allowed to mar it, and the windows sparkled in the sunshine. His wife's hard work was evident everywhere. Perhaps he had made a mistake yesterday, forbidding her to do more . . .

"Well?" Melissa said, breaking into his thoughts, and in her voice he heard just a touch of fear. "What did you wish to see me about?"

Justin straightened. "Been looking over the account books," he said, tapping the ones that lay piled on his desk with his finger.

"Oh? Oh."

"Correct me if I'm wrong. The Jenkinses were stealing?"

Melissa hesitated, and then slowly nodded. "Yes."

"Why the devil wasn't I told? No, don't answer that," he said, getting to his feet and waving his hand. "That is why you dismissed them?"

"I had to." Melissa looked up to where he stood by the window. "I've found out since that they had arrangements with the local shopkeepers, to pay more for inferior goods and to split the profits. And they would dismiss staff on their own authority, then pocket the wages. And—Well, I could go on, but it was clear they were bleeding the estate, and we couldn't have that! Besides," she added, "they wouldn't listen to anything I said."

Justin thrust his hands into his coat pockets. "Didn't think of bringing charges against them?"

"Well, I did, of course, but you know Sir Percival. I met him at church, and I'm afraid he thinks I'm dreadfully empty-headed." Justin smiled. Sir Percival Dutton, the local magistrate, did believe every woman

105

was empty-headed. "I didn't feel I could go ahead without support, my . . . Chatleigh, and so I dealt with it as best I could. If I could have reached you—"

"Pray do not reproach me any more on that score," he said, his voice icy, and Melissa sat back, her spirits sinking. When he spoke again, however, his tone had moderated. "You did the best you could."

"That's generous of you."

"But in the future you won't make such decisions alone."

"Oh, good." She smiled at him as he sat down again, which was not at all the reaction he had expected. "I must confess I had my doubts, but we are so much better off without them. They really were difficult to work with."

"I see. So, madam?" He looked at her hard. "What did you plan to do next?"

Melissa's spirits rose. It seemed she would have some influence in the running of this house, after all. "Hire more staff. I have the money—"

Justin crashed his hand on the desk and stood up again, very fast. "Damn, I wondered how long it would take you to bring that up."

"But it's foolish to ignore it! I do have it, there's nothing I can do about that, but as your wife surely I can use it to help you with the estate? I know you didn't want to marry me," she went on. "Perhaps this will make it easier."

Justin's back was to her, and so she couldn't tell his reaction. "I cannot be bought," he said, coolly.

"I didn't think you could," she retorted, her tone matching his. "But it's obvious the estate needs money."

"Damn it, I am not a damned fortune hunter."

"No, just a seducer of innocent young girls," she said, and he turned to stare at her. "That's what

106

you said."

Justin just looked at her for a moment, and then, to her surprise, let out a bark of laughter. "So, madam," he said, sitting down, "what do you propose to do?"

"Well, I really would like to hire more staff." She leaned forward, baffled and encouraged by his sudden affability. "We certainly need it! Heavens, this house hasn't been cleaned for years."

"I know," Justin murmured. "M'father preferred to spend his time in London, and m'brother and I were always away."

"Yes. Well, whatever the reason, it does need a lot of work, and I was hoping to redecorate." She looked up at him through her lashes. "If I could."

Justin let out another laugh. If she were using her wiles to influence him, he didn't mind. It was oddly pleasant. "Very well," he said, and leaned back, stretching out his legs and crossing them at the ankle. "What have you in mind?"

"Nothing drastic, I assure you. But there are so many repairs that are needed, and so much painting, if nothing else. There's damp in the music room, I'm afraid, and some of the windows need repairs, and as for my own rooms—"

"Spare me, madam." Justin held up his hand and Melissa subsided, looking up at him with such hope in her eyes that he found, to his great surprise, he could not disappoint her. "Very well. I'll give you carte blanche for the house. But," he said, at her exclamation of surprise, "no gilt." He ticked the remaining prohibitions off on his fingers as he spoke. "No Chinese things, no Egyptian, no Gothicky stuff. Understand?"

Melissa nearly bounced in her chair from excitement. "Yes, my lord!"

Justin gave her a look at that. "And I want the portrait of my mother removed from the drawing room."

"But," she began, and then stopped. "Oh, very well. But I will not put that hideous hunting painting back up."

"What, don't you like it?" he said, in so even a tone that she had to look at him twice to realize, by the glint in his eyes, that he was teasing her.

"You, sir, are a complete hand, and if you are not careful I will put a painting of the Regent himself there instead!"

"God forbid." Justin rose, as did Melissa, who was rather sorry that this odd interview was at an end. He was much more approachable than she had realized.

"Sir?" she said, pausing at the doorway, and Justin, seated behind the desk again, poring over the accounts, looked up. "Thank you."

"Go on now," he said, brusquely. "Got work to do."

"Yes, sir." Melissa closed the door softly behind her, but in the corridor outside she executed a spontaneous dance step. There was hope for the future, after all.

Christmas was fast approaching. The thought of spending the holiday without any of her beloved family, especially her mother, was enough to depress Melissa's spirits, but she had her pride. No one could guess at the grief hidden behind her impassive face as she supervised the placing of greens over the windows, garlands of laurel around the doorways, and then the construction of the kissing ball and the preparation of the Yule log. Staff there was a-plenty, now; Mr. Elliott, her man of affairs, had sent down a veritable army of servants, kitchen maids and footmen and a proper cook. With Mrs. Barnes to serve as housekeeper, the house was at last functioning as it should. Everything is going well, Melissa thought, standing back to study the garland she had just draped on the balustrade of the grand staircase: If only life weren't so lonely . . .

She saw little of her husband. He was busy, learning about his estate, and he had no time for a wife. Melissa suspected that he saw her as a nuisance; he never smiled at her, never spoke to her except on trivial matters, never seemed to want her company. Oh, that was fine with her, she assured herself, because she surely did not want to be close to him. It was, however, also frustrating. In the past weeks she had come to know and love the estate, and she was bursting with ideas on how to improve it, but she had no way to tell him. She, who had feared few people in her life, was oddly reluctant to approach this one man. Though he had shown her no violence, he had the power to inflict on her a hurt greater than any physical pain.

The fact that she was an heiress should have helped, but it didn't. Instead, he seemed to resent her money, and the uses to which she wished to put it, which only made matters more difficult. It was not the kind of marriage she wanted. Just what she did want, she wasn't sure, but when she'd been young, before she had met *him,* she had dreamed of a real marriage, a marriage for love. Though that wasn't possible now, surely she and her husband could deal together better than this? Perhaps she wouldn't mind if he decided to make the marriage real, if he again took her in his arms and—

The sound of the door knocker broke into her thoughts. "Oh, drat!" she exclaimed, hastily retreating up a few stairs, so as not to be visible from below. She was dressed in old clothes and she knew her face was dirty. All she needed at this moment were visitors. "Now what?"

Below her the new porter crossed the hall to open

the door. From her hiding place Melissa couldn't see the visitor, but his voice piped up to her. "I'm looking for Miss Melissa . . . I mean, Lady Chatleigh," he said.

Melissa, for a moment rooted to the spot, suddenly gripped the banister. "Harry," she whispered, and then said it again, in a loud, joyous cry. "Harry!"

The boy who stood in the doorway looked up as Melissa flew down the stairs, and a grin split his face. "Melissa! Oh, famous!" he exclaimed, his voice cracking on the last word.

"Harry." Melissa stopped short a few paces from him. "Your voice is changing." A tide of color, nearly matching the bright red of his hair, flooded into the youth's face. "Next thing we know, you'll be shaving! Oh, sorry, I didn't mean to embarrass you. But you've grown up so." She beamed at him, her brother, five years younger than she and yet, as always, looking oddly adult. Perhaps it was the spectacles that did it, she thought, reaching out and catching him in an enthusiastic embrace that he suffered stoically. "But what are you doing here?"

"I'm here to spend Christmas, if I may," he said, and at that moment the sound of boot heels on the marble tiles made them both turn.

"And what is this?" Justin asked, mildly enough, but brother and sister gave him identically wary looks.

"This is Harry, Chatleigh," Melissa said. "My brother. And this, Harry, is the Earl of Chatleigh."

"How do you do, sir," Harry said, his voice cracking again as he held out his hand. Justin took it, glancing at Melissa, and though he said nothing she read the question in his eyes.

"Harry is here to spend Christmas with us. If that is all right with you, Chatleigh?" she said.

Justin looked from one to the other, and the look on

110

Melissa's face, as if she were frightened of him, suddenly made him feel very tired. He shrugged. "Do as you wish. Doesn't matter to me."

"Chatleigh," Melissa said, as he turned away, but he didn't stop. "Oh, dear."

"Have I caused trouble for you, Lissa?" Harry asked, sounding very young and uncertain.

"No, of course not, I'm afraid that's just Chatleigh's way." She smiled reassuringly at him. "Now. Phelps will show you up to your room so you can wash off the dirt of the road, and then we'll have tea in the drawing room. Is that all you brought?" Melissa indicated his bag.

"No, there's one more in the chaise. Oh, Lissa the driver expects to be paid . . ."

"I'll handle it." She smiled. "Short of funds again?"

"Yes, you know Mr. Elliott keeps me on a short leash."

Melissa nodded. A new idea had just come to her, but now was not the time to mention it, not until she had a chance to talk with Chatleigh. "We'll see what we can do. Do go on upstairs, and I shall see you in a few moments."

"Yes. This will be a capital holiday!"

"I certainly hope so!" Her heart lighter than it had been in many a day, Melissa turned away to instruct Phelps to pay the driver of the post chaise. Christmas would not be so unbearable, after all.

It was late. Harry, exhausted from his journey, was abed, but Melissa could not sleep. Even the novel she had chosen from the library specifically for its soporific properties had failed to work; finally she tossed it aside. Harry's arrival had brought up problems that she had tried to submerge, and now they were preying on her mind. This afternoon she had glimpsed a possible solution. The question now was, did she have enough courage to go after it?

Well, of course she did, she assured herself as she stared at her reflection, running a comb through her curls. Though her hair was darker in shade than Harry's, both had inherited their coloring from their father. Just as Harry was definitely Major Selby's son, so was she his daughter, and she was not going to back down from a fight. The only trouble was, she was tired of the constant struggle.

Tapers in sconces lit the corridors and the staircase as she went in search of her husband. He retired late these days, spending the evening in his study. Melissa's heart was thudding a bit as she stopped before the door, and she took a deep breath before she knocked.

"Enter," Justin called from within.

She did and found the room in darkness, except for the fire in the hearth. Justin sat in an armchair near the fire, a nearly empty bottle on the table near him. Too late Melissa realized that he was probably foxed.

"Well?" he said, when she had stood for a few moments without speaking.

"May I speak with you?" she asked, her voice oddly breathless. Justin did not answers but merely inclined his head, a response she didn't find encouraging. "I've a problem."

"Have you?" He took a sip of his burgundy. "Something your money can't solve?"

"Oh, must you be so odious?" she snapped, and then controlled herself with an effort. "As it happens, it is money that is causing the problem. Harry's money, not mine. Do you know anything of our stepfather?"

Justin poured the dregs of the wine into his goblet. "Not much. Rum sort, isn't he?"

"Most decidedly a rum sort. And that is the problem." She leaned forward, her hands clasped upon her knees. "Mama was quite wealthy, and Papa controlled her money." She smiled, fleetingly. "Grandfather didn't trust aristocrats, you know, but he did like my father."

"Why are you telling me this?" he said, abruptly.

"It's important. Please, be patient for just a moment."

Justin shrugged "Very well."

"You've spoken with Mr. Elliott and so you know how my money was left. It came to me when I married you. Harry will get his when he reaches his majority. He also got Cleve Court." Her voice grew worried. "And that's the problem. When Sir Stephen married Mama he went through her jointure very quickly and then thought he could start on Harry's money. He claimed it was for improving the estate, and I'm afraid Mama believed him. She was one of the trustees, you see."

"Yes. Did he get it?"

"No. Mr. Elliott is the other trustee, and he always refused to give more than he thought necessary for the upkeep of Cleve Court. Unfortunately, Sir Stephen squandered whatever money there was and the estate went to rack and ruin."

"You sound bitter." Justin sounded interested for the first time. "What did he do to you?"

"Nothing very important," Melissa said in a stifled voice, and because her head was averted she didn't see the glance he shot her. "Oh, he wanted my money, too, but he didn't get it."

"I see." Idly Justin stroked his upper lip, not sure he did see. More here than met the eye. "So what, madam, is the problem?"

"The problem is, he's Harry's guardian and, oh, my lord, I'm worried! He can be a vicious man, I'm afraid

113

of what he'll do to Harry—"

"Should think Harry's safe enough at Eton."

"Ha! Did you attend Eton, sir?"

"Yes."

"And were you safe?"

Justin grimaced. "Not at first," he admitted. "But everyone has to go through it. Toughening up process."

"I'm afraid Harry isn't very tough."

"He had better learn how to be, else he won't survive. Boy's not a coward, is he?"

"No! But he has misinterpreted something Papa once said, about fighting never solving anything, so now he avoids it on principle. I'm afraid the other boys see it as cowardice."

"Of course."

"No 'of course' about it! I think it takes more courage to stand on principle than to fight, willy-nilly."

"Perhaps. Boys that age don't understand, though."

"No."

"So, madam?" he said, after a few moments. "What is it you want me to do?"

"About Eton? I suppose there's nothing we can do, short of withdrawing him, and I know his pride won't take that. It's the other problem. Sir Stephen," she said, when he looked at her quizzically. "Sir, do you think you could assume Harry's guardianship?"

"Good God!" Justin drained his glass and set it down with a thump. "You presume a great deal, madam. Not only do you trap me into marriage—"

"I didn't!"

"—but you take over my entire household, and now you think to saddle me with your family! Well, I will not have it. You may have taken over the Hall, but you cannot buy me."

"Oh, your stupid pride," she said, bitterly. "Poor

114

man, you're so put upon, aren't you? I've only brought you the fortune you need to restore this barn of a house—"

"By God, madam, you had best be careful!" Justin exclaimed, starting up from his chair.

"—and all you've done is whine and cry about it, like a little boy! To hear you tell it, nothing that has happened is your fault. Well, my lord, it is high time you grew up!"

"Be careful, madam. I will not answer for the consequences."

"No, you never do, do you? I think it is time you did, my lord, and—"

"If I didn't think of the consequences, madam, I would not have married you."

"And whose fault was it?"

"I warn you, madam, this is a dangerous subject," he said, very quietly. "I do not wish to discuss the circumstances of our marriage."

"But you've been well paid for it, have you not?"

"That tears it." He advanced upon her and, finally realizing she had gone too far, Melissa began to back up, turning only when she reached the door. But he was too quick for her. Before she could escape he caught her up in his arms and swung her over his shoulder, her face against his back and her backside poking in an undignified manner into the air while he held her legs.

"Put me down!" She pummeled his back with her fists as he strode along the corridors of the dark, quiet house and up the grand staircase. "Put me down at once!"

"Cease to struggle, madam, or you will fall on your head," he said, calmly. In spite of the burden of carrying her, his breathing was normal.

"Oh, please!" she wailed. "Put me down, I promise I

115

won't bother you . . ."

"Rather late for that, madam. You were warned."

"Oh, this is so undignified!"

"Now who is the one with pride?" he said, and dumped her unceremoniously on her bed.

Chapter Nine

For a moment, there was silence. Melissa stared up at him, her skirts rucked up to her knees, exposing shapely ankles and calves clad in practical cotton stockings. Her breasts rose and fell with her agitated breathing, and her eyes were huge in her pale face, surrounded by tumbled, disordered curls. The angry frustration that had driven Justin on suddenly died. God, but she was beautiful, and she was his. It was that which had driven him to the bottle these past nights: the frustration of knowing that her soft, sweetly rounded body should, by all rights, belong to him; the agony of knowing that claiming it was folly. He didn't want to succumb to her wiles, but it was hard to remember that now, with the blood thrumming in his veins and the urge to make her his own pushing him on. By God, she was his wife!

He reached out. Melissa, impeded by her skirts, scuttled away. "No!" she gasped. "You promised—"

"You are my wife."

"But I will not be your whore!"

That stopped him. The memory of once calling her that came back to him, and with it the knowledge that what he had been about to do was folly. With an oath he turned, slamming the bedroom door behind him and roundly cursing himself for a fool. And, once again, Melissa was left alone.

The ground, crisp with frost, crunched under Justin's feet as he left the house by a side door the next morning. Early rising was ingrained in him after his years in the military, and still, no matter how late he'd been up, he rarely missed his morning ride. The gallop helped clear his mind and prepared him to face the day ahead. After the events of the past night, he certainly welcomed these benefits. He had bungled things, all right.

The path to the stables turned, and abruptly, through a break in the trees, the valley opened before him, so naturally that it was easy to forget this vista had been planned by a master. His land. In the gray light mists rose from the fields, brown and sere now with the coming of winter. Nothing grew, yet suddenly his heart swelled as he surveyed his holdings, love and pride and a fierce possessiveness welling in him. This was his! He would do whatever he must to hold onto it, everything he could to bring it back to full life. And, when the estate was running well and he was again making an income, he would pay back every penny his wife had expended on it. Perhaps then he wouldn't feel so beholden.

He frowned as he continued down the path, absently tapping his riding crop against his leg. Odd to feel this way. He'd known he'd have to marry money, and by a most unusual turn of events he had found himself with a fortune. Aye, and a wife who was not only beautiful, but hard-working and competent, kind and compassionate, brave and—

Bah! He slashed at a tree with his crop. He sounded like a lovesick moonling. So his wife did have some good qualities. Perhaps. He must never forget, however, the deviousness that lurked behind that pretty face. Women were not to be trusted. He'd learned that long ago.

Voices floated out to him from the stable as he passed under the archway, the clock in the tower above striking the half-hour. He stopped in the doorway a moment. Jeffrey, the groom, had Diablo out of the stall already and was just saddling him, difficult though it was; Diablo was in a restive mood, prancing about and promising Justin a fine ride. Justin's mouth quirked when he saw who Jeffrey's companion was. Perched on a mounting block, chattering away to the groom, was Harry.

"Morning," Justin said, advancing into the stables, and Jeffrey looked up from tightening the girth.

"Morning, milord. Him's proper restless today," he said.

"So I see. Morning, Harry."

"Good morning, my lord!" Harry stood at attention, for all the world like a soldier on parade. Justin glanced at him, feeling an unwilling sympathy. Hard at that age to be at all different from the other fellows. Harry's spectacles, Justin suspected, made life difficult for him.

"Do you ride, Harry?" he asked casually, stepping over to Diablo and running a hand down his flank. The horse nickered and then butted his head against Justin's arm.

"Yes, sir, but I'm afraid I didn't bring any gear."

"Daresay we could fit you up with something."

"Really? You mean it, sir?"

"Yes. Jeffrey, have we any boots that Master Selby could use?"

"I'll see, milord." Jeffrey stepped away from the horse and headed for the tack room.

"Oh, famous! I haven't ridden in ever so long."

"Can't promise you a good ride." Justin reached into his pocket for a carrot, and the stallion nibbled at it eagerly. "Afraid the stables need restocking."

"My sister told me about the Hall," Harry said, so intent on the horse that he didn't see Justin wince. "I have the same problem with Cleve Court."

Justin looked up at that. "Have you?"

"Yes. My stepfather's run it into the ground. Bang up bit of blood, sir," he added admiringly as the stallion suddenly took exception to something only he could see and began to dance about.

"Diablo? Yes, a good mount." Justin, keeping an iron hand on the bridle, smiled at the horse.

"Diablo?"

"Spanish for devil. Good-tempered, for all that."

"You were in Spain, sir?" Harry's eyes grew wide. "Melissa didn't tell me! Did you know my father? Major Selby of the Light Division?"

"Knew him well. I was in his regiment."

"You were? Oh, famous! Were you at Vittoria last June or Talavera or—"

"Talavera, yes, and unless I'm mistaken here are some boots for you." Justin stepped back as the groom came back, carrying a well-worn pair of boots.

" 'Twere Master Philip's, when he were just a lad," Jeffrey said. "Here, Master Harry, try them on."

"Oh, capital!" Harry sat down on a bench and pulled the boots on, and Justin watched him, a little smile playing about his lips. It had been a long time since he had been so enthusiastic about anything, let alone something so simple as a ride. For the first time he wondered just what kind of lives his wife and her brother had led.

Jeffrey led out a bay mare. "Not as prime a bit as that there Diablo," he said, "but a sweet goer all the same." Justin, already mounted, watched the boy dispassionately as Jeffrey gave him a leg up. Good hands, and a good seat.

"Does your sister ride?" Justin asked.

"Yes. Sir, will you tell me about Spain?"

"What?" Justin turned as they walked their horses out of the stableyard. Since his return to England he had spoken little of his experiences in battle on the Peninsula. Most people, he had quickly learned, were far too concerned with their own pleasure to be interested, and until recently support for Wellington's troops had not been widespread. It was rare to see such enthusiasm in anyone's face. "Very well, halfling," he said, and pointed with his crop. "That way."

So it was that some time later Harry, his clothes mussed and his glasses askew, burst into the breakfast parlor, where Melissa was just dealing with the morning mail. She set down the roll she had been about to bite into and looked up at him. "And where have you been?" she asked, her dancing eyes belying the sternness of her tone. This morning Harry looked like a boy again.

"It was famous, Lissa!" Harry pulled out a chair. "Chatleigh let me ride with him!"

Melissa wrinkled her nose at the smell of horse. "I might have guessed."

"Chatleigh told me all about the Peninsula and all the battles he was in, and all about Papa! Why didn't you tell me he knew Papa?"

Melissa's startled eyes met Justin's as he paused in the doorway, and he had the grace to look ashamed. She looked at him for a long moment before turning away. "It must have slipped my mind. Have you breakfasted, my lord?" she asked, coolly.

"Yes, before riding. Hope you don't mind I took Harry along?" he said, in milder tones than she had

121

yet heard from him. The circles under her eyes were dark this morning, and Justin felt an unaccustomed sense of guilt.

"No, of course not. I was worried about finding ways to entertain him."

"Enjoyed it. Excuse me now. Got work to do." He inclined his head and turned away, and Melissa glared at his back. What had happened last evening was something she would not soon forget.

" . . . and he said I could ride with him whenever I wanted, and oh, Lissa, he offered to teach me how to box!"

"What?" Melissa came out of her daze. "He did?"

"Yes, he said it's true, fighting doesn't solve things, but sometimes you have to fight, whether you want to or not."

"But that's what I've been trying to tell you for years!"

"Yes, but you're a girl. And he says that you have to stand up to bullies or they think you're a coward, and where would we be if we hadn't stood up to Napoléon?"

"True." Melissa brought her napkin to her mouth to hide her smile. It seemed her husband had listened to her last night, and had chosen to do something about it. It wasn't like him, but she was not going to question it. "I'm glad, Harry." She rose. "You could have a worse teacher."

"You don't like him much, do you?" Harry said, his eyes suddenly penetrating behind his spectacles.

"Why, what a question! Would I have married him, else?"

"I don't know. You hardly talk to each other, and he didn't even know you rode." Harry's gaze was accusing. "And he's the most capital fellow."

"That's enough out of you, young man!" Melissa

122

said, sharply. "What happens between the Earl and me is not your concern. Do you understand?"

"Yes." Harry stared sullenly at his plate. "You never used to be this bossy."

"Times have changed." Melissa looked down at his bent head and forced herself not to ruffle his hair. He was growing up, she thought wistfully. "What do you plan to do today?"

Harry looked up. "Read, I suppose. I have a lot to do before next term and Chatleigh says his library is excellent."

Melissa suspected that she would soon grow tired of hearing what Chatleigh said, but she only nodded. "Don't wear your eyes out," she said, and this time she did ruffle his hair.

Harry ducked his head and applied himself to his breakfast. *Girls!* he thought in disgust.

Sometime later Justin leaned back in his chair and glanced out the window. The morning's clouds had burned off, and the day was bright. Won't be many more days like this before winter, he thought, and reluctantly turned back to the estate account books spread over the leather surface of his desk. Melissa had been right, though it pained him to admit it. His agent had done his best, but the Hall had felt the lack of a master's presence over the years. Justin had never had much interest in an estate his father would not let him manage, but now he felt an almost primeval urge to control his land. He wanted to walk over his holdings, learn about them and the people who worked them. Instead, he seemed fated to obtain his knowledge second-hand.

There was a discreet knock on the door and Phelps came in, holding a silver salver. "Forgive me for disturbing you, my lord," he said, bowing, and Justin fleetingly reflected that this was another instance in which his wife had been right. In spite of a few mistakes, Phelps was turning into an excellent butler. "Are you receiving visitors?"

Justin held out his hand for the salver. "Who is it, Phelps? Anyone I know?"

"I couldn't say, my lord. But her ladyship told me never to admit him to the house."

Justin had taken the black-bordered card from the salver, and he now looked questioningly up at Phelps. "Does she know he's here?"

"No, my lord. She's in the music room with the builder."

"Good. Don't tell her. And I will see him."

"Very good, sir." Phelps bowed and left the room, and Justin got up, to look out the window. So, he was finally to meet the infamous Sir Stephen Barton. After what Melissa had told him last evening he had to admit to more than a passing curiosity about the man. What had Barton done to make her so bitter and fearful?

"Sir Stephen Barton, my lord," Phelps announced from the door, and Justin turned. Immediately he felt a wave of distaste so strong it stunned him. Never in his life had he taken so quick, or so unreasonable, an aversion to anybody.

Years of army staff life stood him in good stead as he came forward, hand outstretched. "How do you do?" he said, formally, quickly assessing the other man. On the surface there was nothing out of the ordinary about him, nothing to cause that clenching of Justin's muscles. Dressed conventionally in mourning, he was tall and thin almost to the point of emaciation. Thinning hair of an indeterminate shade between blond and gray was brushed back from a high forehead, and his face with its sunken cheeks was dominated by a hawklike nose, giving him the look of a cadaver. Only his mouth, unexpectedly full and red, gave the lie to that impression. "I am Chatleigh."

"Good of you to see me," Sir Stephen said, taking his hand.

"Not at all." Justin motioned the other man to one of the armchairs flanking the fireplace. "Care for a cigarillo? Bad habit of mine. Picked it up on the Peninsula."

"Thank you, don't mind if I do." Sir Stephen looked up at Justin again as he chose a cheroot from the mahogany box held out to him. "So you're an army man, are you?"

"Yes." Justin blew out a cloud of smoke. "Knew your predecessor, as it happens."

"Excuse me?"

"Major Selby."

Sir Stephen's pale eyes darkened for just a moment. "Is my daughter here?"

"She's somewhere in the house," Justin said, dismissing her with a wave of the cigarillo. "Believe Harry's in the library."

"Harry!" Sir Stephen straightened. "Harry's here? I thought he was at Eton."

"Came to spend Christmas with us." Justin studied the tip of his cigarillo. "Putting up at the Crown?"

"What? Oh, no. I'm staying with friends."

Bad luck for the friends, whoever they were, Justin thought, and reached a decision. It did not matter why Melissa and Harry disliked their stepfather, Justin didn't want him in the house either. He would not invite him to stay. "So what can I do for you?"

"I wanted to see how my daughter's settling in. How is she, by the by?"

"Quite well. Keeping busy." Justin gestured about

the room. "House needs a woman's touch."

"Quite so. And her money as well." Justin looked up sharply at that, but Sir Stephen went on before he could say anything. "Did you know, I didn't even realize you and my daughter were acquainted?"

"Met through her father," Justin said, easily.

Sir Stephen's eyes darkened at this obvious lie. "That's not what I heard. I understand you met in an inn."

Justin drew in on his cigarillo. "Oh?"

"Yes. The Hart and Hind, to be precise."

"We met there, certainly. But not for the first time."

"Do you take me for an idiot?" Sir Stephen's eyes suddenly blazed. "I heard what happened there. She's made me the laughingstock of the village. I deserve some recompense for that."

Ah, now we come to it. Justin had been expecting this since the beginning of the interview. No longer, however, did he believe that Melissa was behind it. "Harry's money not enough for you?"

"What!" Sir Stephen sat bolt upright. "Are you implying—"

"Speaking of Harry, I'd like to talk to you about him. Or, rather, my man of affairs will talk to your man."

"About what?" Sir Stephen looked wary.

"About assuming Harry's guardianship. Well really, old man, you can't wish to be saddled with another man's brat—"

"Never!" Sir Stephen had jumped to his feet. "That is a sacred trust his mother placed in me, and I will never give it up."

"I see." Justin drew on his cigarillo and then looked up at the other man, his eyes suddenly keen. "Nevertheless. plan to pursue the matter."

"Want all the money for yourself, do you, Chatleigh? I'll fight you on this."

"Do so." Justin rose. There was nothing menacing in his aspect, but Sir Stephen shrank back. "But I warn you. You'll not see a penny from me."

"No? And what, sir, will people say when they learned how you seduced my daughter? You'll be singing a different song then, I'll wager!"

Justin crossed to the bellpull. "I don't give a damn what you do, Barton, but I will not tolerate you bothering me. Or mine."

"Are you threatening me?"

"Take it as you like. Phelps, please call for Sir Stephen's carriage."

"Yes, my lord. If you'll come this way, sir?" Phelps said.

Sir Stephen looked indecisively from one to the other, and then turned. "Very well. But we are not finished, my lord." He gave Justin a look. "No. We are not finished."

Justin bowed, looking bored, and went back to his desk. He was half-turned, looking out the window, when Phelps knocked again on the open door. "Yes, Phelps, what is it?" he asked.

"Excuse me, my lord. Is Sir Stephen to be admitted in future?"

"No. On this, I agree with her ladyship."

"Very good, my lord." Phelps went to the door, and then turned. "My lord?"

"What the devil is it now?" Justin said, looking up from the account books.

"Jeffrey, the groom, says as how he's seen Sir Stephen on the estate once or twice."

"Really." Justin leaned back, tapping his pen against his hand. "Does Lady Chatleigh ever ride out alone?"

"No, my lord."

"Good. Inform Jeffrey she's never to go out alone."

127

"My lord, you don't think—"

"That Sir Stephen would try to harm her?" An unbidden memory came to Justin, of Melissa on that fateful night at the inn, willing to marry a stranger rather than return to her own home. For some reason, she was terrified of Sir Stephen. The thought infuriated him. "I don't know, Phelps. Best to be safe, though, isn't it?"

"Yes, my lord." Phelps bowed and closed the door behind him, and Justin was left alone with his thoughts.

". . . but I tell you, Lissa, he was here."

"It couldn't have been him, Harry," Melissa said, and in the corridor outside the drawing room, Justin paused, his hand on the knob of the half-open door. "Surely he's back at Cleve Court by now?"

"I don't know, Lissa, but it looked like him."

"It can't have been!" Melissa's voice was shaky with panic, and Justin deemed it time to intervene. Pushing the door open, he walked in, and brother and sister looked up at him, wearing identically startled, guilty expressions.

"Mind if I join you?" he said.

"There, he'll tell you!" Harry jumped up. "Was our stepfather here today, sir?"

Justin's eyes sought out Melissa. "Yes, Harry, he was."

"I told you so, Lissa!" Harry said, triumphantly.

"What . . . what did he want?" Melissa's hand was at her throat, and her voice sounded strangled.

"Merely to make my acquaintance, I believe. Are those rock cakes I see?" Justin sat on the sofa across from Melissa.

"Yes, they're capital, and the scones! Shall I toast

one for you, sir?" Harry said, jumping up again.

"If you like. I sent him away." Justin said, his eyes never leaving Melissa's face. "He won't be back."

Melissa's tense shoulders suddenly slumped. "Are you sure of that?"

Justin nodded. "Yes. Tell me," he reached for the cup of tea she handed him, "why does he frighten you so?"

"Melissa's not scared of anybody," Harry said, scornfully, coming back from the fire with the toasted scone. "But we both think Sir Stephen's a toad."

"Harry!" Melissa said.

"Well, he is. You think so, too."

"A snake, more like." Justin spread jam and clotted cream on the scone and bit into it. "You're right, Harry. Capital."

Melissa looked from one to the other. Men! The world could be falling to pieces and all they would care about would be their precious stomachs. "I'm glad you enjoy your tea, my lord," she said, frigidly.

Justin glanced at her. "Always did," he said, his tone mild. "Been a long time since I had it in this room, though." His eyes roamed around, noting with approval the changes she had made and stopping briefly at the spot where his mother's portrait had once hung. A landscape hung there now. "M'father wasn't much for tea. Not much for anything, besides his hounds and his gambling."

"Did he hunt, sir?" Harry asked, his eyes suddenly eager.

"Indeed he did. Kept the best stables and the best kennels around. Boxing Day hunt used to meet here all the time. Now Sir Percival hosts it."

"But now you're here, sir. Couldn't we have it again?"

"Afraid not, Harry." Justin smiled at him. "For one

thing, I sold him m'father's hounds. Had no use for them myself."

"No use!" Harry stared at this bit of heresy, and his adoration of Justin, his hero, slipped a little. "But, sir—"

"I couldn't afford to feed them, Harry. And, no, I won't house them again," he went on, before Harry could speak. "Money could be better spent elsewhere."

"But a hunt would be capital, sir," Harry protested.

Justin glanced over at Melissa, who was struggling with a smile. "Perhaps. But perhaps your sister has other ideas?"

Melissa looked up. "Excuse me?"

"Been thinking. Been a long time since we entertained guests here. With Christmas almost here—"

"We could have a party!" Melissa exclaimed. "Oh, I wish you might have thought of this sooner, there's so much to do, invitations to send and the menu to plan, and should we just have dinner or dancing afterwards, and—"

"Melissa." Justin was grinning at her, but it was his use of her name that stopped her. "Plenty of time to plan something. For Twelfth Night, perhaps?"

"Oh, splendid!" Melissa clapped her hands. "We could have a masque, with people coming as Twelfth Night characters . . . that is, if you don't mind?"

"Don't mind at all." Justin was still smiling. "Time we have some life back in this house. M'father used it only during hunting season, and Philip and I have been gone for years."

"I'd like to meet your brother," Melissa said. "Do you think he'll get home on leave soon?"

Justin looked down into the fire, and his smile faded. "Maybe. With Wellington in France, the army will likely be home soon," he said moodily, kicking the fender. In October Wellington's troops had invaded

130

France, and there was talk that peace negotiations would begin soon in Vienna. The long war was nearly over, and all England was excited.

Harry looked up from toasting another scone. "You don't sound happy about it, sir," he said.

"Well, no matter," Melissa said quickly. If Harry didn't know the reason behind Justin's sudden silence, she had an excellent idea. "It's a shame none of your family can be here, Chatleigh, but perhaps we could invite your Aunt Helmsley?"

"Is that supposed to make me feel better?" Justin asked, his eyes gleaming.

"I like her."

"Yes, well, she doesn't bully you."

"She tried. She means well, Chatleigh."

"God save me from people who mean well."

Melissa smiled. "I know. She does like to have her own way. But I think that underneath she's a very lonely lady —"

"Ha!"

"Oh, think what you will! I think we should invite her."

Justin stared at her a moment. He was getting a very different impression of his wife than he had had, and it disconcerted and intrigued him. Perhaps she was not as self-seeking as he had thought. "Oh, very well, madam, you win this round! Invite her, if you will."

"I shall. It will be good to have guests here. The house is so large, one tends to rattle around."

"Mm." Absently Justin raked through his hair, and Melissa had the odd urge to smooth it down. "Been a long time since there were parties here. Not since m'mother's time."

"What was she like?" Melissa asked impulsively, and the shuttered look she so disliked came on his face.

131

"Rather not discuss her." He stood away from the mantel, dusting his hands together. "Now, if you'll excuse me, I have those account books to look over."

He strode from the room, and Melissa looked after him in dismay. "Oh, dear!"

"What was that all about?" Harry said, looking up from the fire.

"I don't know, Harry," she said, frowning, and sat back. Oh, dear, and just when things had been going well between them. He had been friendly, approachable, and in spite of herself hope had risen in her that perhaps matters could be improved between them. But that wouldn't happen if he continued to hold her at arm's length. Something, she decided, would have to be done.

Justin was dozing, sitting upright in a chair in his room, when a noise, the cry of a woman in trouble, jerked him out of his sleep. He stumbled to his feet, bumping against a nearby table, and the bottle of wine that stood upon it slowly tipped over, falling to the floor with a crash and rolling away. It threatened to trip him as he shambled across the floor, and for a moment he teetered dangerously, his arms flailing. Then, overbalanced, he stubbed his stockinged foot and was hopping on the other when at last he managed to open the door that connected his room with his wife's. He nearly fell through it, then came up short. The room was empty, except for Melissa, tossing restlessly in her bed.

God, she was just having a bad dream, he thought, plunging his fingers into his hair, and he would have turned to go had she not cried out again. His lips briefly set in a straight line. *Damn, suppose I ought to do something about this.* Maybe she wasn't in danger physically, but a nightmare could be an unpleasant thing.

"Melissa," he said, calling her name softly. When there was no response he crossed the room and stared helplessly down at her. Why must she be so damned attractive? he wondered, and reached out, finally, reluctantly, to touch her shoulder. "Melissa."

She jerked awake, her breath drawing in sharply, her whole body pulling back from his hand. "Don't touch me, don't you dare touch me! Oh! Chatleigh!" She stared up at him, her eyes dark and wide with fear.

"Yes, who did you expect?"

"I . . . no one," she said, but her eyes refused to meet his. "Just a dream." She shook her head, and, mesmerized, he watched her curls, unbound and tangled, sway with the motion. "I'm all right, Chatleigh. You can go back to bed."

He stood, uncertainly, in the middle of the floor. If he just reached out, just a little bit, he could touch her, feel the soft silk of her skin under his fingers. The urge was so strong that he couldn't help himself.

She flinched as he raised his hand, and he let it drop. "Wish you good night, madam," he said, and stalked back into his room.

His lips twitched with annoyance as he stared at the spilled wine. All that, and it had been just a dream. But he couldn't help wondering, as he straightened up the mess, just what it was his wife feared. And he wondered, now that he had seen her and so nearly touched her, how he would make it through the night.

Sir Stephen was not a forgiving man. He never forgot an insult, and he never missed a chance for revenge. He had expected that evening to be sleeping between fine linen sheets, dining on the choicest of viands and sampling the vintage in the Earl's wine cellar. Instead, he had eaten a rough supper of brown bread and crumbling cheese, and then had sought his bed in the small, rudely furnished room that was all this hedge tavern had to offer. The sheets, he was certain, hadn't been aired in months, let alone changed, and he feared the bed was infested. He would not soon forgive the Earl of Chatleigh for this.

The rough straw mattress crackled as he turned over, staring into the darkness and fuming at the treatment he had been accorded that afternoon. He was Sir Stephen Barton, damn it! What right had his lordship, the high-and-mighty Earl, to treat him so? Were it not for the Jenkinses, Sir Stephen would not have a place to sleep. He had not lied when he'd told Chatleigh that he stayed with friends; just now the Jenkinses, who had procured these lodgings, were the best allies he had.

But not for long. They would serve his purpose admirably, but once they had, they would have to go. Sir Stephen had no intention of associating with such rough company once his fortunes had been restored. And restored they would be. Chatleigh would pay, he assured himself, and so would Melissa. And with more than money.

At last, he thought, grinning evilly and fell asleep contemplating his revenge.

Chapter Ten

The crunching of gravel on the newly raked drive heralded the arrival of visitors. From his study window Justin glanced out and then ran his fingers through his hair. "Oh, damn," he muttered, and pulled on the coat he'd discarded during his session with the estate books. It was Christmas Eve. Lady Helmsley had arrived, and would be with them until at least Twelfth Night. How Justin was going to survive the next fortnight, he didn't know.

"Made some changes, haven't you, girl?" Augusta's voice was booming out, accompanied by the thump of her cane, as Justin came into the hall.

"Some. Not many." Melissa's voice was light and musical in contrast. "The main thing was getting everything clean."

"About time. There you are, boy. High time you came to greet me."

Justin took a deep breath and stepped forward. "Hello, Aunt. Good to see you again."

"Hmph." Augusta raised her cheek for his kiss. "Look like a country squire. Weston never made that coat."

"No, as a matter of fact, he didn't," Justin said, his affability unimpaired. "Have a pleasant journey?"

"No, I did not, much you care! Just you take care you don't get too comfortable, here in the country," she continued as she made her stately progress towards the stairs. "London's where you should be."

"London?" Melissa said.

"Of course. Parliament opens next month. High time you took your seat there." She directed this last observation to Justin.

He looked at Melissa before answering. "Been thinking about that, Aunt, and—"

"Don't think, boy. Always get into trouble when you do."

Justin's face darkened. Melissa cast a hasty look back at him and then propelled the old lady towards the stairs. "You must be tired after your journey, Aunt. Let me show you to your room."

"Thank you, you're a good girl. Don't know what that nevvie of mine did to deserve you."

There was a stifled expletive from the floor below. Melissa looked down to see her husband turn on his heel, and smiled. Chatleigh, she suspected, was in for a rough time.

Melissa had just reached the bottom of the stairs a few moments later when Justin suddenly loomed up before her. She was briefly annoyed that, in all the space of the hall he still managed to get in her way, and then her annoyance faded. It was rare that she was this close to him, so she sometimes forgot just how tall he was, how broad his shoulders were.

"Sorry," Justin said, and stepped back, his voice breaking into her thoughts. Melissa's face colored furiously. "Got the old dragon settled?"

"Chatleigh!" she exclaimed, but her eyes danced. "Yes, she was going to rest for a while. I think she is not so strong as she pretends."

"She'll outlive us all." His voice was gloomy. "When I'm old she'll still be telling me what to do."

"Nonsense. Though what was that about London?"

Justin looked down at her for a moment, and then made his decision. "Come," he said, turning, and Me-

136

lissa had no choice but to follow.

He led her to his study, indicating a chair by the fire. "I wish you would let me do something with this room," she said, looking around at the clutter, the shabby furniture, the threadbare carpet. "At least let the maids in to clean."

"It's fine. Now." He sat across from her, feet planted firmly on the floor, elbows resting on his knees. "About London. M'aunt has me pegged for a political career."

"What? You?"

He stared at her. "Not that funny."

Melissa controlled her mirth with an effort. "No, of course not. But you don't like to talk, and isn't that what politicians do?"

"Damned windy lot, most of 'em. Never have been too interested in taking it up." He leaned back, staring into the fire. "Though sometimes I've wondered if I could do some good, at least shake 'em up a bit. The way they behave, wouldn't even know there was a war on."

"But surely they're behind Wellington."

"Yes. Now, when he's winning. Where were they when he needed them?"

"Papa used to say the same thing."

"Your father talked to you about such things?"

"Papa talked to me about a lot. He had to. Mama wouldn't have understood." She glanced away, blinking rapidly.

"And how old were you?" he asked, softly.

"I was fourteen when he died. But that's neither here nor there." She straightened. "The question now is, are you going to do as your aunt wishes?"

Justin looked into the fire. "Easiest thing, I suppose."

"That's no reason!"

"It is if you know my aunt. Once she gets the bit between her teeth, hard to make her stop. She even chose . . ."

"What?" Melissa asked, when he didn't go on.

137

"A bride for me," he said, unwillingly. "Before I knew you, of course."

"You were engaged?" She stared at him. "No wonder you were so angry with me!"

Justin shifted in his seat. "Not that at all. Truth is, don't know if I would have married Eleanor. Wasn't a love match, if that's what you're thinking."

Melissa let the silence lengthen. Perhaps theirs wasn't a love match either, but she felt a sudden, unreasoning jealousy of the unknown Eleanor. Whoever this woman was, Melissa was going to prove that she could be just as suitable a wife. "What do you want to do?"

Justin looked up. "Truthfully? Go back to the army." Melissa didn't want to analyze the pain that went through her. "But I can't. I am the Earl, now. Owe something to the name."

Melissa lowered her head to hide the color that flooded into her face. To get an heir, she supposed he meant. "But even so, Chatleigh," she said, when she had command of herself again, "you couldn't stay in the army forever. The war will end someday, and what then?"

"I don't know." He leaned his head against the back of the chair. "Can't see myself doing nothing, like some damned dandy. Trouble is, I don't have any training, except for the military."

"But you went to university."

"Yes." He glanced over at her, deep in thought, gnawing on a fingernail, and unaware of his look. Been a long time since anyone had put so much thought towards what he might want to do rather than what he should do. It was oddly warming.

"Chatleigh," she said, and straightened. "You must know a lot of people? From the military and from school?"

"Yes, so?"

"Well, wouldn't that help you if you took your seat in

Parliament? No, hear me out." She held up her hand to forestall his protest. "I think you'd be better at it than you believe, and you might like it. At least, perhaps you should try."

"M'aunt put you up to this?"

"No, of course not, this is my idea. Chatleigh, don't you see? You owe it to yourself to try. At least go to London—"

"I see," he said, his voice odd. "You want to go to London."

"Well, yes, of course I do." Her eyes grew dreamy. "I've always wanted to go there."

"And you'd use me to get there." Foolish of him to have thought, even for a moment, that she was actually concerned about him. He should have remembered what she was, a conniving little witch willing to do anything to achieve her own ends. Like all women.

Melissa was staring at him. "That's not it at all!"

"Isn't it?"

"No! Oh, for heaven's sake, I don't do things like that!"

"As I recall, you did at the inn, like a common—"

Melissa eyes flashed as she jumped to her feet. "Like a common whore," she said, bitterly. "Oh, believe what you want. You will, anyway."

Justin held her gaze for a few seconds, and then turned away, kicking at the fender. "Sorry, princess," he said. "This time you won't get what you want."

Melissa's hands clenched into fists, and then she whirled, whisking out the door. Justin sank back into the chair, staring into the fire. He had been foolish to let his guard down, to forget what she was, but it was a mistake he wouldn't make again. He would keep his distance from her. It was better that way, he told himself, and almost believed it. Almost.

* * *

139

Christmas morning dawned frosty and cold. The party from the Hall attended services at St. Mary's, arriving in Lady Helmsley's barouche and sitting in the black leather-lined pew that had long been reserved for the Chatleighs. All around them was the stir of movement and murmuring. That the Earl was in residence with his new Countess was no longer a source of wonder to the villagers, but they were still curious. The estate and, to a certain extent, the village had suffered under the old Earl's proprietorship. It remained to be seen just what his successor would do.

The staff was assembled in the hall to greet them when they returned, and for the first time in years Justin felt that this really was his home. It had been a long time since anyone had welcomed him so warmly. It had been a long time, too, since the house had been decorated, with velvet ribbons of red and green festooning long ropes of greens, and the kissing ball hanging in a doorway. Melissa paused briefly under it as she handed her pelisse and gloves to a maid. Justin looked at her speculatively and then turned away, to go to the drawing room.

"The fire feels good," Augusta admitted, sinking onto the sofa nearest the fireplace. Today her turban was of red and gold brocade, and her gown of cherry red satin, decked with cascades of lace at throat and sleeves, had a holiday air. By contrast Melissa, in the unrelieved black of mourning, looked pale and colorless. "Demmed cold out there. Took down Amelia's portrait, I see."

"Who?" Melissa turned from the table in the corner.

"My mother," Justin said quietly, as he came into the room and sat on the sofa facing his aunt. "Asked her to."

Augusta favored him with a long look. "I see."

"Harry, will you help me, please?" Melissa requested, and her brother went over to her. In a moment both were back, their arms piled with gaily wrapped packages. Justin's heart sank. Presents! Giving presents at Christmas was a custom just recently made popular by the Duchess of York; he had been away for so long he had forgotten about it.

And what would he have given to his wife, he wondered, watching her as she knelt on the floor, as enthusiastic as a child. He knew nothing about her, her likes or dislikes, her hopes or fears, and though that was by choice, there were times when he was filled with an overwhelming curiosity about her. What was it that had driven her to so desperate an act as trapping a stranger into marriage? Surely she could have found a husband without resorting to such measures. She was warmhearted — one had only to see her with little Georgie Turner, still recovering from his injury, to know that — lively and likable, and too damned attractive for his peace of mind. He had almost begun to believe that he had done well in his choice of a wife. Perhaps that was why yesterday's reminder of her opportunism, her willingness to use him to get what she wanted, had struck him so hard.

". . . and this is for you, Lady Helmsley," Melissa was saying, as she laid a package on Augusta's lap. "I know it isn't much, but — "

"On the contrary, child," Augusta said, with such a note in her voice that Justin looked up, distracted from his thoughts. She lifted a woolly, lacy shawl from the box. "Thank you, child, and how did you know that these old bones are always cold?"

Melissa smiled. "From my grandmother, ma'am."

"Not Lady Townsend!"

"No, my grandmother Honeywell," Melissa replied, still smiling. "The one who was in trade."

"Hmph. And did you make this?"

"I did."

"Hmph. Should be making baby clothes." Melissa turned pink, and Augusta turned her eyes towards Justin, who was studiously avoiding her gaze. "Well, boy?"

"Sorry, afraid I forgot about presents," he said hastily, before his aunt could quiz him on the prospect of an heir.

"Hmph!" Augusta glared at him. "About what I expected, boy."

"It doesn't matter," Melissa said, reaching for a small package. After much debate with herself she had decided she would give him his present, after all, though what he had said to her yesterday still hurt. Withholding his gift would only make her look petty, the greedy opportunist he thought her. "This is for you, Chatleigh. From Harry and me."

She held a small, square box out to him. Justin looked at it for a moment without speaking, and then took it. Still without words, he opened it, and pulled out a fine gold hunter's watch, hanging on a chain.

"It was my father's," Melissa said, "given him by Wellington. Harry and I think you should have it."

"I see." Justin held the watch up to read the inscription on the back, and then replaced it in the box. "And is this supposed to make me change my mind about London?"

Melissa drew back as if she'd been struck. "Must every gift have a price, my lord?"

"It generally does."

She got to her feet. "Then I pity you," she said, and walked out of the room.

"Not well done of you, boy," Augusta said into the heavy silence that followed Melissa's departure.

Justin put the box into his pocket, avoiding Harry's hurt gaze, and rose. "Stay out of it," he said to Augusta crisply, and stalked out of the room.

Early the following day Justin came down the stairs and paused in the hall, tapping his riding crop against his leg. "Where is everyone, Phelps?"

Phelps stood stiff and still near the door. "Her ladyship and Master Harry have left already, my lord," he said.

"The devil they have!" Justin stared at him, noticing the butler's stiffness and coolness. In the mysterious way of servants, the entire staff seemed to have learned of what had transpired yesterday morning. "They were to meet me here, and we were to go together."

"Yes, my lord."

Justin looked at him again, and then turned. "Never mind," he said, as he walked towards the breakfast room. Not that it really mattered, he thought, sitting at the table, but he had wanted the party from the Hall to arrive at Sir Percival's for the Boxing Day hunt together. Absurd to feel as if he had been abandoned.

"There you are, Master Justin," Mrs. Barnes said, bustling into the room when he was nearly done with his breakfast.

"Here I am, Nanny," he said, mildly.

"I've been wanting a word with you."

Justin put down his fork. "If it's about yesterday, Nanny, it's not necessary."

"How could you, Master Justin?" she went on, as if he hadn't spoken. "Surely I taught you better than that."

"You did, Nanny, but—"

"The poor girl was in tears, so I heard."

"Who told you that?" he said, startled.

"Her maid. At least," she said, scrupulously honest, "she said she thought her ladyship had been crying."

"Huh." Justin rose to his feet. "Her ladyship is tougher than anyone thinks."

"But not as tough as you think, Master Justin. If you're not careful, you'll lose her."

Justin's shoulders stiffened as he stalked out. Damn, everyone meddles in my business, he thought as he strode towards the stables. Only he really knew what the situation was; only he knew why he had been so churlish

143

about the gift.

Slowing down, he put a hand in his pocket and withdrew the watch, letting it dangle on its chain. Fine piece of jewelry, but what made it more valuable to him was the fact that his wife had thought enough of him to give it to him. And he had thrown it back into her face, but not for the reasons anyone had thought, not for the reason he had given. He had refused to accept the watch graciously because he didn't want to be caught in his wife's toils.

Alfred was just finishing saddling Diablo when Justin walked into the stables. "Morning, Alfred."

"Morning, sir." Alfred didn't look up at him, and Justin frowned. It was unusual for Alfred to act as a groom, now that there were others to perform that function, but Justin knew from long experience that Alfred liked to work with horses when he was upset.

"Well, Alfred?" he said, when the silence had stretched quite long enough.

"Well, sir?"

"Out with it, man. What's troubling you?"

"You shouldn't have done it, sir!" Alfred burst out.

"Oh, God, not you, too?" Justin swung up into the saddle, and Diablo, sensing his annoyance, danced about.

"It was wrong, sir." Alfred stood his ground. "Her ladyship didn't deserve it."

"For God's sake, Alfred, whose side are you on?"

"Yours, sir. You're wrong about her. She's Major Selby's daughter."

"Doesn't make her perfect, Alfred."

"No, sir, but she's not what you think either."

"I wish everyone would mind his own business," Justin said, wheeling around.

"Only thinking of you, sir," Alfred called after him as he rode out of the stable yard, and Justin gritted his teeth. God save him from well-meaning people! Still, he supposed, drawing back on the reins to slow Diablo's pace, he would have to apologize. Alfred had been right about one thing. Melissa hadn't deserved it.

Sir Percival Dutton's stableyard was a scene of noise and confusion when Justin reached it. Melissa and Harry were nowhere in sight as he joined the milling restless crowd of men in pink coats and ladies in riding habits, fine horseflesh and baying hounds. By God, he'd forgotten how stirring a good hunt could be. Conditions were perfect for it, too, cold enough for the ground to be hard, and clear enough. For the first time since returning home Justin felt his blood leap to life.

He was talking to Sir Percival when, out of the corner of his eye, he saw three riders emerge from the stables. There was Harry, astride a roan gelding that looked big for him; Richard Dutton, the squire's son; and a woman Justin didn't recognize immediately, until she turned her head. For a moment, he forgot to breathe. It was Melissa.

Good God, he thought, blankly, staring at her. Good God, he hadn't realized she was so attractive, but then, he'd never seen her in anything besides black before. Her high-waisted riding habit of forest green velvet, trimmed with epaulets and frogs of gold braid, clung to her curves and changed the color of her eyes to bright, vibrant emerald. Her skin glowed from the cold and from the excitement of again being astride a horse, which, he noted, she sat very well, and against the dark green of her hat, a dashing military shako, her auburn curls blazed like flame. Justin wondered why redheads had never come into style, and then Melissa, responding to something her companion had said, turned, and the moment was gone.

Justin shook his head, much as a man awakening from a dream, and then, clucking softly to Diablo, made his way through the crowd. "Good morning, sir!" Harry called when he spotted him, yesterday's hurt and disap-

145

pointment apparently forgotten. "Capital day for a hunt!"

"It will do," Justin agreed, turning Diablo so that he was next to Melissa. She was mounted on a sweet-tempered, fineboned chestnut mare, whose glossy mane was only several shades darker than her hair. "Morning, my lady. Dutton."

"Good morning, Chatleigh," Melissa said easily, but the smile that had been on her face a moment before was gone, replaced by a wary, shuttered look.

"Morning, Chatleigh," Richard Dutton said, across Melissa. "Glad to have you back with us."

"Glad to be here. Must thank you for mounting m'wife and her brother. Stables at the Hall aren't what they should be."

"Our pleasure. In fact, I've told Lady Chatleigh she may have free use of our stables whenever she wishes."

Melissa turned and gave Richard a piercingly sweet smile. A bolt of white-hot rage shot through Justin, and he tightened his hands on the reins. Diablo, in response, danced about, and it took Justin a moment to get both his horse and himself under control. Damn, she never smiled at him like that!

He became aware that Richard was looking at him, awaiting some sort of response, and he pulled himself together. "Of course," he said, and lightly flicked the reins, setting Diablo to a walk. "Excuse me."

"Of course." Richard's eyebrows went up a bit. "Taciturn fellow, ain't he?" he remarked.

Melissa shrugged, watching Justin with a puzzled frown as he easily maneuvered Diablo through the crowd. Now what had that been about? Certainly there was strain between them just now, but it was not her doing. Chatleigh, she had thought, had better sense than to advertise their problems to the world.

Sir Percival's groom blew on his horn at that moment,

146

and the people who had been milling aimlessly about stilled, some leaning forward in their saddles, some straightening in expectation, eyes bright with interest and excitement. Marianne Dutton, Sir Percival's daughter, turned to say something to Justin, who had just come level with her, and the same anger that had assailed Justin a few moments earlier struck Melissa as she saw him smile and answer her. She had no time to dwell on it, however, for at that moment the hounds took the scent and were off, with a mighty chorus of barks and howls. Melissa's mount stirred under her, and her hands in their Limeric gloves gripped the reins a little harder as the participants began to stream out of the stableyard. The hunt was underway.

Past the Duttons' house, through the gate, onto rough, stubbled fields brown and bare with winter. Melissa had forgotten the exhilaration of a hunt, and the camaraderie of riding with a group of people, all intent on the same goal. Occasionally she caught a glimpse of Justin, ahead of her, wearing a black riding jacket instead of a pink, but nevertheless unmistakable because of his height. Marianne Dutton, she noted with malicious satisfaction, had deserted him for the moment.

There was a fence ahead. She leaned forward, gathering the reins, and they were up and over, flying, soaring, the stone fence passing below, to land with a thud on the turf on the other side, kicking up clods of dirt and grass. The countryside went by in a blur of trees bare of leaves and a lowering sky. Ahead of her ranged the lead riders, Sir Percival hot in pursuit of his anxious, baying hounds, with Marianne, the witch, not far behind, and Harry, his flaming hair a beacon, bent low over his horse's neck. Another fence was coming up, the lead riders taking it easily, though some of the ladies turned away to find a gate. Not for her such weakness, Melissa thought, preparing herself to make the leap.

Justin, several paces ahead, soared over the fence easily, and in spite of her annoyance with him Melissa watched in admiration as he and Diablo seemed to become one. Heavens, he could ride, she thought, aware only on some subconscious level of a sharp crack of noise off to the right. Something happened then, Justin jerked to the side, and when he landed, Diablo seemed to stumble. Melissa opened her mouth in a silent scream as Justin tumbled from the horse's back, and she no longer cared about the hunt, no longer cared about keeping up the pace. She wanted only to reach her husband. She gathered her mount to make the leap and they soared over, gracefully and easily. Wheeling around, she dashed for the spot where she had seen Justin fall. *There!* He lay by the fence, sprawled on the ground, his eyes closed and his face white as death, save for the blood that trickled from the wound on his forehead.

Chapter Eleven

"No, oh no!" Melissa gasped, dropping the reins and sliding off her horse. "No, no, no, no, no!" She fell to her knees beside Justin and lifted his shoulders, cradling his injured head to her bosom. "Justin, oh, Justin, no. No."

"Lady Chatleigh!" Melissa looked up sharply as a horse loomed up before her, and then Richard Dutton was dropping down next to her. "My God, what happened?"

"I don't know, I think he's dead, oh, Justin!"

"Good God!" Richard stared blankly at the unconscious man. "He's been shot!"

"What?" Melissa snatched her hand, covered with blood, away from Justin's face, and stared down at the wound. "Oh no—"

"He's alive." Richard dropped Justin's wrist and glanced up at the little crowd of people that had gathered around, his eyes fastening on his brother. "Roger, ride back to the house and get a litter, and have someone go for the doctor. And tell them we'll need a room prepared."

"No," Melissa said, her firmness in sharp contrast to her hysteria of the moment before. Her fingers, probing the wound, had found it to be superficial;

149

the bullet, if there had been one, had only grazed the skin. Justin had had a lucky escape. "We'll bring him back to Chatleigh."

"But, my lady—"

"Melissa?" Harry threw himself off his mount and raced towards her.

"Harry, thank God!" Melissa raised her head. "I don't think he's badly hurt."

"But what happened?"

"I don't know. Harry, I need you to ride to the Hall and tell everyone. If he can borrow the horse, Mr. Dutton?"

"Of course," Richard said, "but I think—"

"Yes, I know, but he'll do better in his own home."

Richard looked as if he were about to argue, but just then the litter arrived. Melissa stood back as Justin was placed upon it, and she walked by his side as he was carried back to the Duttons' house. The distance that had flown by on horseback proved to be very long, indeed, and the men carrying the litter were straining under their burden by the time they reached the stableyard. The barouche already stood waiting, the horses put to, and though Sir Percival, who had heard of the incident and actually cut short the hunt, remonstrated with her, Melissa was adamant. Justin would recover in his own home, in his own bed; and she intended to oversee every moment of that recovery. Because, when she had seen him lying so still and pale upon the ground, when she had thought she had lost him, Melissa had at last realized the truth. She was in love with her husband.

The fighting raged around him. They had thought to win

this battle easily, but Soult, the wily French marshal sent by Napoléon to retake Spain, was close to victory here at the small town of San Sebastian. Wellington had galloped hell-for-leather in time to order his forces where they were needed, a close-run thing. Now Justin rode through the chaos of crashing cannons and the screams of men dying in agony, the precious dispatches from Wellington to General Picton tucked into his saddlebag. Good God, Jocelyn had been hit! He watched in horror as Arthur Jocelyn, his good friend since school days, fell before the determined onslaught of the enemy. And then he felt a jolt, and Diablo buckled under him, and he was falling, falling. . . .

"Best to keep him quiet for a few days," a man's voice was saying. "The wound's not deep, but he'll have a nasty headache when he awakes."

"Should he be on a special diet?" a woman asked. The voice was unfamiliar, but something about it compelled him, made him strain to hear more.

"Beef broth and gruel would be the best. No spirits, though I expect he'll argue with you on that."

"I suspect he'll argue about the gruel! But no matter. You're certain he will be all right?"

"Not to worry, my lady. The concussion wasn't severe, and his constitution is sound. He may not remember what happened, however."

"I fell off my damned horse," Justin said, opening his eyes as memory came back to him. Not a battle, after all.

"Justin!" Melissa spun around and flew over to the bed, and he realized that it was her voice he'd heard. "My heavens! How are you feeling?"

"Never saw you in green before," he said, smiling crookedly at her.

"I'm afraid I don't have a black riding habit." She smiled back at him, briefly erasing the lines of worry

151

from her face. "Does your head hurt?"

"Damnably. Diablo all right?"

"Diablo is fine. You'll have a scar, I fear." Her smile became strained. "Very dashing. People will wonder how many duels you've fought."

"Huh."

"Must let the patient rest now," the doctor said, bustling over, and Melissa stepped back.

"Of course," she said, and turned to smile at him.

"Damned leech," Justin muttered, but he closed his eyes. The truth was, he was very tired. Damn, he thought as sleep overtook him. Of all the foolish things to do.

Melissa stood by the side of the bed until Justin's breathing fell into the easy rhythm of sleep, and then turned away, her shoulders sagging. Thank God, he was going to be all right. Until he had spoken to her, she hadn't been certain he would be, in spite of what the doctor had said. Now there was the period of convalescence to get through, but she wasn't concerned about that. Justin was strong and would heal quickly, if he would allow himself. Chances were he would be a very impatient patient.

Alfred turned from Justin's wardrobe, where he had just hung up the riding coat. "You don't mind me saying so, m'lady, you look done in."

Melissa looked up in surprise, and then smiled. "I feel done in, Alfred. It's been quite a day."

"Best you get some rest now, m'lady. I'll look after the master."

Melissa hesitated, then nodded. She would not do Justin any good if she wore herself out, and Alfred was more than capable. Looking down at her husband, she reached out her hand, as if to touch his cheek, but pulled back. "Very well, Alfred. But you'll

MORE PASSION AND ADVENTURE AWAIT... YOUR TRIP TO A BIG ADVENTUROUS WORLD BEGINS WHEN YOU ACCEPT YOUR FIRST 4 NOVELS ABSOLUTELY *FREE* (AN $18.00 VALUE)

Accept your Free gift and start to experience more of the passion and adventure you like in a historical romance novel. Each Zebra novel is filled with proud men, spirited women and tempestuous love that you'll remember long after you turn the last page.

Zebra Historical Romances are the finest novels of their kind. They are written by authors who really know how to weave tales of romance and adventure in the historical settings you love. You'll feel like you've actually gone back in time with the thrilling stories that each Zebra novel offers.

GET YOUR FREE GIFT WITH THE START OF YOUR HOME SUBSCRIPTION

Our readers tell us that these books sell out very fast in book stores and often they miss the newest titles. So Zebra has made arrangements for you to receive the four newest novels published each month.

You'll be guaranteed that you'll never miss a title, and home delivery is so convenient. And to show you just how easy it is to get Zebra Historical Romances, we'll send you your first 4 books absolutely FREE! Our gift to you just for trying our home subscription service.

BIG SAVINGS AND FREE HOME DELIVERY

Each month, you'll receive the four newest titles as soon as they are published. You'll probably receive them even before the bookstores do. What's more, you may preview these exciting novels free for 10 days. If you like them as much as we think you will, just pay the low preferred subscriber's price of just $3.75 each. *You'll save $3.00 each month off the publisher's price.* AND, your savings are even greater because there are never any shipping, handling or other hidden charges—FREE Home Delivery. Of course you can return any shipment within 10 days for full credit, no questions asked. There is no minimum number of books you must buy.

4 FREE BOOKS

TO GET YOUR 4 FREE BOOKS WORTH $18.00 — MAIL IN THE FREE BOOK CERTIFICATE T O D A Y

Fill in the Free Book Certificate below, and we'll send your FREE BOOKS to you as soon as we receive it.

If the certificate is missing below, write to: Zebra Home Subscription Service, Inc., P.O. Box 5214, 120 Brighton Road, Clifton, New Jersey 07015-5214.

FREE BOOK CERTIFICATE

4 FREE BOOKS

ZEBRA HOME SUBSCRIPTION SERVICE, INC.

YES! Please start my subscription to Zebra Historical Romances and send me my first 4 books absolutely FREE. I understand that each month I may preview four new Zebra Historical Romances free for 10 days. If I'm not satisfied with them, I may return the four books within 10 days and owe nothing. Otherwise, I will pay the low preferred subscriber's price of just $3.75 each; a total of $15.00, *a savings off the publisher's price of $3.00.* I may return any shipment and I may cancel this subscription at any time. There is no obligation to buy any shipment and there are no shipping, handling or other hidden charges. Regardless of what I decide, the four free books are mine to keep.

NAME

ADDRESS   APT

CITY   STATE   ZIP

(   )
TELEPHONE

SIGNATURE   (if under 18, parent or guardian must sign)

Terms, offer and prices subject to change without notice. Subscription subject to acceptance by Zebra Books. Zebra Books reserves the right to reject any order or cancel any subscription.   039102

GET
FOUR
FREE
BOOKS
(AN $18.00 VALUE)

ZEBRA HOME SUBSCRIPTION
SERVICE, INC.
P.O. Box 5214
120 BRIGHTON ROAD
CLIFTON, NEW JERSEY 07015-5214

let me know if there's any change?"

"Of course I will, ma'am." He hesitated a moment. "My lady," he said, just as Melissa reached the door. She turned, a question in her eyes. "Did you see what happened?"

"No." She came back into the room, glancing over at the bed, and her voice lowered. "That is, I saw him fall, but I didn't see anybody aiming a gun at him, if that's what you mean."

"Didn't hear anything neither, milady?"

"No. Yes! I don't know." Her brow furrowed in concentration. "It seems to me," she said, slowly, "that I did hear something that could have been a shot, but I'm not sure when. I'm sorry." She gave him an apologetic smile. "So much happened at once, you see."

"Yes, of course, ma'am. Didn't really think you saw anything."

Melissa, heading towards the door again, turned as a nasty suspicion struck her. "Alfred, you don't think . . . do you think someone did it deliberately?"

"I don't know, my lady."

"You can't be serious!" She stared at him in horror. "Who would? In the middle of a hunt —"

"That's just it, ma'am. Everyone around here knows about the Boxing Day hunt. Who would be out shooting?"

"But it had to be a mistake! It had to be." Her fist was to her mouth. "Couldn't it have been a poacher? Someone who knew everyone would be too busy to try to stop him?"

"It could, m'lady," he said, reluctantly, "but . . ."

"It must have been," she decided. To think otherwise was madness. "Alfred, you won't say anything of this to his lordship?"

Alfred hesitated, and then shook his head. "No, ma'am. Not until he's better. But he'll have to know," he said, stopping her at the door again. "If some-one's trying to do for him, he'll have to be on his guard."

Melissa stood still for a moment and then nodded. "Yes, Alfred," she said, and walked out.

"Oh, my lady, your pretty riding habit," Liza said in dismay when Melissa reached her room, and Me-lissa looked blankly down at herself. On the bodice and the sleeves, where she had cradled Justin to her, the velvet was matted and stained.

Her first reaction was an instinctive recoil against the dried blood; her second, the realization that this habit was precious to her. Justin had said he liked seeing her in green. No matter that he seemed to need to be out of his head, whether foxed or hurt, to speak nicely to her, she thought as she peeled the habit off. If something good came out of this morn-ing's near tragedy, it should be cherished. "See what you can do with it, Liza," she said, slipping into her dressing gown, "and I'll require a bath."

"Yes, my lady," Liza said, whisking the habit out of the room. Melissa sank onto the chaise longue, her arm over her eyes as a reaction overtook her in long, shuddering waves. The day's tumultuous events crowded in on her: the excitement of the hunt, the horror when she had seen Justin go down, her own stunning realization of what she felt for him. Dear God, and she had nearly lost him! If whoever had fired the gun had been a better shot, she would be a widow by now, a widow who had realized too late what she really felt.

Liza came back in, carrying cans of hot water, and Melissa rose, glad to be distracted from her thoughts. A few moments later, sinking back into the deliciously warm water of her bath, she let her tired, sore muscles relax. It had been quite a day, and she was exhausted from the physical activity and the firestorm of emotions. Lord help her, she loved her husband.

Briefly, she closed her eyes. It was true. She loved him, a man who thought only the worst of her, a man she had no desire to love. But then, if she were honest with herself, she had no desire to love any man. What she had seen at home had cured her of that. Papa had been wonderful, a loving husband, an understanding father, but she had since learned that not all men were like him. She had learned that, to her cost, when she had met *him*.

Melissa abruptly sat up and reached for the bath sponge, scrubbing herself vigorously, but after a few moments she dropped the sponge back into the water. The stain was there, and nothing she could do would erase it. It was amazing that no one else had noticed it, but someday someone would. Someday, probably Justin would. Until that day, she would keep quiet about it, holding back the urge to confide in someone. No one must ever know, because the shame was in her.

Liza came back in with fresh water, and Melissa rinsed her body, staring into space. A hard road lay ahead of her, and there were too many obstacles to overcome: a husband who mistrusted her, a serious flaw within herself, her own very real fears. She didn't want to love Justin, but the fact remained that she did, and, she would have to do something about it. And that meant, she thought, slipping her arms into the dressing gown Liza held out for her, that Justin had better watch out. She was going to make him love her.

Several days later, Melissa was wondering about that resolve. As she had suspected, Justin was a very poor patient, and not all the love in the world could dampen her exasperation with him. He tested the limits of her patience, never her strong suit, by insisting on following his usual routine, and then growled at her when his strength failed him. By the second day after his accident, Melissa threw up her hands in defeat and left him to Alfred's questionably tender mercies. Why in the world, she wondered, striding away from Justin's room, did she love that man?

Alfred stared after Melissa as she left, a thoughtful expression on his face. Then he turned. Justin, sitting in bed, propped up by pillows, looked a most improbable invalid, with his broad shoulders and obviously healthy physique; only the bandage around his head and his pallor proved otherwise. "Well?" he said, sardonically. "Going to scold me, Alfred?"

Alfred gave him a look, and then went over to the wardrobe, where he had been sorting through Justin's coats. "Didn't ought to have ripped up at her ladyship that way, sir," he said.

"I will rip up at anyone who insists on feeding me that disgusting stuff." Justin pushed at the tray that lay across his lap, and gruel, thin and gray, slopped over the side of the bowl. "That includes you or her ladyship or my aunt. Do I make myself clear, Alfred?"

"Admirably, sir." Alfred bit back a smile. Unlike Melissa, he had seen Justin through several convalescences, and he could accurately gauge his temper.

"Weren't her ladyship's fault, though. Just doing what she thinks is right."

"Alfred," Justin said in a dangerously quiet voice, "do not try me."

"No, sir." Alfred smoothed down the arm of the riding jacket Justin had worn during the hunt, and a frown furrowed his forehead. He cast a quick look back at Justin, then made his decision. His lordship was strong enough to hear the truth. "Sir, who hates you enough to want you dead?"

Justin, idly stirring the gruel with a spoon, looked up. "Dead?" he said. "What the devil are you talking about?"

Alfred left the wardrobe and pulled a chair close to the bed. "What happened to you weren't no accident."

His eyes narrowed. "What are you saying? I fell off my horse."

"No, sir. You were shot."

"The devil I was!" Justin sat bolt upright, an action he immediately regretted. His pallor had deepened when he sank back against the pillows, and his hand was pressed to his forehead, against the sudden pounding.

"Sorry, sir." Alfred removed the tray from harm's way. "No doubt about it, I'm afraid. You didn't get that wound from the fall."

Justin lowered his hand and glared at him. "Who shot me?"

"Don't know, sir. I was hoping you'd remember something."

"No, damn it, not a thing." Justin's brow furrowed in concentration. "We were well away on the hunt. The hounds had a good scent, and we were riding fast. There was a fence coming up, a high stone

one, and Diablo jumped it, and—good God!" His face went blank with surprise. "Damn, there was a shot, I remember it now. And then, nothing." No wonder he had dreamed about a battle. "Whoever it was, was a damn poor shot."

"Or a good one, sir." Justin stared at him. "Maybe it was meant to miss."

"But why? For what reason?" If he had been healthy, he would have risen and paced the room. Being bedridden only increased his frustration.

"Don't know, sir. You don't know of anyone you might have crossed?"

"Since I returned? No." He thought fleetingly of Sir Stephen's mention of revenge, but then dismissed the thought. Absurd. "I've been gone for five years. Who would hate me that much . . . ?" His voice trailed off. "Where was my wife?"

"Sir, you don't think—"

"Where was she?"

"Behind you, sir," he said, "and to your left."

"I see." Justin put his hand to the wound at his right temple. "She could have had an accomplice."

"Sir!"

"She didn't want to marry me, Alfred."

"No, sir, I'll not believe it of Major Selby's daughter," he said stoutly, and considered telling Justin what he had heard, that Melissa had cried over her husband's prostrate form. A quick glance at Justin's face decided him otherwise. "No, I don't believe it, and I don't think you do, either."

"Who else would it be?" Justin said, and then sighed. "No, I don't really believe it. But, damn! Who would want to kill me?" He leaned forward, this time ignoring the pounding headache. "Was there any investigation?"

158

"Sir Percival sent men into the woods, but they didn't find anything."

"I see." Justin leaned back. "It must have been a poacher, Alfred."

"Take a lot of guts to be out poaching when the hunt's going by."

"Yes, but the hunt wouldn't necessarily have gone that way. Am I supposed to believe someone was lying in wait in the woods, on the off chance I'd go by?"

"No, sir. But perhaps someone followed the hunt. Someone who hasn't given up."

Justin's head jerked up, and his eyes narrowed again. "You think I'm in danger?"

"Might be, sir. I think you'd best be on your guard."

"Yes, Alfred." Justin's face was grim. "I intend to be."

"There you are," Melissa said, walking down the long gallery towards Justin. All the anxiety she had felt when she had found him missing from his room translated itself into annoyance. Here she had been picturing him lying unconscious somewhere, when in reality he looked disgustingly healthy. The fact that she had searched nearly the entire house only exacerbated her feelings. "What do you think you are doing?"

Justin glanced towards her, and then turned back towards the portrait he had been contemplating. "Desist, madam. I cannot abide your fussing over me."

Melissa's eyebrow rose at that. "Cranky, are we?"

"Don't patronize me," he growled.

159

"The fact remains, Justin, that you should be in bed."

"I'm fine." He glanced at her again for her unexpected use of his name. "I don't need you or Alfred to nursemaid me."

"You and your stubborn pride! You'll make yourself sick before you'd admit to any weakness."

"If I get tired, madam, I will return to bed. Will that satisfy you?"

Melissa stopped a few feet away from him, peering anxiously into his face. He certainly didn't look sick, but instead exuded an air of almost overpowering masculine strength and power. She had to step back, lest her feelings betray her. "It will have to, won't it?" she said, her tone softening. "I can't force you."

"No, madam, you cannot," he said, and turned back to the painting.

Melissa followed his eyes, and she gave a little gasp of dismay. He was looking at the portrait of his mother. Since he rarely came into the long gallery, where the other family portraits were hung, she had thought it safe to place it there. "I'm sorry, Chatleigh, but I couldn't relegate it to the attics. She's much too beautiful."

"Yes, a beautiful whore," he said, absently. "Like you."

Pain struck Melissa with such stunning force that for a moment she couldn't see, and her breath drew in, sharply. Now, when his good opinion meant so much to her, hearing what he really thought hurt with an intensity she had never felt before. Blindly, fighting tears, she turned away.

"Melissa." Justin's hand came down on her shoulder, and though she stiffened, she didn't struggle when he turned her towards him. "I'm sorry," he said, with what sounded like genuine regret. "I didn't mean that the way it sounded."

"Never mind, I know what you meant. It's what you've thought of me all along."

"Maybe once, but I was wrong, God help me. I'm sorry."

Melissa stared up at him through wet lashes. "Are you? Do you mean that?"

"Yes, of course." He gestured impatiently, and she realized how difficult this confession was for him. "I was wrong. Of course, you have to admit, the circumstances—"

"You were foxed."

"I was foxed," he admitted, and turned to look down at her with an odd intentness. "And you were the most—"

"What?" she said, when he didn't go on.

"Nothing." The most beautiful, enticing thing he had seen in a very long time, he had nearly said. The blow to his head must have addled his brain more than he'd realized. "You're not like her at all," he said, more to himself than to her.

"Did you expect me to be?" Melissa turned to look at the portrait, surprise in her voice.

"Mm." He shifted his weight, his hands shoved into his pockets. At the moment he looked so like a guilty little boy that Melissa had to resist the impulse to hug him.

"Tell me about her."

"M'mother? What do you want to know about her for?"

"Because she was your mother, silly. I don't know anything about your family."

"Then you are lucky."

"Surely you don't mean that!"

"But I do."

"But she was so beautiful."

"Do you really think so, madam? You wouldn't, if you knew her." He shoved his hands deeper into his pockets. "It was a famous love match, you see, she and my father. Except the love didn't last. My mother was incapable of being faithful. So was my father, but she was worse."

"Why? Because she did something only men are supposed to do?" Melissa asked tartly.

"No. Because she did so much more of it, and she didn't care who knew." He stared up at the portrait. "She would come into the nursery to see us, m'brother and me, smelling of perfume, and kiss us and then go off to some rout or ball, the only time we saw her all day. And then she and m'father would come home, and there'd be dreadful rows, about who she flirted with, who she left the ball with, and how long she was gone. . . ." His voice trailed off. "I heard her tell my father once I wasn't his son."

"No!"

"Then she denied it, but I'm not so sure. My father believed it."

"Oh, Justin." Melissa laid a hand on his arm, her heart aching for the lonely little boy he must have been. "Perhaps she just said it to make him mad."

"Oh, undoubtedly. But I've wondered. I'm not much like him, you see." His eyes flicked over to the portrait of the seventh Earl. "I never was the son he wanted."

"She must have been a dreadful woman."

"Oh, no. She could be quite charming. When she wanted to be."

"What a shame." Melissa studied the portrait.

162

Somehow her mother-in-law no longer looked quite so beautiful, now that she knew the truth. "When did she die?"

Justin glanced down at her. "What makes you think she is dead?"

"Isn't she?"

"No."

"Heavens!" She stared at him. "Then where is she?"

Justin ran a hand through his hair. "God knows. When I was sixteen, she ran off with the butler. The butler, mind you. When it was over she wanted to come back, but m'father wouldn't let her. Last I heard, she was living on the Continent with a man who makes his living gambling. Once in a while, she'll write to me, asking for money."

"Dear God." Melissa breathed out the words. No wonder he had so distrusted her in the beginning. It would be a wonder if he trusted any woman. "Justin, I'm sorry."

Justin looked down at the hand she had laid on his arm, and, after a moment, she pulled away. Damn, why had he told her all this? No one knew of these things, not even Aunt Augusta, and certainly not Philip whom he had tried to shield from the worst of their mother's excesses. "Well, no matter, now. But you'd best be prepared, if we go to London. There'll be people who remember, and you might hear whispers."

"Are we going to London?" she said, surprised.

"Don't know." He scuffed at the gleaming parquet surface of the floor. "Been thinking, you know, about what they would want me to do." The jerk of his head indicated the other portraits. "Not m'father, of course, but my grandfather and the others. And I

163

think they'd want me to do it. It's what we've been bred to do, to serve the country."

"You've already done that, Chatleigh."

"Yes. But I wonder if I shouldn't do more?" He looked down at her. "And I think you might be right. Maybe I should try."

"You'll never know if you'll like it, if you don't," she offered, timidly. "Justin, I do hope you're not doing this on my account? I'd like to see London, but it doesn't have to be now. I'm happy here at Chatleigh."

"I know." He smiled down at her. "Very well. London it is, then. On one condition."

"What?"

"Want you to start wearing colors."

Melissa's face sobered. "I can't. My mother's recently dead."

He studied her face. "And you miss her."

"Yes. I miss her."

"Well, no matter," he said, after a few moments. "Think about it."

"Perhaps. Justin." Her brow furrowed, and Justin, who had turned away, looked back at her. "Before we go to London, something will have to be done about Harry."

"He'll go back to Eton soon," Justin said, and Melissa shook her head.

"No, I didn't mean that. I meant, Sir Stephen."

"I see." Justin's eyes narrowed. "Why does he frighten you so?"

"I'm not scared of him," she said, but she didn't meet his eyes. "At least, not for me, but for Harry." She looked up then. "I know you don't want to, but if you could assume Harry's guardianship—"

"I've tried," he said, interrupting her, "or, rather,

my solicitors have tried." Melissa stared up at him in surprise. "But we can do nothing so long as Sir Stephen refuses to give up the guardianship."

"Oh." Melissa turned away, her shoulders slumping. "Then he could come and take Harry away whenever he wants."

"He could try." There was such an odd note in Justin's voice that Melissa turned back, to see him flexing his fists. "Said to be handy with my fives, you know."

"No, I didn't know." She broke into a smile. "Oh, dear, wouldn't Sir Stephen hate that! He's quite a coward, you know."

"Is he? Suspected as much." Justin's gaze softened. "Don't worry, m'dear. Harry will be all right."

The effect of that endearment, spoken for the first time without mockery or icy politeness, was out of all proportion to its meaning. Joy shot through Melissa, and she had to restrain herself from beaming at him. "I know he will."

"My lady." A footman appeared at the end of the gallery.

"Yes, what is it?" Melissa asked, as the servant approached, bowing.

"Begging your pardon, my lady, but the builder would like a word with you."

"Oh, bother! Very well. I'll be there in a moment." She turned back to Justin. "They're working in the music room, and if it's going to be in shape before our party I'll have to go. As for you, you should be in bed, sir."

"Yes, madam, in a moment." He nodded to her as she turned to go, smiling shyly at him. "By the by, Melissa." She turned. "Liked the watch."

Their eyes held, and then Melissa smiled. "I'm

glad," she said, simply.

Only when she had turned the corner and was, she was certain, out of sight of her husband, did she allow her smile to spread. He'd liked the watch! And he no longer mistrusted her. Melissa executed a little dance step. There was hope, after all.

Chapter Twelve

1814 came in cold. In London there was a heavy fog that didn't let up for days, so that people went about their business in a perpetual gloom; in the north, snow blanketed the ground. In Surrey, it was merely cold, and the inhabitants of Chatleigh Hall assured each other that they could not remember such a winter. It was not the best weather for traveling to the capital, Melissa reflected as she supervised the packing, but she would be glad to leave.

She had seen little of Justin since he had recovered from his injury. He had been busy about the estates and in local affairs, joining the militia and the Volunteers. Though the harvest had been good, he had also ridden to meet with his tenants, finding out what needed doing and who would need additional food and clothing to survive this unusually cold winter. While Melissa approved his activities, sometimes she deplored the results of them. She saw him now only at the dinner table, and then he seemed never to wish to talk. Even at their Twelfth Night party, which had been a success, he had managed to spend little time with her. It was almost as if he were avoiding her, and that held her back. She had no desire to proclaim her love for him if he were only going to reject it. She loved him, and she didn't have the slightest notion what to do about it.

She was glad, then, when the day came for their departure. Since London was only a few hours distant, it had been decided to take the trip in easy stages rather than change horses at each stop. Justin had elected to ride Diablo, and so, except for her maid, Melissa was alone in the coach. She was not bored, however, particularly when they reached the outskirts of the great city. London! All her life she had heard of it, and had wondered if she would ever go there. Since she was old enough she had dreamed of having a season, whirling about in glittering ballrooms on the arm of a tall, handsome gallant, who had tousled brown hair and warm brown eyes and a direct way of looking at one, a man who looked oddly like her husband. . . .

Melissa shook her head. "Are you all right, my lady?" Liza, who was sitting opposite her, asked.

"Yes. Heavens, look at all this, Liza!" The coach was passing through a section of mean little houses and grim, dark factories. Melissa and Lisa looked at each other in dismay, fearful that this was what the city would be like, but then the coach trundled onto the bridge crossing the Thames, and they were at last in London.

The air was smoky and sooty, the streets crowded, but the city pulsed with life. They went through Westminster and down Piccadilly, past the Pulteney Hotel on one side, Green Park on the other, and the great houses of the aristocracy. There were people everywhere, and traffic such as they had never seen. Melissa, trying to hold on to her composure in the face of such wonders, nevertheless swiveled her head back and forth so as to miss nothing, and Liza's exclamations of amazement echoed her own thoughts.

She was in London, at last! Perhaps here Justin would finally notice her.

The coach turned down a side street lined with neat houses, some unpretentious, others set back behind high iron fences. At last the coach drew up in a courtyard and came to a stop. When a footman came to hold the door, Melissa clambered stiffly down onto the cobbled yard, glancing up at her new home with some disappointment. In comparison to many of the mansions she had seen, the Chatleigh town house was plain and rather small, made of Portland stone, with black shutters. But the brass railings gleamed and the steps had been recently swept, and as the door opened she had an odd feeling of being welcome. No fear that her husband would leave her here, to deal alone with hostile servants.

Justin came over as Diablo was led away to the stables, in time to catch Melissa's look of dismay, and he grinned. "Come, madam," he said, holding out his arm. "I assure you it's much worse on the inside."

Melissa gave him a startled look, but had no time to reply before they had reached the door and Phelps was welcoming them. Inside, the entrance hall was an oasis of calm and order. The parquet floor was highly polished, and on a table beneath a heavy, gilt-framed mirror stood a silver bowl filled with roses, an impressive sight in this cold weather. A large covered vase of bone china rested at the back of the hall, its colors echoing those of the Brussels carpet. "It isn't so bad," she said to Justin as they climbed the stairs after greeting the assembled staff. "Perhaps a bit old-fashioned, but everything seems to be in good repair, and good taste."

"Oh?" Justin said, and flung open a door that lay to the left of the second-floor landing. "The drawing room. After you, madam."

"Thank you," Melissa said as she stepped into the room. Then she stopped abruptly. "Oh—my heavens."

Justin came to stand by her. "M'father rather liked the Egyptian look, when it was in vogue."

"Really!" Melissa recovered her poise with an effort. To the left of her a sofa, upholstered in velvet—the nile green she so hated—curved and flowed in sinuous lines, and across the room a large table with a glass top was supported by gilded legs in the shape of crocodiles. Serpents writhed around the legs of chairs, and lotus leaves curled around the frame of the mirror that hung over the mantel. "Oh, heavens," Melissa said, weakly. "I need a cup of tea."

Justin grinned and crossed the room, splashing some brandy into a cut-glass tumbler. "Quite sympathize with you, madam," he said, and saluted her with the glass. After a moment, Melissa returned his smile.

"You are a complete hand! Is the rest of the house like this?"

"Not quite so bad." He sprawled into a chair facing her as, after a moment of fastidious disgust, she perched on the edge of the sofa. "Feel free to do whatever you wish with it."

"Oh, I shall." Melissa glanced around the room, and shuddered. "I shall."

After washing her face and lying down for a bit, she was ready to go on a tour of the house with Mrs. Herrick, the housekeeper. She didn't know what to expect after the drawing room, but to her pleased surprise the rest of the house was more than passable. Her own suite of rooms was pleasantly old-fashioned, its furniture cherrywood; the curtains and bed hangings were of a floral chintz, softly faded, with a plain fringe edging; and the rug underfoot was deep and luxurious. There was a cozy breakfast room where, Melissa decided instantly, they would take most of the their meals, and a grand dining room to be used for entertaining. The morning room, on the ground floor, appropriately caught the sun and was furnished with Chippendale and Hepplewhite, and the drawing room, in spite of its hideous decoration, was well proportioned. At the back of the house there was, much to Melissa's surprise, a grand ballroom, with French windows opening onto a terrace overlooking surprisingly large gardens. Though now nothing bloomed, there was a greenhouse, and she suspected that the garden would be a riot of color in the spring. She was suddenly very glad she would be there to see it.

She turned at the footstep behind her, to see Justin. "It isn't so bad, Chatleigh," she said. "Of course the drawing room will need to be redone, but the rest of the house is passable."

Justin passed a hand over his hair. "Might have you take a look at my rooms, while you are about it."

Melissa looked at him swiftly, but she could find no double meaning in his words. Certainly nothing to make her heart start pounding. "Why, are they that bad?"

"Serpents crawling up the bedposts." He shuddered. "Never did like snakes."

She smothered a grin. "Well then, we must do something about that."

"Actually, that's not what I wanted to see you about," he said, putting a hand on her arm. The warmth of his touch seemed to spread through her entire body. "Had a note from m'aunt. She wants to see us."

"Oh, dear. Well, we can't refuse, can we?"

"Hardly. Aunt Augusta's summons are in the nature of a royal command."

"Very well. I'll get my pelisse, and then we can go."

"Take your time," he muttered. Melissa turned and

171

flashed him a sunny smile, and he stood for a moment, watching her progress across the parquet floor. Paying a call on Aunt Augusta was suddenly a much more tolerable prospect.

Sometime later their carriage drew up in front of Lady Helmsley's imposing town house, and the Chatleighs emerged onto the pavement. "Could we not have walked?" Melissa asked, as Justin escorted her up the stairs. "It's not very far."

"Not done, m'dear. Afternoon, Fitch."

"My lord. And my lady." Fitch bowed as he held the door open to them. "And may I congratulate you again, my lord, on your nuptials?"

Justin, holding out his hat and gloves, glanced up in time to catch a gleam of amusement in the old man's eyes. "Thank you, Fitch," he said dryly. "Believe my aunt's expecting us?"

"Yes, my lord, in the drawing room. If you'll just follow me?"

"So it's not done to walk from one's house to another, even if it's just a few steps?" Melissa went on.

Justin, ascending beside her the broad marble staircase, shook his head. "Not in town."

"How very odd. Well, I suppose there are a number of things which are not done, which I will have to learn?"

"Many." Justin's voice was gloomy. "And if you don't learn them, my aunt will be certain to teach you."

Melissa flashed him that smile again, and, as before, it had the curious effect of making him forget, just for a moment, about all else. He had little time to think about that, though, as Fitch opened a door just ahead. "The Earl and Countess of Chatleigh, my lady," he announced.

"And about time, too," Augusta grumbled, coming forward. "Took your time getting here, didn't you, boy?"

Justin mumbled something, and Melissa shot him a glance brimming with amusement. "No such thing, Aunt," she said, firmly, bending to kiss the old lady's rouged cheek. "It's good to see you again, ma'am."

"Tush, I never did hold with sentiment," Augusta said, but the color in her cheeks was not strictly due to her *maquillage*. "Sit down, sit." She waved them impatiently towards a sofa. "We have a lot to discuss and not much time if we're to be ready for the season."

"Season doesn't really start for another few months," Justin said, sitting upon a chair, of red velvet and gilt, that creaked ominously each time he moved.

"No, but Parliament will be opening soon," she retorted, "and that is what you need to prepare for." The look she gave her nephew held no affection. "You will have to overcome your aversion to speaking, boy."

"Nonsense, Chatleigh speaks quite well when he wants to," Melissa said coolly, and the others looked at her in surprise at this unexpected defense. "I think we can assume that he will not disgrace you, ma'am, or himself. But may I ask why it is so very important to you that he enter politics?"

"Why, to restore the Chatleigh name, of course, what else?" Augusta said, sounding surprised. "And what else is he suited for? Can't be a soldier forever. Not cut out to be a farmer, and I will not let him turn into a rake like his father!"

"I don't think that's likely, so kindly stop cataloging my faults and tell me what I should do?" Justin said, and though his voice was quiet it had the effect of stopping Augusta. She glared at him and then, surprisingly, chuckled.

"So, boy, got some gumption after all? I wondered if you'd let your wife do your fighting for you. Very well. You've got acquaintances from school and the army.

173

Cultivate 'em, find out where they stand. Then when it's time to make your maiden speech we can discuss the topic—"

"No." Justin spoke firmly. "If I am to speak, it will be on something I care about."

Augusta glared at him again, but she was the first to look away. "Very well, I'll give you that. But mind you don't turn Whig on me."

"Not a chance, ma' am."

"There had better not be." She gave him a hard stare, and though his look was bland, again she looked away first. "Now, miss, as for you."

Melissa looked up from her teacup. "I'll help in any way I can, ma'am."

"Of course you will. A pity that Townsend has gone to the continent with Castlereagh. Having him acknowledge you as his grandchild would do much for your consequence. However, we shall contrive. And the first thing you will do, miss, is get out of that dismal black."

Very carefully, so that it wouldn't clatter, Melissa set her cup on the table, and then raised her chin. "No."

"No?" Augusta's eyebrows rose. Seldom had anyone ever defied her so directly. "What do you mean, no?"

"I am in mourning, ma'am."

"And what has that to say to anything?"

"I will not show disrespect to my mother's memory by going into colors!" This time the teacup did rattle as she rose, pacing over to the windows. "She has not been dead six months. Can you not let it be, ma'am?"

"No, I cannot!" Augusta's cane thumped sharply. "Come, it don't do to be missish about this. No one in the *ton* knows or cares about your mother."

"I care! I am sorry, ma'am, but I cannot put off my blacks."

"Will not, you mean. And you prattle to me of

174

wishing to help your husband's career." Augusta's eyes were cold. "Well, miss, if you will not be guided by me in this, then I cannot help you. Will you listen to me, or will you not?" Melissa, standing at the window with her back to the room, turned her head but did not speak. "Bah!" Augusta rose. "You're a pair, the two of you. Well, you deserve each other, and I wash my hands of you—"

"Aunt." Justin rose also and placed a hand on her arm. "Just a moment. Might be a solution to this."

Augusta looked him up and down. "You've thought of something, boy?"

Justin's lips twitched. "Amazing, isn't it, Aunt? You see, Melissa," he said, ambling across the room, his hands in his pockets, "think I know what m'aunt is getting at."

Melissa turned her head a bit, and sniffled. "What?"

"Maybe you don't understand that a lot of politicking is done outside Parliament. Here." He handed her his handkerchief. "Lot done at parties and dinners and such. Think that's what my aunt wants you to do. Socialize, you see."

Melissa delicately wiped her eyes. "I see. But can I not do that and remain in black?"

"Mm, yes." Justin shot a look back at Augusta. "But not so well, you see. Be more restrictions on you. You couldn't socialize so much. If you did, might cause a scandal."

"I see. Another thing that's not done?"

"Afraid so." He smiled, fleetingly, at her bent head. "Wouldn't consider going into half-mourning, would you?"

"Gray and lavender, you mean?" Melissa looked up at him. "It seems so soon, but—"

"Would that satisfy you, Aunt?" Justin tossed over his shoulder.

"Hmph. But it might serve," Augusta said. "Yes, it just might serve. If the gowns are from Celeste's. Oh, don't wince, boy, you can stand the nonsense now."

Justin winced again, this time for real, but Melissa didn't see. "Are Celeste's gowns so very expensive, then?" she said.

"Very," Justin said, smiling. "But I wouldn't want you in anything less. Have we a bargain, then?"

Melissa looked at the hand he held out to her and then slowly extended her own. "I believe we do, sir," she said, placing her hand in his. His grip was unexpectedly gentle and yet firm, warm and comforting but somehow exciting, the pulse of it spreading up her arm and thrumming through her body. Surely he must feel it too? She looked up at him through her lashes, to see him regarding her with an expression she could not interpret, and she was disappointed when he moved away.

"Well, ma'am?" He turned to face Augusta. "That all you need of us?"

"For now," Augusta conceded, and watched as they made their farewells, pleased and surprised at the way her nephew had handled the situation. *Huh,* she thought, *the boy might make a politician yet.*

The air was brisk as Justin strode along slate sidewalks slippery with melting snow, having just come from a most interesting meeting with his man of affairs. Melissa's money was her own, to be used as she wished, when she wished. However, because he was her husband and the laws were what they were, he was in control of her fortune. He was a very wealthy man, and the thought made him scowl.

It was just that there was so much money involved, too much, and though he needed it to tow himself out of the river Tick, still he resented it. And that surprised him. Once, he had seriously considered marrying an heiress; now he had. Why should it bother him so?

Because of who the heiress was, damn it. He raised a hand to rake his fingers through his hair, remembering just in time that his curly-brimmed beaver was upon his head. If it had been anyone else, perhaps he wouldn't have minded, but he didn't want Melissa thinking he was a fortune hunter. Much as he needed the money, he hated taking it from her. It touched his pride too deeply, perhaps, living off his wife, put him too much in her power. To her credit, Melissa had not yet tried to exercise that power, and he didn't really think she would. But the fact that it was there galled him.

Well, it wouldn't last, he assured himself, swinging up the stairs to his house. He would take her money, yes, and use it to restore his estates. And, once they were profitable again and he was solvent, he would return every damned penny. Standing on his own, he would at last support his wife. Only by exerting such a resolve could he salve his pride.

Across the street, two men who had been leaning against a lamp post came to attention as Justin reached his house. "That him?" one said. He was short and broad, his features coarse, and he had an eye that showed a tendency to wander.

Jenkins nodded. "Him, all right, Ott," he said, and spat. "Bloody bastard."

Ott grunted, staring at the town house with his good eye, the other wandering to the side. "A big man, though. Might not be so easy to take him."

"Are you going back on your word?"

"You saying my word ain't worth nothing?"

Jenkins looked hastily away from the wandering

eye. Trouble was, you never knew where Ott was looking. "Your word had better be worth something. You said you'd do it."

"Aye, and I will. But I'll need help. Can't expect me to take him alone."

Jenkins opened his mouth to say that was exactly what he wanted, then shrugged. Weren't his money, after all. "All right. Hire who you need. I'll square it with the guv'nor."

"Right. Tell him I'll want more, while you're at it. Another half-crown, like."

"Highway robbery," Jenkins grumbled. "All right. But not a penny till you do the job. He's not to be killed, mind."

"He won't be." The squat man flexed his fists thoughtfully. "I'll do the job, or my name's not Ned Ott."

"Stand still, my lady," Liza said, as she struggled with the lacings of Melissa's gown.

"I am trying to, Liza!" Melissa snapped. She shifted onto her other foot. "Oh, are you sure this gown will be all right? I do so want to make the right impression."

"Tch, my lady, what have you got to worry about? Here, look." Grasping Melissa's shoulders, Liza turned her towards the pier glass. Melissa gave herself a long look. The gown of lavender watered silk was deceptively simple, falling from the newly stylish higher waist to the floor in a soft whisper of fabric, with neither flounce nor ruffle to ruin the classic line. Silver lace trimmed the short, puffed sleeves and the low neckline. Melissa studied herself for a moment longer and then reached up to her shoulders, hitching the dress up higher. "Now tell me you don't look fine?"

"The neckline is too low!" Melissa wailed, and her hands went to her shoulders again.

"Now, my lady, you'll see worse than that. Come, sit down and I'll finish your hair. Come on, now." Liza grasped Melissa's hands and led her back to the dressing table. Reluctantly Melissa sat and watched as Liza gave her curls, now fashionably cropped, a final brushing, polishing them to the sheen of burnished copper.

"I'm so pale," Melissa murmured, leaning forward just as Liza was about to thread a lavender satin ribbon through her curls. "Do you think I should try some rouge?"

"No, my lady, you'll do fine." Liza finally managed to fasten the ribbon. "I don't know why you're so nervous."

Melissa's eyes met their reflection, holding a faint violet sheen to match the gown. Nervous was not the word for it. Tonight she would finally make her debut, at a ball given by Lady Helmsley, and she was terrified.

Melissa hadn't realized how unprepared she was to move in the exalted circles of the *ton*. These past few weeks, spent under Augusta's tutelage, had quickly shown her how much she had to learn. There were so many things one must do, and even more that weren't allowed. She must always patronize the best dressmakers, the best milliners; stay on the good side of such powerful hostesses as Sally Jersey or the Princess Lieven, no matter how annoying they might be; and she must never do anything to jeopardize her husband's career. To a girl who was used to being in control of her own destiny, the restrictions chafed, and by the day of the ball Melissa was certain of only one thing. She was sure to disgrace herself somehow.

There was a knock on the door and Justin stepped

in, the first time he had been in her bedroom. Melissa stood up quickly, almost knocking the stool over. "That will be all, Liza." Her hands fluttered up to her shoulders again before she remembered and forced them back down. Justin looked remarkably fine, she thought, unable for the moment to tear her eyes away from him. His evening coat was of black velvet, his shirt a pristine white, and though there was lace at the cuffs, there was nothing the least bit feminine about him. The coat almost seemed molded to his broad shoulders, so perfectly did it fit, the matching black pantaloons hugged the muscles of his thighs and calves. He was so handsome that all her love for him swelled up, and she had to turn her eyes away.

How he reacted to her own appearance she could not tell, because he simply stood there and stared. "Well, Chatleigh?" she said, when the silence had stretched on quite long enough. "Will I do?"

Justin didn't answer, so she looked up from drawing on the gloves dyed to match her gown, to see him regarding her in a new, and somehow unnerving, way. "Yes, m'dear, you'll do," he said, finally, and began to walk towards her. "Wish you'd wear colors, though."

"I think it's a beautiful gown." Melissa held out her dress on either side, then let it fall with a whisper of sound.

"So it is. Just as well it's lavender."

"Oh? Why?" she asked, as he stopped a few paces away from her. For the first time she realized he was carrying a long, flat box.

"M'father," he cleared his throat, "well, it seems that when m'father went into debt the first thing he sold off were the jewels. Afraid most of them are gone, m'dear." The eyes he raised to her were so filled with regret that Melissa was touched.

"It doesn't matter, Chatleigh." His hair was unruly,

as usual, and she had to resist a wifely impulse to reach up and smooth it.

"Doesn't it?" He shrugged, and thrust the box at her. "Here. Should match your gown, anyway."

Melissa glanced up at him and then back down at the box. Inside, nestled on a bed of black velvet, lay a necklace of teardrop-shaped amethysts, set in gold. "Oh, Justin," she breathed out as she drew the necklace from the box, draping it over her hand. "I don't think I've ever seen anything so lovely."

"No? Afraid it's not very valuable, or m'father would have sold it." Little enough to give her, with all the Chatleigh jewels gone. She was, after all, his countess, if not his wife, and something was due her. Bitterness at the fact that he had nothing again rose to gall him.

"That doesn't matter!" She glanced up at him, to see him watching her with that same odd intentness. Feeling suddenly shy, she undid the catch and slipped the necklace on. "You're right, it matches my gown perfectly," she said, after glancing into the mirror. "And earrings, too."

"Sorry there's not more," he said, abruptly, and Melissa shook her head.

"Don't be. I like these very much." For the first time, as she walked back across the room towards her husband, she felt like a countess. That Justin thought of her that way too, if not as his wife, was borne out by this gift. "Thank you," she said, and, before she could lose her nerve, stretched up on tiptoe to kiss his cheek. "It means a lot to me."

Justin didn't say anything. He only watched her as she picked up her shawl of fine white cashmere and then crossed to the door. He was still standing there when she turned. "Aren't you coming?" she asked.

"What?" He shook his head, as if just awakened.

"Yes, of course."

Much later Melissa slipped out of Augusta's ballroom and made her way to the ladies' retiring room. Heavens! she thought as she climbed the stairs and glanced down at the milling mob below. She had been assured that this, her first social affair in London, would be small and quite manageable. Instead, it had become, as Augusta said with satisfaction, a sad crush. And this at a time when town was said to be thin of people! Melissa's lips twitched in amusement as she sat before a mirror and smoothed her hair. Londoners certainly did have different ideas about things.

Not that she was complaining. In fact, as far as she was concerned, the evening had been a success. She had been introduced to many people, and she hadn't disgraced herself. Of course, she hadn't had the chance to exchange much above a few words with anyone, either. She suspected the real test would come once the ritual of visiting began, as Augusta had assured her it would. She was, it seemed, a success. How very odd.

Her fingers stilled in the act of tweaking a curl into place, and she studied her reflection objectively, as she rarely had before. Was she really so attractive? She'd never thought so, having always been envious of her mother's pastel prettiness. Her own coloring was too vivid, too strong; redheads, so she'd been told, were rarely in style. And yet, this night, she'd heard more than one extravagant compliment on her appearance. A girl's head could be turned quite easily by such flattery, except for one thing. Her husband was not, apparently, in the ranks of her admirers.

Her lips tightened just a bit. She supposed it shouldn't surprise her. After all, it was quite the thing for husband and wife to spend the evening apart; she didn't think Justin had even signed her dance card. Quite a fashionable marriage, she thought, picking up her reticule. She hated it.

The ballroom was no less crowded when she went back in, searching the crowd for her husband. He was nowhere in sight, and neither was her partner for the next dance, whoever he was. The signature on the dance card was illegible, a large *E* followed by a scrawl of letters. Melissa was frowning down at it when a smooth, urbane voice spoke behind her.

"Who would ever have thought," the man said, "the last time we met, that we would be meeting again under these circumstances?"

"I beg your pardon?" Melissa said, and, turning, saw her partner for the next dance regarding her through his quizzing glass. The Marquess of Edgewater, whom she had last seen in the corridor of the Hart and Hind, in what seemed like another life.

Chapter Thirteen

"Good evening," Edgewater said, when Melissa merely stared at him. "I don't believe we have been introduced. I am Edgewater."

"Yes, my lord, I remember you," Melissa responded, finding her voice. She must not let this man see how much she disliked him.

"I thought you might. This is my dance, I believe."

Melissa looked down at the illegible scrawl again. "So it is." Placing her hand on his arm, she allowed him to lead her to the crowded floor, where the sets were just forming. She thanked God it was a country dance, not a waltz. With luck, she wouldn't have to exchange much conversation with him.

She was wrong. "So you were married to him, after all," he said when the steps of the dance briefly brought them together.

Melissa stumbled, but made a quick recovery. "Did you doubt it?" she asked, coolly.

"You must admit, the circumstances were suspicious."

Which you were no doubt pleased to tell everyone, she thought, fuming, as she whirled away from him again.

To her relief, the next time they met, Edgewater appeared to be concentrating on his steps, but when they came together again he returned to the attack. "So now you are a countess," he said. "And Chatleigh, I hear, is going to take his seat at the Lords."

"What is it you want, sir?" Melissa snapped, tired of his baiting.

His eyebrows rose at such direct speaking. "Want? Why, I don't wish Chatleigh to take his seat."

"What?" Melissa stumbled again, and he reached out to grasp her elbow.

"Come, we can't talk about this here." Still holding her arm, he led her off the floor and into the hall, which was marginally less crowded.

"Why is it any concern of yours whether Justin enters politics or not?" she demanded when she could, and again Edgewater's brows rose.

"Quietly, my dear, no need to make this a public event."

"But—"

"Smile, as if you are enjoying yourself. Need I tell you how to flirt?"

Melissa stared up at him, and then, to his surprise, burst into laughter. "Chatleigh was right about you."

"Why? What did he say?"

"He called you a damned dandy."

"Did he?" Edgewater paused in the act of reaching for his snuffbox. "He has always underestimated me."

"And I believe you underestimate him. Or do you?" Her eyes suddenly narrowed. "Why does it matter to you what Chatleigh does?"

"Because, my dear, he is a Tory."

Melissa raised a delicately arched brow. That hardly seemed reason enough. "Yes, so?"

185

"And the government is backwards enough and re-actionary enough without adding another Tory to it."

"I hardly think one more would make so much difference."

"Ah, but you never know, do you?" This time he did reach for the snuffbox. "These are dangerous times, my lady. Such times call for boldness, not the timidity of our government."

"Are you saying you're a revolutionary?"

"Hardly. Do I look like one?"

"No, you don't," she said, slowly. "But then, isn't that the idea?"

Edgewater looked up sharply as he was just about to inhale the snuff from the back of his hand. The little countess was no fool. "You are his wife," he said, abruptly. "You could convince him his talents would be wasted in Parliament."

Melissa shook her head "No, I don't have that much influence with him, and wouldn't presume to tell him what to do. Besides, I think he might have something worth saying."

"Do you?" Edgewater studied her and then smiled. "You surprise me, my lady."

"Do I? Why?"

"There is more to you than it appears."

"I am the daughter of a soldier, sir." Her voice was quiet. "And I don't give up a fight easily."

"I believe this is a battle I may enjoy," he murmured.

"Evening, Edgewater. M'dear." Justin suddenly loomed beside them. Edgewater, slim and dapper, looked effete and puny next to Justin's robust frame. "Believe this is my dance."

Melissa consulted her card. It was a waltz, and Justin had definitely not requested it, but she would not argue. "So it is. Good evening, sir," she said to Edgewater, and he inclined his head.

Justin led her out onto the floor, and his arm went about her waist, drawing her closer to him than she had been since that fateful night at the Hart and Hind. Melissa shivered, though the room was not cold. Far from it. She felt warmth creeping up into her face, and as Justin whirled her across the floor, it invaded her limbs, making them feel curiously heavy, so that she leaned towards him for support. Feeling the movement, Justin glanced down, and she met his questioning, silent look with eyes wide and startled. "I . . . I've never danced like this before," she said, breathlessly.

"No? Wouldn't have thought it." Justin swung her about, and her hand, resting on his arm, tightened. Through her kid glove she could feel the tactile warmth of his velvet jacket, the strength of his arm; and she shivered again.

"Shouldn't we be having a conversation?" she asked, when he didn't speak.

"Why?"

"Why? Everyone else seems to talk while they dance."

"Oh, we've plenty to talk about, madam," he said, softly, "but we will not do so here."

"To talk about?"

"Your *tête-à-tête* with Edgewater."

"What!"

"Pray lower your voice."

"But it wasn't—"

"We will not discuss it here."

"We will not discuss it anywhere!" she snapped, and would have pulled out of his grasp had he not held on to her.

187

"Easy, m'dear, don't want to cause a scene."

"I don't care!" she said in a furious whisper. "Of all the ridiculous things to say—you know I'm not like that!"

"Do I?" he said. All the old doubts, the old suspicions, had come rushing back when he'd seen her deep in what appeared to be intimate conversation with Edgewater. His gaze, cool and impassive, caught hers and held for a long moment. Then she jerked away from him. "Come." He took her arm. "I'll bring you to my aunt."

Melissa threw him a fulminating glance as he escorted her across the floor to where the chaperones sat. So he thought her a flirt? Very well, then, she thought. She would be a flirt, and see how he reacted.

And so she was. She did not stay with the chaperones, as she suspected Justin wished, but instead took to the floor with any man who asked her. And there were many. Her beauty and freshness, her delightfully frank way of looking at one, were novelties to the jaded members of the *ton*. She was young, yet without any of the gaucheries of a girl fresh from the schoolroom, and unusually pretty. By the time she and Justin climbed into their new barouche it was late, and her feet in the thin satin slippers were aching. No wonder, she thought with satisfaction. She hadn't sat out one dance. Let Chatleigh make what he would of that.

The barouche swayed gently as it traveled over Mayfair's cobbled streets, and in the light from a passing streetlamp she saw her husband's face, turned a bit to the side, wearing an abstracted look. He'd said little to her since they had left Lady Helmsley's. It was time to change that.

"I have been invited to go driving tomorrow," she said, and Justin's eyes opened.

"By whom?" he asked.

"By Lord Beverley. I trust you won't approve."

"Would it matter?"

"Perhaps. Of course, if I thought you would ask me . . ."

She let the words hang, and though he was quiet, she sensed his surprise. "Can't," he said finally.

"I see." She managed to sound bored. "Well, no matter. If not Lord Beverley, then someone else."

"Melissa—"

"Ah, here we are. It's good to be home. I'm tired, aren't you?"

Justin didn't have a chance to answer, as the carriage drew up to a stop. "About tomorrow, Melissa," he said, catching up to her in the hall.

"What? Are you still thinking about that? But don't bother!" Her laugh was high and tinkling. "I assure you, I will do quite well without you." She turned towards the stairs. "Good night."

Justin stayed where he was, watching her go, raking his fingers through his hair, and then turned. "Phelps, I want brandy brought to the book-room," he called over his shoulder.

Melissa glanced down just as he turned, and she smothered a smile at seeing the look on his face. So, the Earl was confused and frustrated. Good. It was high time he had more to think about than his work. It was high time he noticed her.

The cold that had started the New Year continued, making travel hazardous and stopping the stages, so that no mail could get through. Ice frosted

189

the windows of homes and shops, and by the end of the month the Thames was frozen solid. To the delight of the Londoners, a fair sprang up on the ice, a wonderful Frost Fair, with booths selling everything from beer and trinkets to broadsides printed on presses set up on the ice. Naturally such a novel affair drew many people, and early one afternoon a landau with a ducal crest pulled up on a bank of the river. Melissa emerged as a footman came to open the door. Attired in half boots and a gray pelisse trimmed with fur, and carrying a large fur muff, she was comfortably warm. Behind her came Sabrina, Duchess of Bainbridge, and the Duke, who wore a faintly bemused air. Melissa had known the Bainbridges only since Augusta's ball, but already she and Sabrina were on their way to becoming fast friends. The young duchess was pretty and charming, but what Melissa liked best about her was her openness. Like Melissa, Sabrina had not been born into the *ton;* she was an American, and her attitude was a refreshing change from the stilted formality Melissa had already encountered.

"Oh my, Oliver, just look at this!" Sabrina exclaimed as they stepped onto ice that had been cleared of snow, to form a path reaching to the other bank. A sign nearby read Freezeland St.

"Yes. Careful on that ice," Oliver said, taking her arm. "I shouldn't have let you come. Especially not now."

"Oh, pooh!" Sabrina flipped her hair, long and golden, over her shoulder. "You worry too much. Is the Earl like that?" she asked, leaning forward to address Melissa who was walking on the Duke's other side.

"Oh, no," Melissa murmured, and a little pang

went through her. Her attempts to make Justin notice her had come to nothing. With Parliament in session he spent most of his days away from the house, and often at night they attended different affairs. It was the way of life in the *ton*. Husbands and wives did not live in each other's pockets.

Which was why the Bainbridges had been such a revelation to Melissa. Their marriage was decidedly unfashionable, and yet no one would deny their place in society. The Duke's position at the Foreign Office kept them in town, where they had a wide range of acquaintances. Today he had left his office to escort his wife; the Frost Fair was said to be rife with pickpockets and other undesirables, and he was concerned about her safety. It seemed a little silly to Melissa, since nothing looked more harmless, but again she felt that pang of envy. It must be wonderful when one's husband cared that much.

They stopped at different booths, one selling gingerbread, another toys, and by such progress they eventually reached the intersection with the lane that was called the Grand Mall. Even Bainbridge looked impressed. From here one could see the broad sweep of the river, to London Bridge in one direction, Blackfriars in the other. "Oh, heavens," Melissa said. "I've never seen anything like this."

"Yes," Sabrina said in an odd tone.

Bainbridge glanced down at her. "What is it?"

She looked back, frowning. "I don't know. That man—"

"What man?" he said, instantly alert.

"There was a man, but he's not there now."

"So?"

"I thought he was following us. Oh, but it must have been a coincidence."

"Many people here are going the same way," Melissa said.

"Yes, but he stopped whenever we did. I noticed him a few booths back." Her face grew serious. "He was looking at you."

"Me! Heavens, whatever for?"

"What did he look like?" Bainbridge asked.

"He was, oh, not very tall, with pointed features, but I don't see him now, Oliver."

Bainbridge glanced around. The intersection, thronged though it was, seemed an open and safe enough space. "Wait here," he said, and plunged back into the crowd.

"Oh, dear." Sabrina's brow puckered. "I wish I hadn't said anything."

"But if someone is following us . . ." Melissa protested.

"Yes, but I'm not at all sure that he was. And Oliver tends to be too protective. Especially now."

"Why is that?"

"Oh, dear, I shouldn't have said anything." She glanced around. "Promise you won't tell a soul?"

"What?"

Sabrina glanced around again, and her voice dropped to a whisper. "We're to be parents."

"Why, Sabrina, that's marvelous!" Melissa exclaimed, ignoring the sudden sharp stab of envy and loneliness. To have a child. To have Justin's child. As things were, it would probably never happen. If she thought it would do any good she would approach him, but she was scared. If she came too close he would see her too clearly, the flaw that was inside her.

Bainbridge came back then, and at his wife's look shook his head. "I didn't see anyone," he said.

"I didn't imagine it, Oliver. You know I'm not prone to such fancies. Not even now."

"Yes, I know." He smiled down at her. "But I think we've seen enough for today, don't you?"

Sabrina looked up at him and then sighed. "Very well. I am starting to feel a trifle cold. Melissa, you don't mind?"

"Oh, no," Melissa murmured, though she felt a little resentful at having the expedition cut short because of Bainbridge's overprotectiveness. Justin would certainly never treat her that way. Unfortunately.

Although the outing had been cut short, Melissa was glad to reach the warmth of her own home. "Phelps, bring the tea tray, please," she called as she climbed the stairs. She turned into the drawing room and then stopped. "Justin!"

He turned from the window through which he had been looking out. "Yes, m'dear?"

"Nothing." Melissa crossed the room to stand before the closed stove. "I didn't expect to see you."

Justin turned back. Not for the world would he tell her that he had come home, thinking to give her a treat by escorting her to the Frost Fair. Nor would he admit, even to himself, how disappointed he had been when he'd learned she'd gone with someone else. "Was that Beverley you were with?" he said, sharply.

Melissa's eyes widened slightly. "No, the Bainbridges. Do you disapprove?"

He smiled. "Whigs, m'dear."

"Oh, dear, so they are. Would you like tea?" she asked, as Phelps brought the tray in.

193

Justin shook his head. "No, thank you. Got work to do. Excuse me."

"Of course." She watched him go with a little frown on her face. Drat, and just when they had been talking amicably enough. This would have to stop. If only there were some way to hold him.

Her eyes fell on a pile of square envelopes lying on a salver, invitations to various events, left there that morning. It was a prodigious pile, and her heart sank at the prospect of dealing with it. And the season hadn't even begun! She couldn't imagine what it would be like when everyone returned to town and began having balls and routs and soirées. It was hard enough deciding which to attend now.

She glanced at the invitations again, sharply this time. Usually she consulted Augusta on which events to attend, trusting that lady to choose the best. Chatleigh always went along with the choice, though he often went off on pursuits of his own. That, Melissa thought, was something she could change. If she needed an excuse to see her husband again now and in the future, she had it at hand. It would only take courage.

Before she could stop herself, she had scooped up the invitations and was running lightly down the stairs to knock on the door to the book-room. After a moment Justin, within, spoke. "Enter."

Melissa pushed the heavy door open and went in. The room was long and wide, the recessed shelves with glazed doors set between the long windows holding thousands of books in morocco bindings. Cushioned seats were set in the window embrasures, and comfortable leather armchairs were scattered about, some near the fireplace, others grouped together as if for a *tête-à-tête*. It was probably the most inviting room in the house, but Melissa had rarely been inside. Justin had appropriated it since he'd taken up politics. Here he was close to any books he might need, and the large table gave him plenty of space for spreading out his papers.

He rose from behind that table now, a questioning look on his face. "Yes?"

"I think you need a secretary, Chatleigh" Melissa said, gesturing towards the papers. Justin looked down, and smiled.

"Almighty mess. Trouble is, can't seem to find anything worth speaking out on." He gestured her towards a chair and sat down himself, linking his hands behind his head. "Nothing that hasn't been taken, that is."

"Surely there's something?" Melissa said, putting the invitations down.

"Don't know what. I don't know, Melissa." He got up and began to pace the room. "If I thought I was doing some good I'd stay with it, but nothing ever seems to get done. There's too much concern for party, and if you're a Tory, you'd better not agree with the Whigs. Never mind they have some of the right ideas. And neither side seems to care about the war."

"Maybe that's what you should speak about."

"Maybe."

"No, I'm serious, Chatleigh. You were there. You know what it's like. Perhaps they need to hear it."

Justin shrugged. "Perhaps. What did you wish to see me about?"

"These." Melissa handed the invitations across to him. "I'm afraid I need a secretary, too."

Justin glanced through the invitations. "Want to know what to accept?"

"Yes. Well, I really want to know which ones you'd like to attend."

"Hm. Well, I'd like to go to the Bainbridges' ball, even if they are Whigs."

"Sabrina assures me it won't be at all political."

"Sabrina, is it?" Justin glanced up. His wife was a social success. On the days when she was at home, their drawing room was thronged with visitors; at the various parties she attended, she was always surrounded by a small crowd of admirers. How he felt about that, he wasn't sure. Sometimes he looked at her, flushed with laughter aroused by a compliment paid her by one of her gallants and felt sharp, cold anger. At other times, however, he felt a curious pang of loneliness, as if he'd lost something precious. There were times, as now, when they seemed to get along well. Perhaps if he attended more events with her, she would remember that she had a husband. "Very well. The Bainbridges, it is. And this one." He tossed a card onto the table. "And this. And . . . this."

"What is it?" Melissa asked, leaning forward.

"A political do, at the Prime Minister's. We'll have to go, I'm afraid."

"Of course." Melissa gathered up the invitations he had selected, her hand just brushing his, and rose as Justin's hand quickly drew away. "I'll go write the acceptances. Will you be home for dinner?"

"No, m'dear, afraid not." He sounded genuinely regretful. "Another time, perhaps."

"Of course," Melissa said, and left the room.

Justin stayed still for a few moments and then turned in his chair, looking out the window without seeing anything. He had hoped that by coming in to the book-room he would be able to concentrate on his work and forget about his wife, but it hadn't worked. He thought about her too much, damn it, when he was supposed to be working, and at night, when the thought of her sleeping just a few doors away, available to him should he wish to go to her, had kept him awake more than once. Sometimes only a liberal dose of brandy or wine helped him find surcease from his powerful, incomprehensible yearnings. He longed to take her in his arms, lower his face into the sweet scent of her curls, run his hands along her soft curves, and . . .

Bah! He threw himself into a chair. He sounded besotted. He was not going to be caught in her toils. It would not do to dwell on her beauty, longingly and lovingly, and wonder how she would look suitably attired. *Or unattired* . . .

Justin sat up quickly, clearing his throat. Dangerous thoughts, these. Think about other things, he told himself. Be grateful she is in half-mourning, which dims her beauty, though it does not discourage her admirers. And he realized, suddenly sitting upright, there was something he could do. She was a woman, and that meant she could be bought. A cynical thought, but a true one. And he knew just what would do the trick.

He grinned, sitting back with his hands behind his head. His wife's money freed his own for use on such extravagances, and that almost reconciled him to having married a wealthy woman. Doubtless Madame Celeste had Melissa's measurements and would be happy to create a new wardrobe for her. And once Melissa saw it, she would forget about other men for a time. If he had to buy her loyalty, so be it. She was his!

Melissa settled back against the squabs of the barouche, tired but happy with the events of the day. It had occurred to her that she and Justin would want to start entertaining. Her only experience in doing so had been the Twelfth Night party, and though it had been a success, she had to admit that had partly been due to its novelty. In London, standards would be much higher.

The thought had made her take a second look at the house, and she had realized how much there was to be done. Fortunately the structure itself was sound, but several of the public rooms were in urgent need of redecoration. The dining room was much too dark, with its heavy oak furniture and wine velvet draperies; the drawing room remained an Egyptian nightmare. In the past weeks she hadn't been able to see to them, but now she made time.

The weather had moderated somewhat. After what people were beginning to call the Great Freeze had ended, a heavy fall of snow had blanketed the land for days on end. Now it was turning warmer, and though the streets were wet and muddy they were passable, allowing Melissa to go out on her errands. She visited Gillow's warehouse to look at furniture, linen drapers to settle on fabrics for draperies and upholstery; and carpeting shops to select floor coverings. She also consulted with Augusta on a date for her own ball. Once the season began, the social calendar would be so filled that it would be difficult to find a night when some other major event didn't conflict with theirs.

There was just one more place for her to visit today; a printer's, to order the invitations. The footman came to open the door of the barouche for her.

As Melissa descended she glanced down the sidewalk and then froze. Coming towards her was her stepfather.

She almost ducked back into the barouche, but it was too late. He had seen her. Schooling her features to present a calm facade, Melissa stepped back against the coach, her chin held high. "Sir Stephen," she said.

"Well, daughter." She turned her head as he moved to embrace her, and he pulled away, his gaze filled with reproach. "What, don't you even have a kiss for your father?"

"What do you want?" Melissa's gaze was cold.

"Merely to have a word with you. Are you going in there?" he said, indicating the printer's shop.

"Yes."

"Pity. We cannot be private there."

"I don't wish to be private with you!" she snapped, and the footman, who still held the door, glanced towards her. "What is it you want?"

"Merely to have a word with you, daughter. Would you deny your father that?"

By a great effort of will, Melissa held her temper. "Oh, very well, if we stay here we'll likely cause a scene. Come." She turned back towards the barouche. "Tell John Coachman to return home," she said to the footman as she climbed in.

"Ah, this is more like it," Sir Stephen said, settling in. "Better than those hacks I've been chasing you in."

"You've been following me?" Melissa exclaimed, and a sudden memory of the Frost Fair came into her mind. But the man Sabrina had thought she'd seen didn't resemble her stepfather at all. A coincidence.

"Yes, of course. I had to reach you. Really, daughter, you should tell your butler to allow me in."

"What do you want?" she said again.

"You know what I want, daughter." His eyes bored into hers. "What I deserve.

"I'll not give you any money!"

"Ah, but it's not money I want, is it?"

Chapter Fourteen

Melissa's caught her breath when she heard the silky menace in his voice. Her eyes never leaving his, she reached up to bang on the ceiling of the coach. After a moment the equipage stopped and the footman came to the door. "Yes, my lady?"

"Sir Stephen is getting down here," she said.

"Now, daughter —"

"I am not your daughter!"

Sir Stephen's face grew ugly with anger. "I grow tired of you and Chatleigh, and of your high-handed ways," he growled, leaning forward so far that she shrank back. "But you'll pay." He climbed out of the coach. "Remember that. You'll pay."

"Tell John Coachman to drive on," Melissa said to the footman, and she leaned back against the squabs, shaking. She had no doubt that he meant what he said. His threat against Justin, she discounted; that had been empty words. The threat against herself, however, had been all too real. The feeling of safety, which she had treasured since her marriage, evaporated, leaving her feeling alone and defenseless. Unless she found a way to stop him, Sir Stephen would, indeed, make her pay.

* * *

"Has her ladyship returned home yet?" Justin asked, striding into the hall, and Phelps shook his head.

"No, my lord, but—"

"Damn!" Justin turned away, raking a hand through his hair. "Of all days for her to be late. Let me know when she does come in, Phelps."

"Yes, my lord. I think that it is her now," he added, glancing out one of the sidelights, and Justin turned from the back of the hall.

"Good." He leaned against the wall as Phelps went to open the door. A few moments later Melissa came in. Her gray pelisse was usually flattering, but today her color was missing and her eyes had a haunted look. In spite of his resolve to behave coolly, Justin stepped forward. "My dear, what is it?"

Melissa jerked away from his outstretched hand, wrapping her arms about herself. "Nothing."

"No?" Justin let his hand drop, absurdly disappointed that she had not let him touch her. "Are you ill?"

"No! Just tired. If you'll excuse me, I'll go up to my room—"

"Wait." Frantically Justin searched his mind for some pretext to keep her with him. He didn't want her going upstairs while she was in this mood. "Come into the bookroom. Got something I want to ask you."

"Can't it wait, Chatleigh?" she responded, sounding so miserable that he had the odd urge to enfold her in his arms and rock her back and forth, comforting her.

"Won't take a minute. Come on."

"Oh, very well." With slow, heavy movements Melissa took off her bonnet and pelisse and handed them to Phelps. "But just for a minute."

Somewhat more than a minute later, Melissa climbed the stairs to her room, glad at last to be seeking sanctuary. After the incident with her stepfather all she wanted was to take a bath, scrubbing herself clean of his presence, and then climb into bed, pull the covers over her head, and shut out the world. It had been unfortunate that Chatleigh had chosen today, of all days, to ask her advice on topics he could speak about. At any other time she would have been more than pleased, but not today. Today she was beginning to think that it was just as well he'd kept his distance. She couldn't bear to be touched by him, by anyone, because if he came too close, he would know.

"Oh, my lady!" Liza exclaimed when Melissa came into her room.

"What is it?" Melissa asked, crossing the room to place her reticule on the dressing table.

"Nothing, my lady. I just didn't expect to see you. Would you be wanting to choose a gown for tonight?"

"Tonight?" Melissa's fingers, poised to remove the ribbon that held back her curls, stilled. "What is tonight?"

"His lordship told me you're dining with Lady Helmsley."

"What? He didn't tell me." Melissa scrubbed at her face with her hands. "All I want is to have a bath and then go to bed."

"Yes, my lady, you do look done in. Just tell me which gown you want and then I'll draw a bath for you."

"Oh, very well." Melissa walked across to her dressing room and then stopped as Liza flung open the wardrobe doors. "What!" Inside was a rainbow, a profusion of colors and fabrics such as Melissa had never seen before. There were evening gowns of silk and satin in emerald and bronze and turquoise; morning gowns of peach muslin and ivory wool; a new pelisse, of teal blue velvet, with a dashing little hat to match; and even a riding habit, of forest green velvet. Melissa stared, mouth agape. "What in the world—"

"Aren't they beautiful, my lady?" Liza said, shyly stroking the pelisse.

"Yes, but—where in the world did they come from? I never ordered all this."

"No, but I did," Justin said from behind her, and she turned, to see him lounging in the doorway, grinning. "Merry Christmas, a little late."

"But, Chatleigh—"

"Went to Celeste's and had her make all this up for you," he said, waving a hand towards the gowns. "Hope she picked the right colors."

"Yes, she did, but Chatleigh—"

"High time you started wearing colors, m'dear," he said, his voice softening. "Time to put the past behind you."

Melissa quickly glanced up from fingering a satin evening gown. Justin was smiling, but his eyes were anxious. He looked so like a hopeful little boy that she couldn't bear to disappoint him. She remembered all too well how she had felt when he'd refused her gift. "They're lovely," she said, going on tiptoe to kiss his cheek. "Thank you. They must have cost a fortune."

Justin smiled down at her, a look in his eyes she'd never seen before. "Worth it," he said. "Which are you wearing tonight?"

"I don't know!" She turned back to the gowns. "You might have warned me we're dining at Aunt Augusta's."

"Just came up. She wants to see me about something." He lounged against the doorjamb. "The green, I think."

"What, this one?" Melissa held the gown of green watered silk against her. "Yes, I think so, too. It's a lovely present." Her eyes softened as she looked at him. "Thank you."

Justin nodded, and his cynical motive for providing her with this wardrobe was forgotten. All the expense and the time had been worth it, if only to remove that bleak look from her eyes. "You'll do me proud," he said, and, bowing, turned.

"Really!" Melissa exclaimed, but he was gone. She stared after him, and then, in spite of her pique, laughed. That was Justin, and she might just as well accept him as he was. He was right, she thought, turning back to the gowns. It was time to put the past behind her, time, in spite of her stepfather's veiled threats, to concentrate on the future. And, after today, that future looked much brighter.

The line of carriages in Whitehall, all bound for the home of the Prime Minister, was prodigiously long. Melissa, outwardly composed, inwardly very nervous indeed, sat across from Justin in the barouche. This night would mark her debut as a political wife. She hoped she would measure up.

At last the barouche came to a stop, and the Chatleighs emerged from within. Justin's attire was, as usual, faultless; his evening coat of black superfine sat on his broad shoulders with nary a wrinkle, and even his normally unruly hair had been tamed. It was Melissa, however, who caught the eye. In a gown of bronze satin trimmed with gold braid, she was dazzling. The gown fit her perfectly, the *décolletage* lower across her youthful bosom than she was accustomed to, the short, puffed sleeves revealing slender, rounded, arms. The heavy satin fell straight nearly to the floor, where slippers dyed to match peeped out. Topazes, borrowed from Lady Helmsley, sparkled at her ears and throat, and a filet of gold banded her forehead. The color, an unusual shade, caught the highlights in her hair and made them blaze, and her eyes held a faint golden tinge. Justin was very proud of his wife as he walked beside her into the house. There, knew she'd look good in colors, he thought.

Although the official residence of the Prime Minister was in Downing Street, Lord Liverpool chose instead to live in his own residence, Fife House. Melissa and Justin slowly made their way up the crowded staircase and, after being greeted by Lord Liverpool, passed into a drawing room already filled with ladies in brilliantly colored gowns and gentlemen in evening clothes. Justin stopped a passing waiter and procured champagne for each of them, and they smiled at each other over the rims of their glasses. "So this is the sort of thing a political wife attends?" Melissa asked.

"Afraid so, m'dear," Justin said, taking her arm and leading her deeper into the room. Tonight all the members of the Tory establishment were present, Lord Sidmouth, the Home Secretary; Eldon, Lord Chancellor; and Lord Palmerston, Secretary of War among them, people Justin would have to impress, if he were to stay in politics. "No dancing, I'm afraid, and no music."

"As long as there's food."

Justin grinned down at her. His dainty little wife had a trencherman's appetite. "There'll be food. Come, there're some people I'd like you to meet."

"Justin?" a feminine voice said behind them, and they both turned. "You are here! Daddy said you would be."

"Eleanor." Justin ran a hand over his hair, the first time he'd done so that evening, and Melissa looked at

206

him curiously. What was there about this woman that made him uncomfortable? "Evening, Eleanor. Your father here?"

"Yes, over there." Eleanor gestured carelessly over her shoulder as she came forward, her eyes never leaving Melissa's face. "Is this your bride, Justin?"

"Yes." Justin cleared his throat, acutely aware that this meeting was the focus of much interest. "Melissa, m'dear, like you to meet an old friend, Miss Eleanor Keane."

"Miss Keane." Melissa held out her hand, smiling politely as she studied the other woman. In a gown of ice blue satin that matched the expensive simplicity of Melissa's attire, Eleanor looked regal and icily beautiful. Her golden hair was plaited into a coronet atop her head, and an ornate, heavy necklace of sapphires and diamonds glowed brilliantly from her neck. She was so beautiful, Melissa thought wistfully. Eleanor Keane had the height Melissa lacked, and the proud bearing to go with it. She seemed a veritable goddess, and at that moment Melissa took a decided dislike to her.

"Lady Chatleigh." Eleanor's voice was cool as she took Melissa's hand and, after one brief glance, dismissed her. "So, you are going into politics after all?" she said, taking Justin's arm. "Daddy told me, but I wasn't certain I believed him."

"Yes, well, thought I'd try it." With a woman on either arm, Justin couldn't give in to the desire to run a hand over his hair again. *Damn, what a coil.* "In fact, I was just going to introduce my wife to some people she hasn't yet met, Eleanor, if you will excuse us?"

"Of course." Eleanor stepped back. Her smile did not reach her eyes, which were as icy as her dress. "But I must insist you talk to Daddy later on."

"Of course," Justin replied, and turned away, aware

that Melissa was looking curiously up at him.

"Is Daddy anyone of importance?" she asked.

"Hm? Oh, Mr. Keane. Yes, he's an M.P. Not as important as he'd like to think. Found out money can't buy everything."

Melissa's hand tightened on his arm. "Oh."

Justin glanced down at hearing the colorless monosyllable. "Sorry, m'dear," he said, patting her hand with his free one, and she looked up at him. "Come, let's get some food."

Melissa smiled. "First sensible thing you've said all evening."

Later in the evening, she was standing with Lady Rutherford, the wife of the Earl of Rutherford, and trying hard not to yawn. Never before had she realized that parties could be such hard work when a career was at stake. Justin appeared to be doing quite well, though, she thought fondly, seeking him out as he made his way through the throng. He seemed to be well liked and respected by his peers. The foundation had been laid for his future. Now they would just have to find some way for him to make his mark.

". . . and I must say, Chatleigh is doing better than I expected," Lady Rutherford said, paralleling Melissa's thoughts. "I've heard good things about him tonight, my dear."

"I'm glad," Melissa said absently, for across a small clearing in the crowd she could see that Justin had stopped near a small group of people that included Miss Keane. With them was an older man, short and running to fat, his bald pate glistening. Mr. Keane? He didn't look as if he could have produced the beauteous Eleanor, who had her hand on Justin's arm and was smiling up at him. Melissa had a sudden urge to scratch her eyes out.

"Yes, he's shown more shrewdness than I would

208

have guessed. Talking with the Keanes is a particularly good idea. Think of the scandal there might have been!"

"What?" Melissa turned back. "Why?"

"Why, my dear, because he and Miss Keane were so nearly engaged, of course. You knew about it, did you not?"

It was as if she had been struck. "Of course," Melissa said through frozen lips, aware that Lady Rutherford was watching her closely.

"Quite a surprise when Chatleigh turned up married to you, but then, I daresay he's done better for himself. They call her the Ice Princess, you know. I daresay it's well earned."

"Oh?" Melissa hoped her face didn't betray her shock. Justin and Eleanor. Now she remembered where she had heard the name. She should have known, just from the way the woman looked at him. The question now was, what was she going to do about it?

Lady Rutherford murmured some excuse and moved away, and though Melissa nodded at her, she was hardly aware of her going, so intent was she on the tableau across the room. Justin must have said something amusing, for at that moment Eleanor put back her head in a laugh, displaying her long white throat and emphasizing her bosom. Primitive rage suddenly surged through Melissa. *She shan't have him!* she thought, grabbing a glass of champagne from the tray of a passing waiter and swallowing it in one gulp. Justin was hers, and she was not going to give him up to some blond hussy.

Melissa would never afterwards remember how she made it through the rest of that evening. It dragged on interminably as she talked and laughed with various people in the interest of furthering her husband's ca-

209

reer. Fortunately for her peace of mind, he didn't stay much longer with the Keanes, but that incident made her look at him in a new way. Lord, he was handsome, and so well built, she thought, swallowing another glass of champagne. Almost graceful, in spite of his height and bulk. And he was hers! She remembered, with a little shiver, how his arms had felt when about her, and suddenly she longed to feel them around her again. And soon. Her fingers clenched around the stem of her glass. Miss Keane had best watch out. Justin was hers!

It was late when they finally arrived home. Justin stifled a yawn as they climbed the stairs towards their rooms. "Well, m'dear, if you'll excuse me, I'm for bed—"

"No, don't go just yet." Melissa laid a hand on his arm and gazed up at him, her eyes tawny in the dim light. "Surely you can spare a few moments to talk about this evening?"

"Of course," Justin said, a bit puzzled. She had been quiet since leaving the Prime Minister's, and this request was unprecedented. "Are you feeling all right, m'dear?"

"Certainly. I may have had a bit too much champagne," she added over her shoulder as she preceded him into the drawing room. For the life of him, he could not take his eyes from the gentle sway of her hips.

"I believe many people did." Justin tugged on the bellpull, and a moment later a footman came in, to build up the fire and light the remaining lamps. Melissa had worked hard on redecorating this room, and its color scheme of blue and white and gold was relaxing and comfortable. "What was it you wished to talk about?" Justin asked, when the footman had gone.

"Will you have a brandy?" she asked, her voice

husky.

"I wasn't going to, but—"

"I'd like one, Justin."

"Very well." He turned away, startled by her use of his name. "Though it won't make you feel any better tomorrow," he added as he handed her the cognac.

"I daresay I shall survive." She sipped from the glass, her eyes never leaving his, and then, almost abruptly, turned. "Come sit with me," she said, leading him over to a pair of gold striped-satin sofas. He waited until she had chosen one, and then sat on the other, his long legs stretched ahead of him, crossed at the ankles. He thought he saw a spasm of annoyance cross her face before she rose and came to sit by him, curling her legs up under her. Of all the things that had happened this night, this was the most startling. Justin wondered if he was dreaming.

Melissa took a sip of the cognac and then reached down to untie the satin ribbons that fastened her slippers. With nudges from her toes she pushed both slippers off and stretched out one leg. The sight of her foot, slender and elegant in the white silk, and of her delicately turned ankle, had an odd effect on him. "I dislike wearing shoes," she said, with the careful pronunciation of the tipsy. "I would go barefoot all the time . . . if I could."

"I dislike neckcloths," he said, tugging at his. "Whoever decreed this ridiculous fashion—"

"Here, my lord, let me help you." Setting her glass down on the sofa table, she leaned forward and began working at the knot. The neckline of her gown gaped, and Justin had to force his eyes away from the soft white mounds presented to his view.

"Melissa." His voice was firm as he grasped her hands. "I can manage."

"Can you?" she said softly, her fingers reaching up

211

to stroke his cheek.

He swallowed, hard. "Melissa, stop. If you don't know where this leads—"

"But I do." Her eyes met his, and held. "Justin."

Justin stared at her, his head reeling, and then he very careully reached over to set his glass down. All the nights he had paused at her door, thinking of her lying soft and warm in her bed, all the evenings when he had sought comfort in a bottle, needing surcease from the desire raging within him. But she was his wife! There was nothing wrong in this, in taking what was offered. "Melissa. Are you sure—"

Melissa suddenly pressed against him, reaching up and kissing him full on the mouth. Caught by surprise, he pulled back, but then his arms came down of their own accord, pulling her across him, onto his lap. Her fingers wound into his hair as he bent to her, deepening the kiss. "Ah, Lissa," he whispered, his lips now trailing kisses over her cheeks, her nose, her eyes. "My wife." He found her lips again, parting sweetly under his to allow his tongue entry. They kissed for a very long time, his fingers stroking restlessly up and down her back, hers now touching his face, now clutching at his shoulders. He bent her backwards, one arm supporting her, and his free hand came around to trace the lines of her jaw and throat, to stroke her shoulder, and finally, at last, to slip below the gold braid-trimmed neckline of her gown. Melissa moaned low in her throat as his warm hand cupped her breast, and she tightened her hold around his neck, pressing closer to him and kissing him with greater abandon. When they finally broke apart, his breathing was as shaky as hers.

They regarded each other for long moments, her eyes glazed and her lips swollen. He reached out to trace the outline of her lips with his fingertips and then, slipping his arm under her knees, stood with her in his arms. There was no one in the hall to see the Earl carrying his wife up to bed, no one to notice the way she nestled against his shoulder or pressed kisses into his throat. Justin was breathing heavily by the time he reached her room, though she was as light as a feather in his arms.

At her door Justin reluctantly set her down, while she whispered that she would send her maid away. A little while later, he knocked on the door that connected their rooms. Melissa had removed her jewels and taken down her hair, but she was still dressed. Swiftly he crossed the room to her and pulled her against him, hard, claiming her mouth in a fierce, triumphant kiss as the blood sang in his veins. She was his! His hands slid over her satin-covered curves, and then his fingers fumbled at the laces at the back of her gown. At last they came free, and he impatiently pushed the material off her shoulders, letting it fall into a molten pool at her feet, leaving her clad only in shift and stockings. As he reached for her, she gave a little giggle, which unexpectedly turned into a hiccup.

"Oh, dear," she said, and hiccupped again, as he swung her into his arms and carried her over to the bed, invitingly turned down for the night. She hiccupped yet again, and as he stood gazing down at her, a nasty suspicion struck him. She had had too much champagne, and then the cognac. Damn, she was foxed, and therefore not responsible for her actions. If he took advantage of her now, he would be a cad, the veriest bounder. She would never forgive him, or herself.

"Justin?" Melissa said softly, when he made no move to join her, and he came out of his thoughts. All his instincts, his very soul, demanded he give in to the desires raging through his body, but he couldn't. Not like this. It was a difficult decision, but it was for the best.

He took a deep breath. "Best get some sleep, m'dear," he said, bending and swiftly kissing her on the forehead as he pulled the covers up. "Likely to have quite a head tomorrow."

"Justin!" Her voice came out as a wail as he crossed the room. He stopped for a moment, his shoulders stiffening, but then resolutely went on. This was for the best, he told himself, and closed the door, cursing himself for a fool. There'd be no sleep for him this night.

"Good morning, my lady," Liza said, opening the curtains and letting brilliant sunshine flood the room. " 'Tis a fine day."

Melissa groaned and turned her aching head into the pillow, sick with shame and the effects of too much to drink as memory came back to her with a rush. Somehow, perhaps because of exhaustion or the combination of brandy and champagne, she had managed to fall asleep. Now, unfortunately, it was morning, and she had to face her husband. It would be difficult, indeed. "Go away," she muttered.

There was the sound of a door opening, and someone spoke in a low voice. "Here, my lady, drink this," Liza said a moment later, and Melissa looked with undisguised loathing at the tumbler in her hand.

"What is it?" she said, revolted by the murky brew.

"It will make you feel better, my lady. 'Tis his lordship's idea."

Melissa looked up sharply, which she immediately regretted, and she realized for the first time that Justin stood at the foot of her bed. "Good morning," he said, quietly.

Melissa glared at him. "You!" she said, bitterly.

214

"Yes. Liza, leave us, please."

"No, Liza, stay. His lordship will be leaving."

Liza looked from one to the other and then made her decision, hastily scuttling out of the room with this titbit of gossip. Melissa looked after her resentfully and then dropped her head into her hands. "Go away," she said in a muffled voice.

"We must talk," Justin said, bringing a chair near the bed and turning it around, so that he straddled it.

"I don't want to talk to you—ever again."

"I understand you're upset—"

"Upset? Upset?" Melissa's hand flew to her temple in response to the renewed pounding there. "Go away!"

"Melissa—"

"Go away. Get out! Get out!" Her voice rose. "I don't want to talk to you. Get out!"

Justin gazed at her for a moment and then rose. "Very well. I can see you're in no shape to talk right now. We'll talk when you're feeling better."

"I don't want to talk to you, not ever again!" she yelled after him as he crossed the room. Then she sank into the bed. *I wish I were dead,* she thought as she turned her head into the pillow, and shame brought on by the memories of last night's events washed over her. *I wish I were dead.*

Justin paused at the door as he heard her sob, and his eyes briefly closed. He could bear almost anything but a woman's tears, particularly this woman's. He thrust a hand into his hair as he went into his bedroom. What he'd done, he'd done for the best, difficult though it had been for him, and all he'd accomplished was to make matters worse. In trying to spare Melissa pain, he had only caused her more.

He crossed the room and stood at a window, looking out. The streets below were busy as usual, private carriages and tradesmen's vans going by, and as he watched he felt a sudden revulsion for the city scene. He wanted to be back at the Hall, walking over his own lands, living a life unfettered by the conventions of the *ton* and the demands of a political career. He wanted to choose his own way of living.

Idly stroking his upper lip, Justin turned away from the window and sank down into a chair. So. It was time for him to think about what he really wanted, instead of letting fate, or other people, dictate to him. Did he want a political career? Oh, he was good enough at it, better than he'd thought he'd be, but he detested the machinations and scheming necessary to get things done. That wasn't how he wanted to spend his life. No. He sat up straighter as the force of his decision hit him. He would not stay in politics, no matter what Aunt Augusta might have to say. He would make his maiden speech, for which he was beginning to have some ideas, but after that, he would live his life as he saw fit. And that did not include politics.

As for his wife. Justin shifted uneasily in his chair. She, too, had proven to be a revelation to him, not the hussy he had once thought her, but a lovely, enchanting woman he might well have chosen, had he had the chance. That led him to another question. What kind of life did he want with her? For certain he didn't want the arid, lifeless marriage all too common among the *ton*, but, on the other hand, he was still wary of being ensnared by her. Not that, after last night, that was much of a possibility. He suspected it would be a very long time before Melissa let him get close again. He was, he reflected dispassionately, the world's biggest fool.

Alfred came into the room and stopped short. "My lord," he said in surprise. "Thought you were out."

"Not yet, Alfred," Justin said, and rose while Alfred watched him covertly. Word was in the servants' hall that something had happened between the Earl and his lady, but try though he might, Alfred could see no hint of it in the Earl's face. "I plan to ride out to Richmond later today," Justin stated as he crossed the room. "Care to accompany me?"

"Won't you be taking the barouche, sir?"

"No, I'll leave that for her ladyship. Diablo and I need the exercise. Well?"

"Yes, sir, of course. Be good to be out riding together, sir. Like the old days."

Justin's brief smile didn't reach his eyes. "Quite," he said, and left the room to begin the day. The old days were gone. Ahead of him was only the confusing, perplexing future.

The days were growing longer, but still it was dusk, footpad hour, when Justin and Alfred at last started home from Richmond. It had been an enjoyable afternoon; Justin had looked over the set of matched grays Lord Radcliffe had for sale, and was interested enough to consider buying them. Perhaps Melissa would like to drive her own team and would take it as a peace offering. Lord knew what else he could do.

Beside him, Alfred stirred uneasily in the saddle. "My lord," he began, and at the same time a shot rang out up ahead.

"Stand and deliver!"

"Good God!" Justin exclaimed, wheeling Diablo around. This stretch of road was not known for highwaymen, but it appeared that was what they faced. His first thought was to run, but there were four of the ruffians, too many to outrun. They would have to fight. He reached into the pocket of his greatcoat for the pistol he kept primed and loaded for just such eventualities, and came out shooting. The shot went wild, but its report startled one of the ruffians' horses into bolting. That left only three, two of whom were advancing upon him. A quick glance showed that Alfred was busy with the remaining ruffian, and so Justin wheeled Diablo around again, pulling back on the reins so that the big horse reared. But one of the ruffians caught at the bridle, and there was no choice for it. Justin swung off the horse, his foot catching the ruffian squarely in the face. The man yelled and went down, and Justin whirled, dropping into a crouch to face his other attacker. The second pistol was in the saddlebag. If he could reach it. . .

The ruffian suddenly kicked out, and Justin jumped back. There, Diablo was just to his right. Justin's hand fumbled at the saddlebag as the ruffian kicked again, this time connecting with Justin's kneecap. Pain exploded in his leg and he bent double, unwittingly jerking the trigger of the pistol still in the saddlebag. There was a deafening report, and even Diablo, seasoned campaigner though he was, danced away as the ruffian fell to the ground. Good, he'd got him!

Justin turned then to see Alfred struggling with his attacker, and as he pulled his arm from the saddlebag he was only dimly aware of motion to his side. There was a rush of movement, then a sudden, stunning, blinding pain in his head, and he knew no more.

Chapter Fifteen

"My lord! My lord!"

Hands pulled at him. He was at Talavera again and the surgeon had just told him he would lose his leg. The pain, the pain . . . had anyone seen Major Selby? Justin had seen him go down, attacked by four ruffians. But, no, that was Alfred, he thought, and opened his eyes.

"Oh, m'lord, thank God, thought they'd done for you!" Alfred exclaimed, pulling at Justin's arm. Pain lanced through Justin's head, and he put a hand to his eyes. "Come, m'lord, best go. No tellin' how many more of them there are."

Justin got to his feet, barely able to stand for the pain. "What the devil happened?"

"You did for one of 'em, m'lord," Alfred said, in tones of great satisfaction. "Diablo went for the other."

"Did he!"

"And the third, when he saw what happened to his mates, why, he just ran right away."

"I see." The pain in Justin's knee was settling into a steady, throbbing ache as he stood and surveyed the carnage. "I think we'd best go to Bow Street with this, Alfred."

Spring was coming, and more and more people were returning to town from their estates, where they had spent the winter. That meant more parties, more routs, more balls. Melissa was growing adept now at separating those affairs into the ones which would do Justin's career some good, those at which the Chatleighs' presence meant little, those they'd be most likely to enjoy. So it was that she, in a gown of turquoise silk, stood chatting with several other acquaintances at the Bainbridges' ball, on the surface enjoying the evening but inside a mass of uncertainties and unhappiness. Some two weeks had passed since the evening Justin had rebuffed her advances, and in that time they had spoken little to each other. He kept busy in Parliament; she, with plans for their ball, scheduled for a week hence. Sometimes she looked up, from her plate at breakfast or from reading a novel after dinner in the drawing room, to see him watching her, but she always looked away again before he could speak. Sometimes she wished he would approach her; at others she was glad he did not. What had happened had struck hard at her self-esteem, not strong at the best of times, and the hurt went deep.

"Good evening, Lady Chatleigh." The voice was at her side, and she turned to see the Marquess of Edgewater. He was as neatly turned out as ever, his evening coat fitting faultlessly, his shirt points so high and so starched that he was in danger of cutting himself if he dared to turn his head. "Strange to find you here."

"Good evening, sir. In the enemy camp, you mean?" Melissa said coolly. "But the Bainbridges are our friends. If you will excuse me, I was about to return to the ballroom—"

"Let me escort you, then." Edgewater deftly took her arm, and they began strolling down the corridor. "I gather Chatleigh intends to stay in politics, then?"

"Yes, of course. Why would you have thought otherwise?"

"I had thought perhaps you had convinced him to change his mind."

"No, sir, I wouldn't do that. I believe Chatleigh has something worth saying."

"Do you? Well, I very much fear, my dear, that you are in for a sad letdown. I'm afraid the only thing Chatleigh is likely to do is fall on his face. It won't be the first time."

Melissa pulled away from him and glared at him, her hands on her hips. "Why do you persist in belittling him?" she demanded. "You make him out to be a clumsy fool."

"But he is, my dear. At Eton he was always falling over his own feet. Quite the laughingstock, I'm afraid."

"And you, I suppose, laughed the loudest."

Edgewater bowed. "Much as it pains me to admit it, dear lady, I am afraid so. But then, he was so deliciously laughable. And there was such scandal about his parents."

"I see," Melissa said, her lips tightening. In spite of her feelings towards Justin at the moment, she couldn't help feeling a pang of pity for the boy he must have been, tall even then, and probably not used to handling his height. Of course he would have been clumsy, and if he had already been in the habit of downplaying his talents, few would have guessed what he was really like. "You, I take it, were never clumsy yourself?"

"Perish the thought!"

"And, of course, you never made a mistake."

"I won't go that far, my lady." His tone was smug. "But I must admit I did quite well at school."

"I see. Do you know what I think, sir?" Melissa ran her finger along the edge of her glass. "I think you are not nearly so secure as you seem. In fact, I'd wager that you dislike yourself so much that you must set down other people to feel good about yourself."

Edgewater's eyes blazed for a moment. "Do you, my dear?" he drawled. "I assure you, you are far out there."

"Am I? I don't think so. I think you're afraid he'll show you up."

"I don't care what you think. Chatleigh will regret it if he stays in politics. You may tell him I said so."

"Tell me you said what, Edgewater?" Justin said smoothly, coming up and taking Melissa's arm. She started, then relaxed, though she was very conscious of his touch.

"I'll leave it to Lady Chatleigh to tell you," Edgewater said, and he bowed. "My lord, my lady. If you will excuse me."

"Damned fop," Justin muttered as Edgewater walked away. "I will not have you seeing him behind my back."

"It's no such thing!" Melissa exclaimed indignantly.

"Isn't it? Best listen to me, madam. You will not take up with another man."

Melissa stared at him and then smiled in pleased surprise. "You're jealous!"

"Of that coxcomb? Hardly."

"Yes, you are. Oh, Justin!" She laughed. "As if

I would!"

Justin looked uncomfortable. Not so long ago he would have believed it of her. Now he was not so sure. "What did he want, then?"

"He would like you to get out of politics," she said, and told him the gist of the conversation. "He said something like that once before. I think he means it, Justin."

"Man's a lightweight," Justin said.

"But, Chatleigh just now he sounded threatening."

Justin looked briefly startled and then shook his head. "Don't worry about him, m'dear. It's nothing new."

"Oh?" She glanced up at him as they began walking towards the ballroom. The glorious strains of a waltz filtered out into the hall.

"No. Been going on since Eton. Once I got used to the place I didn't do so badly, and that was what he didn't like." It was Justin's turn to sound smug. "He didn't like not being at the top."

"I thought as much." Melissa glanced into the ballroom. The waltz was in full swing, and the floor was a swirl of jewel-like colors offset by the darker tones of the gentlemen's evening clothes. For just a moment a pang went through Melissa because she was not dancing with Justin, but she ruthlessly suppressed it. She did not wish to be that close to him, ever again.

Justin was watching her. "Melissa, I—" he began, and at that moment, Lord Beverley came up to them.

"There you are, Lady Chatleigh," he said. "This is my waltz, I believe."

"Of course it is," Melissa replied, and walked off on his arm, tossing Justin a brilliant smile over her shoulder. His fists clenched in response, but he forced himself to relax. He knew it would take time to repair the damage he had done, and a good deal of patience, however, he was beginning to think the prize would be worth the effort. There was passion in her, waiting to be awakened by the right man, and just the thought of her in his arms was enough to make him ache. She was his wife, and someday she would be that in more than name.

"There's money behind it, my lord, that's for certain." The man who sat across the library table from Justin was thin, small, and nondescript, but his chin was firm and his eyes were steady. When Justin had gone to talk to the magistrates at Bow Street, Alfred had suggested hiring a runner to look into the attack by the ruffians. Justin had at first refused, but on second thought, remembering the incident on the hunting field on Boxing Day, he had changed his mind. If someone wished him dead, he wanted to know who it was.

"Your informants tell you this?" Justin asked quietly, his fingers toying with a pen, and Lawton, the runner, shook his head.

"Not in so many words, no, sir. Don't know they're talking to a runner, neither," he said. He had already detailed to Justin the places he had looked, the rough dives and kens of London's underworld. "There's them that admit they know Ott, that's the one you shot, my lord, was up to something. Won't admit to being in on it themselves, acourse, but will say they saw Ott talking with a sharp-featured man. Face like a ferret, they said." Justin frowned. "Bring anyone to mind, sir?"

"No. He is the leader?"

"No, sir, I doubt it. From what I hear he didn't look near prosperous enough. No, there's someone else behind him." Lawton leaned back, folding his hands. "Who hates you enough to want you dead, my lord?"

"Damned if I know." Justin ran a hand through his hair. "All I know is there have been two attempts. And now you tell me there is a plot?"

"Aye, sir. Weren't no accident you were shot during the hunt." Lawton watched him closely. "Sir, best you think of anyone you've quarreled with, anyone with any reason to want you killed."

"I have. The devil of it is, there's nobody."

"No one, sir? No enemies?"

"No, damn it, none I can think of."

"What about your heir?"

"My brother? No. He'd inherit less than I did. Besides, he's in Spain."

"I see. Sir . . ."

"Yes."

"What about your wife?"

"Nonsense!" Justin burst out, starting up from his chair, and Lawton sat back, impassive. After a moment, Justin seated himself. It was true that his relationship with Melissa had been strained lately; it was equally true that she had not wanted to marry him in the first place. She certainly had the money to finance such a plot, but would she? "No, I will not believe that my wife is trying to kill me, Lawton, and I don't like your saying so."

"Sorry, my lord," Lawton said, imperturbably. "Maybe, though, she knows something." Justin opened his mouth to refute this accusation as well, then stopped. "You've thought of something, sir?"

"Yes. Something that was said to my wife. Hard to believe, though." Justin stroked his upper lip for a moment in silence, and Lawton watched. "There is someone," he said, finally. "Someone who doesn't want me to stay in politics, someone who's been a rival of sorts for years."

"Who, sir?"

"The Marquess of Edgewater."

Lawton whistled. "Money there all right, sir."

"Yes. Mind you, I'm not at all certain of this." It was true they were rivals, but would Edgewater's dislike and contempt actually extend to murder?

"No, sir, but it will bear looking into."

"Yes." Justin rose, tall and resolute. "If this is planned to keep me out of politics, I'm not giving into it."

"No, sir," Lawton said. "But best you be careful."

"I intend to be."

"There, yes, those flowers should go there. Yes, like that." Melissa watched the footmen critically as they placed a large basket of flowers just to the side of the door opening into the ballroom. "Yes, perfect! And that should be it. Well?" She turned to Augusta who was leaning on her cane. "What do you think?"

"Hmph. Place looks like a damned hothouse," she said.

"That's the idea. Thank you." Melissa smiled at the footmen. The decor was perfect for her ball, to be held that night. White-latticed trellises climbed the walls between the French windows, and upon them were twined roses of red and white and yellow, perfuming the air with their scent. More roses climbed the archway that stood before the door that led to the supper room, and the daffodils, set in tubs placed around the dais on which the orchestra would be situated, brought a welcome touch of spring. Carnations in baskets lined the small area for chairs, white and gilt and rose velvet. There the chaperones would sit. And finally, an unexpected touch, a garland of greens and carnations in pink and white and red was draped over the door to the ballroom. It was almost like stepping into a garden.

"I think it's charming," Melissa declared, "and it's not like anything I've ever seen done. Really, I am amazed that more people don't make use of flowers at times like this."

"Hmph." Augusta shifted her weight. "Most people can't afford roses in March, miss."

"No, I suppose not," Melissa said, her good humor unimpaired by this reference to her money. "Are you tired, ma'am? Perhaps you should rest a while before this evening."

"Not a bit of it. Puny things, you girls are today, always fainting and resting. Why, in my time we danced all night, and we didn't sleep the day away."

Melissa's eyes twinkled. "I'm sure, ma'am. Nevertheless, I think I will lie down for a time. There'll be much to do tonight."

"Hmph," Augusta said again, but she did allow Melissa to lead her to the bedroom she would be occupying that night. Melissa smiled as the door closed behind the old lady, then went along to her own room. She doubted she would rest, however. She was much too excited and nervous about her debut as a London hostess.

Some hours later Melissa turned towards her pier glass and gave her reflection a long, unsmiling look. The woman who gazed back at her was almost a stranger. Her hair was caught atop her head in a knot, and her modish, sophisticated gown of emerald silk, with its brief bodice, hugged her curves. A net overskirt embroidered with gold thread sparkled over the slip, and a plume of feathers attached to a jeweled band made up her headdress. Against the brilliant color her skin glowed a milky white and her hair blazed, but what caught Melissa's attention were her eyes, faintly green. They were not the eyes of a girl but of a woman. She had seen a thing or two over the past months. She had grown.

"You look beautiful, my lady," Liza said, and Melissa came out of her thoughts. This was not a night for reflecting about the past or worrying about the future. It was a night to be lived, one when she could hope that Justin would at least waltz with her.

She frowned as she descended the stairs to the ballroom. The last weeks, since the fiasco in her bedchamber, had been difficult. Justin had acted much as he always had; it was her own feelings that confused her. There had been times when she had never wanted a man to touch her, there had been times, and just recently, when she hadn't wanted ever to be touched by Justin. But her emotions apparently ran deep. In spite of everything she wanted to be near him. She wanted to share his life in every way, though he didn't seem to want that. At night in her lonely bed, she speculated endlessly on what it was about her that repelled him; by day, she stared for hours in the mirror, seeking some flaw, some reason for his rejection. And though she could find none, she knew it existed. There was something wrong with her, and Justin could see it.

"Don't frown, girl, it gives you wrinkles," Augusta said tartly, and Melissa looked up to see her and

Justin already standing at the top of the stairs, waiting for their guests to arrive. "Worried about tonight?"

"No. Well, maybe a little." She looked past Augusta at her husband, and he smiled at her. "You look fine, Chatleigh."

"So do you, m'dear. Daresay we'll brush through this tolerably enough," he said.

"Daresay we will," she replied, and after a startled glance Justin smiled again.

The door knocker sounded below, and there was no more time for speech. Their guests arrived, slowly at first, and then in a veritable flood. By ten o'clock the ballroom was filled. The cream of the aristocracy was present, Whig and Tory alike: the Bainbridges, with Sabrina looking lovely in a gown of rose watered silk; Sally Jersey, talking constantly as usual; and many of Justin's political acquaintances. It was even rumored that the Prince Regent might make his appearance, which, as Augusta said, would be quite a feather in their caps. Her nephew was doing well, she thought. Better than she'd dared to hope, but that, she was certain, was due to Melissa. The little countess was shaping up very nicely indeed.

The flood of guests slowed to a trickle, and Justin took Melissa's arm, leading her into the ballroom to open the dancing. A quadrille came first. With four couples to a set, it left little chance for private conversation, and as Melissa went through the steps her mind ranged over the preparations that had led to this moment. The decor was fine, though some of the flowers already appeared to be wilting in the heat; the supper, to be served later, was varied and interesting enough to tempt even the most jaded appetite, consisting not only of the usual lobster patties and champagne, but also of various platters of *entrées volantes,* quenelles of chicken, and an intricate confection of cake and icing in the shape of a fairy-tale castle; and enough people that she had invited had decided to attend. Thank heavens, the ball was a success.

As the music wound to a halt Melissa found herself standing among a group of people. She had no memory of having danced, though she was warm and her heart was pounding. Justin came over to her side. "Looks to be a success, m'dear."

"I hope so," she replied, looking up at him. Something in his eyes caught her, and for the life of her, she could not look away.

Justin pressed her hand. "Save a waltz for me," he said, and, smiling, turned as an acquaintance hailed him, leaving Melissa staring after him in amazement.

Happiness and expectancy lent a special sparkle to her as she circulated among her guests, joining various conversations and occasionally dancing. From time to time she caught a glimpse of Justin, and she was pleased to see the respect with which he was received. Even the Prince Regent, when he arrived shortly after midnight, was seen in conversation with him. Melissa's heart swelled with pride. If this evening were any indication, her husband would be a man to be reckoned with.

Melissa was smiling as she sank down onto a chair near the chaperones and older ladies, next to the Duchess of Bainbridge. "Heavens, I've hardly been off my feet all evening," she said.

Sabrina smiled. "It's a lovely ball. I particularly like what you did with all these flowers."

"Thank you. But you're not dancing, Sabrina?"

Sabrina grimaced slightly. "No, Bainbridge doesn't want me to. He's become so overprotective! He's even talking about returning to the Abbey, and all because I am a trifle unwell in the mornings."

"Men can be a trial," Melissa said, patting Sabrina's hand, and looked up to see Justin, across the room, watching her. A peculiar warmth filled her, and any envy she felt for the Bainbridges' marriage faded. On this night she would not trade places with anyone.

As if her glance had drawn him to her, Justin crossed the room, just as the orchestra struck up a waltz. "My dance, I believe, m'dear," he said, and Melissa, her eyes sparkling, rose.

"Of course. Sabrina, you don't mind?"

"No, of course not, and there is Oliver, in any event." She smiled at the couple as they walked out onto the floor, and her smile deepened as Oliver approached her. He looked in the direction of her gaze and then turned back.

"They seem to be getting along better," he commented as he reached his wife's side.

"Yes. Well, it can be difficult." Sabrina's eyes met his. "As we should know."

Oliver's gaze held hers for a moment before he took her arm, drawing her to her feet. "Come. This is my waltz."

"What? You are actually going to allow me to dance, Oliver?"

"Be quiet, minx," he said, and swung her onto the floor.

Melissa had a glimpse of the Bainbridges joining the swirling group of people on the floor, and then Justin's arm came around her, blotting everything

231

from her mind but the nearness of him. His hand was warm at her waist, and his shoulder, under her hand, was firm and strong. She suddenly felt very warm and rather dizzy as he whirled her around. "Justin!"

"What, m'dear?"

"Nothing." She shook her head, and looked up to see him watching her with an unnerving regard. He had never looked at her like that before, with such intentness and warmth. It made her curiously lightheaded and weak, and yet more alive than she had ever felt before. The sounds of orchestra and conversation faded, the floor seemed to drop away from her feet, and she saw nothing, nobody, but the man who held her, closer than was proper for a waltz. Their footsteps, their quickened breathing, even their very heartbeats seemed to be in unison. Only gradually did they become aware that the music had stopped. Their waltz had ended.

For just a moment they stood, gazing at each other, Justin's arm still about her waist. Then he stepped back, bowing. "We will continue this—conversation later," he said.

"Yes," Melissa replied, dazed. "Later."

He bowed again as her next partner came to claim her. She went through the steps of the country dance in a haze. Later! Later? After all the guests had gone, she supposed he meant. Oh, how can I wait that long? she wailed inwardly. Tonight. It would be tonight. At long last, all the strains, all the tension, were gone. She was going to be his wife.

Time seemed to pass with agonizing slowness after that, and though Melissa chatted and danced, though she seemed normal on the outside, she melted inside each time she caught Justin's eyes on her. Would this evening never end? It seemed that the ball she had earlier delighted in was now an ordeal. She was grateful for the distraction of slipping down to the kitchen to make sure everything was in readiness for supper. The French chef they had recently hired met her questions with his usual Gallic tirade, convincing her that all was well, and she went back upstairs tingling with excitement and anticipation. The sooner the guests were fed, the sooner they would leave; then host and hostess could be alone.

She was nearing the ballroom when she saw a man standing near the door, looking in as if searching for someone. He was tall and thin, dressed in ill-fitting evening clothes, and for a moment Melissa didn't recognize him. Then he turned, and her gasp was loud in the silence created by a pause in the music.

"There you are, daughter," Sir Stephen said, walking towards her. "I've been looking for you."

"But . . . what are you doing here?" she said, her voice high and thin. "I didn't invite you."

Sir Stephen pursed his lips. "No, most unfilial of you, child. Perhaps you believed I had gone back to the country? But I have been here, you see, watching you. And your husband."

There was something vaguely menacing in his words, so that she shivered. "I wish you would leave. Now. Or do I have to call someone to throw you out?"

"You won't want to do that, daughter." He shook his head, sadly. "Think of the scandal."

"I don't care—"

"But you do, child. Or shall I go in there and tell everyone what you are?"

233

Melissa turned white, with anger as well as fear. Damn him for coming tonight of all nights, when matters were finally working out between her and Justin. She would have to speak to the servant who admitted him, she thought distractedly, and then she turned. "Come. We can't talk here."

She led him to a small anteroom, mercifully empty of any guests. Going to the fire and standing before it, Melissa tried to warm herself, though her chill was of the soul. "Well?" she said, when the silence had stretched between them, then turned to see him sitting in a chair, regarding her unblinkingly, like a cat. "What do you want?"

"You know, Melissa."

Melissa shivered at hearing the menacing tone in his voice. "I'll not give you anything!"

"Oh, but I think you will, you know." He made a steeple of his fingers and gazed at it. "You see, I have taken steps to ensure your cooperation."

"They won't work."

"Ah, but they will. You care too much for your husband."

"What do you mean?"

"I mean that for the sake of his health, you will go along with my wishes. Or . . ." He let the word hang, tantalizingly.

"Or?" she said, impatiently.

"I may have to arrange another little incident. Another accident on the hunting field, perhaps, or—"

"What!" She spun around. "That was you?"

He bowed. "Or perhaps another attack on the road. Ah, I see he didn't tell you about that?" Sir Stephen rose and walked to her, leisurely. "Trying to spare you, I suppose. Both attempts failed, my dear. But the next one may not. If . . ."

Melissa swallowed, hard. "If it's money, it will take a few days, but I'll get what you need, just tell me how much."

"Not money, Melissa." His gaze, hypnotic as a snake's, held hers. "You know what I want."

"No." She licked lips suddenly gone dry and backed away. "No!"

"Oh, yes. What I've always wanted." He smiled, a terrible sight, predatory and feral. "You."

Chapter Sixteen

The last guest had finally left. The orchestra had packed up their instruments and gone, the maids had cleared away the remaining food from the supper room, and the footmen, yawning, had sleepily made their way to bed. Outside, false dawn was lightening the sky. Inside, Melissa sat in a chair in her room, wearing her dressing gown and staring straight ahead. The evening was over, and so was the need to pretend that all was well. What was she going to do?

There was a light tap on the door, and then Justin came in from his bedroom, wearing a burgundy silk dressing gown, carrying a bottle of champagne in one hand and two glasses in the other. She continued to stare, hardly acknowledging his presence, and he glanced at her curiously as he crossed the room. "Evening," he said, popping the cork from the bottle. "Or should I says morning?"

"What?" Melissa came out of her daze. "Oh. Justin."

"The same." He bowed slightly, and then walked to her, holding out a glass. "Who did you expect?"

She shivered. "I . . . don't know."

"I believe we have a conversation to finish," he said, drawing a chair closer to hers. "Or are you too tired?"

"I . . . no, but—"

"Good. Fine evening, wasn't it?"

"Y-yes."

"Glad everyone's gone, though." He took a sip from his glass, his eyes never leaving her face. "Tired?"

"No. Yes!" She raised her eyes, imploring and frightened, to him. "Yes, Justin, I'm very tired, maybe I'd should just go to bed—"

"Well, now, that is what I was thinking," he said, and reached out to touch her cheek.

She jerked back, and jumped to her feet, the champagne spilling over her glass. "No! Don't touch me!"

"Melissa." He rose slowly, his hand outstretched. "Don't be frightened, I'll be gentle, I promise."

"Go away, I don't want you near me."

"Damn it, Melissa, what is this?"

"Go, please go. I can't stand you, I don't want you to touch me."

"Melissa." He caught her shoulders, looking down at her in concern. "What is it? What has happened to upset you so?"

"Nothing. I don't want you near me," she said, with a flat calmness that was far more convincing than her earlier shrillness had been.

Justin's eyes narrowed, and he stepped back. "Very well, madam," he said, coolly. "Since my presence is so repugnant to you, I shall leave."

"Justin!" Melissa stood in the middle of the floor, watching him stride across the room. His shoulders stiffened, but he did not turn. A moment later the door closed firmly behind him.

"Oh, Justin," she whispered, and sank down onto the edge of her bed, staring ahead, the champagne glass still in her hands. She couldn't bear to be touched, not now, not after what had happened. She couldn't let him get too close. Though she had known that all along, the night's events had only confirmed it.

She felt dirty, soiled. She couldn't let him be touched by that.

Like a sleep walker, Melissa climbed into bed, her knees drawn up and the comforter pulled over her head. If she could only shut out the world, shut out the reality of what was happening to her, but she couldn't. Sir Stephen wanted her. There was no more escaping that fact.

At first, she hadn't believed it. It had started not long after he had married her mother, with a certain way of looking at her, of talking to her, that made her skin crawl. However, perhaps because Lady Barton had been a caring mother, perhaps because of the money at stake, it had never gone further than that, convincing Melissa that she had imagined things.

Mama's death had changed everything. Sir Stephen had made that plain to Melissa several days after the funeral. Without her mother to protect her, she had known she had no choice. She had to get away from *him*. And so he had run to the Hart and Hind, and ultimately to Justin.

There had been times since when she had wondered if there were something in her that had attracted Sir Stephen. Lately, though, she had begun to realize that it wasn't so. No one else had ever noticed such a basic flaw in her. It must be her stepfather's wrongness, not hers. But it had become her problem. She felt soiled, dirty, and she hadn't wanted Justin to touch her, lest he be soiled, too.

Oh, Lord, Justin. Melissa put her hands over her eyes. What a dreadful coil. She would not, could not, give in to Sir Stephen. Neither, though, could she let Justin suffer for her integrity. There had to be another way, she thought. There has to be. "Please, God," she whispered. "Please. Keep him safe."

"Good boy," Justin murmured softly to his mount. "Good Diablo." The horse nickered in reply, twitching his ears, and Justin took up the reins. "Want a gallop, don't you, old boy?"

"Right frisky this morning, milord," Jeffrey said, as Diablo danced about.

"Right. Should give me a good ride. Let him go!"

"Yes, milord." Jeffrey stood back as Justin walked the horse out of the stable and headed for the park. Since the snow had melted he had begun to ride in the early morning again. Though both Alfred and the Bow Street runner protested, he refused to take along an escort. He was not going to live his life in fear. Besides, he thought better when he was alone, and lately there was a lot to think about.

Justin frowned slightly. There was, of course, his speech before the Lords, which no longer seemed very important. There was the ever-present question of who might wish him dead. And, most importantly and perplexingly of all, there was his wife. He hadn't the slightest idea what to do about Melissa.

His frown deepened as he rode at an easy lope down Mayfair's cobblestoned streets, busy even at this early hour with tradesmen's carts and street vendors. Hard to believe now he had once mistrusted her, disliked her, that he had let the prejudices instilled by his past color his view of her. For she was nothing like what he had once thought; not even her money bothered him very much anymore. She had come to be an important part of his life, and he had thought she felt the same way. There had been no mistaking her reaction to him when they had waltzed; she had been soft and warm in his arms, and her eyes had shone up at him. Yet, when he had come to claim her at last as his wife, she had acted repulsed, revolted. Something had happened, between the waltz and her bedroom, something that had upset her. Otherwise, nothing made sense. Oh, he'd been upset about it at first, angry and hurt and full of injured pride, but he never had held onto anger for long. Once he had calmed down and thought about it, he had realized that what he had seen in her eyes wasn't revulsion. It was fear, pure and simple.

The Stanhope gate was just ahead, and then he was in the park. Once off the city streets he let Diablo have his head, they rode as one, man and beast, a collaboration so automatic that Justin's mind went on with his thoughts. What had frightened her so? He didn't think she was afraid of him; he'd never hurt her, not physically, at least, and though their relationship had had its rocky moments, in the main they got along well. Nor did he think she was really frightened of the physical intimacy. No, it was something else, and so the question remained. What had scared her?

A tree loomed up in their path. Justin tugged the reins to the left, and, suddenly, something gave under him. With the instinct born of years of riding, he grabbed at the reins, but instead of stopping, Diablo, startled by the sudden motion, bolted. The saddle slipped, Justin's grip on the reins loosened, and he was tossed, ignominiously, to the ground.

He came to a few moments later, staring up at the sky through a canopy of branches just beginning to bud with leaves. A quick inventory showed that he wasn't hurt, except for the leg he had wrenched in the fall, the same one injured in the attack several weeks ago. Diablo was contentedly munching grass nearby, so Justin climbed painfully to his feet and went to him, running his hands over the horse's glossy coat and lean flanks to check for injuries. The saddle lay on the ground a few feet away. God, what a foolish thing to do, not to check the girth of the saddle before mounting to make sure it was tightly cinched, he thought as he limped over to it. Somehow it must have come loose. He was lucky his feet had come free of the stirrups, else he might have been dragged quite a distance. He would have the groom's head for this. He picked up the saddle, turned it to examine the girth, and then froze. The leather was broken in two.

For a moment, he simply stared, unable to take it in, and then he brought the girth closer to his face, to study it. The saddle was in good condition, the leather soft and supple. How could it have broken? he wondered. Then his mouth set in a straight, grim line. Not broken. Cut. The break was too clean to have been anything else. Someone had deliberately cut the girth, so that it would let go while he was riding. Someone most definitely wanted him dead, and that someone was in his house.

"We do know a bit more now," Lawton, the Bow Street runner, said a little while later, facing a stony-faced, angry earl in the book-room. "Know who does the hiring, anyway."

Alfred slipped in at that moment, glancing at Justin, who sprawled in an armchair, his injured leg outstretched, while the runner stood before him. Justin raised an eyebrow at him, and Alfred shook his head. "No, my lord," he said, regretfully. "Looks like the new stableboy, one was hired when we came up to town, did it, but he's disappeared. No one admits knowing who he is."

"Of course not. Oh, sit down, man," Justin said, waving the runner to a chair. "Damned inept assassins," he went on, rubbing his leg. "All they've managed to do so far is bang up my leg."

"It might have been worse, my lord," the runner said, quietly. "Might still be. See, the man we found is one has a reason to be angry with you. Or rather, with your wife."

"What? Who?"

"Man name o' Jenkins."

"Jenkins!"

"Sound familiar, my lord?"

"Good God. Yes, he used to be my butler."

"Until her ladyship dismissed him."

"Know about that, do you?" Justin sent him a shrewd look. "So he's hired others to do his dirty work."

"Jenkins?" Alfred, too, looked startled. "But I saw him, my lord."

"When?"

"The day we went to Richmond. I was waiting out front for you, and I saw him across the street. He disappeared soon as he realized I was watching him."

Justin turned to the runner. "You have a man on him?"

"Yes, my lord, of course, and I'd like to put a man on you, too, for your own protection."

Justin raked his hair with his fingers. "Damn! Oh, very well. I suppose it's necessary."

"Or you could leave London, sir. Go back to Surrey."

"No. Not until I make my speech." He glanced at Alfred.

"What is it?"

"Well, sir," Alfred began, "the day I saw Jenkins . . ."

"Yes?"

"Her ladyship was just going out. And, sir, Jenkins was staring at her, and if looks could kill—"

"The devil he was!" Justin started up, and then sank

242

back into his chair. This put a different view on the matter. "Very well, then, we will return to the country. After I make my speech. And I want a man put on my wife, too."

"Yes, my lord, I was going to suggest that," Lawton said. "My lord, she hasn't said anything?"

"About knowing who's behind it? No. I haven't talked to her about it. I don't want her worried. Besides, I believe I know who it is. And he's not going to win this time." His face was grim. "No. Not this time."

Lawton was going out the door as Melissa came downstairs, and she frowned slightly. The man looked so disreputable in his shabby coat and battered hat that she couldn't imagine what business he could have here. "Alfred," she said, and Alfred, who had been on his way back to the stables after seeing the runner out, stopped.

"Yes, m'lady?" he said, his eyes wary.

"Who was that?"

"Someone to see his lordship on business, m'lady."

"Oh?" Melissa continued to descend the stairs, glancing down the corridor in time to see Justin limp into the book-room. "His lordship's leg is bothering him again?"

"No, my lady. Well, yes, but this is something else."

Melissa was suddenly alert. "What? What's happened?"

"Took a tumble off his horse, my lady."

"What?" She grabbed at the banister, going pale. "It was an accident, wasn't it, Alfred? Wasn't it?"

Alfred didn't answer right away. In the past days, her ladyship hadn't looked good, like she was sickening for something. She ate hardly enough to keep a bird alive, her maid had reported, and her face was thin and drawn. Something was bothering her. Alfred hoped it wasn't what he thought it was. "Of course it was, my lady," he said finally. "What else would it be?"

"Oh, nothing." Melissa tried to laugh and almost succeeded. "I am just being foolish. But, Alfred." She laid her hand on his arm, and he looked at it with surprise. "You will watch out for him, won't you?"

"Of course I will, my lady. Got him through Spain. I'll get him through this."

"Thank you." Again she nearly succeeded in smiling. "That does make me feel better." She continued down the corridor. At the book-room she hesitated then went in.

Justin looked up from the table. "Yes? Oh, it's you m'dear. Forgive me if I don't rise," he said, leaning back.

"Of course. Alfred told me what happened," she said, sitting across from him.

"Did he?" Justin's eyes were wary.

"Yes. However did you come to fall off Diablo, of all things?"

He shrugged. "Just clumsiness, I suppose."

"You are not clumsy!"

"Thank you," he said, rather startled by her vehemence. "Tell me, m'dear, something you wished to see me about?"

"No, nothing in particular. If I'm bothering you, I'll go . . ."

"Half a minute, m'dear. Sit. Something I want to talk to you about."

"Yes?" Melissa seated herself, and this time she was the one who looked wary. In the past days she had avoided her husband as much as possible, but she knew quite well that, sooner or later, he would demand an explanation for her behavior the night of the ball. She dreaded that day.

244

"I'll be giving my speech at the Lords next week," he said, riffling the corners of the papers that lay before him. "And then I'll be giving it up."

"What!" Melissa sat up straighter. "Give up politics? But, Justin, you seem to be doing so well—"

"Perhaps." He shrugged. "But I am not happy, m'dear. You told me to try it, and so I have, but it's not the life I want."

"Have you decided what you do want, then?"

"Yes." He leaned back, his hands behind his head. "Decided being a gentleman farmer suits me to the ground. Once I give my speech, we'll be going back to Chatleigh."

"Really!" Melissa exclaimed, but inside a new and fragile hope grew. In Surrey, on his own lands, Justin would be safe, and so would she. Sir Stephen couldn't touch them there.

"Yes. You look relieved, m'dear."

Melissa stiffened, but forced herself to relax. "Of course," she said, striving for lightness. "Anything to keep you away from Miss Keane."

Justin looked startled, and then let out a crack of laughter. "No fear there. But won't you mind leaving London?"

"No, not at all! I'm a country girl, Justin." She beamed at him. "I'll be glad to be back at the Hall."

"Yes, so will I." He toyed with his pen, his eyes never leaving her face. "Anything else you wished to talk about? Must work on my speech, you know."

"Of course. Aunt Augusta won't be pleased, I'm afraid," she said as she rose.

"Aunt Augusta has no say in this." His voice was so firm that she smiled at him. His answering smile faded as soon as she had turned her back and was walking away.

So, his wife was glad, relieved even, to be returning

to the Hall. Vastly relieved, if the look on her face was any indication, and that was curious. It meant that whatever was bothering her was in town, and the suspicion that it was connected with what was happening to him, fostered by Lawton, grew. So, he wondered, making a steeple of his fingers and gazing at them, was she in danger or in league against him? At Chatleigh Hall, he would find out.

"My lady," Phelps called as Melissa emerged from the book-room.

"Yes, Phelps, what is it?" she asked, turning on the stairs. Her spirits were the lightest they had been in days. Soon she would be leaving London, and the threat her stepfather posed.

"This just came for you, ma'am." Phelps held out a salver on which lay an envelope.

"Really? I wonder what it could be." Breaking the wafer, she opened the envelope. Inside was a single sheet of paper, with a brief message: "Are you convinced now?" There was no signature.

Puzzled, Melissa was turning the paper over, looking for some clue, when she suddenly recognized the handwriting. It was Sir Stephen's. What was a worse-jolt was Justin had fallen from his horse that very morning. "Oh, God!" she exclaimed, going white, and grabbed the newel post.

"My lady!" Phelps took a step towards her, but she waved him away.

"No, I am all right, Phelps." She crumpled the paper. "Will you dispose of this—No, never mind, I will."

"Ma'am, are you sure? Shall I call his lordship?"

"No! No." Her tone moderated. "I'm fine, Phelps. Something I ate must have disagreed with me." Forcing a smile, she turned and continued up the stairs,

her mind numb. So Sir Stephen's threats were not
dle. Justin was in danger. Thank God they were go-
ng to Chatleigh soon; there he would be safe. *Please,
God. Let him be safe.*

Chapter Seventeen

The gallery in the House of Lords was only partially filled when Melissa and Augusta, having paid five shillings for admittance to the doorman, came in to take their seats. On the floor below them, those peers who had seen fit to attend the day's session hardly seemed to be attending to business. Some were engaged in conversation, some were leaning back and staring at the ceiling, some even appeared to be asleep. None of them took much notice of Justin as he rose from his seat, but Melissa leaned farther over the balcony to watch him. He glanced up, and she gave him an encouraging smile. An answering smile briefly touched his lips, and then he straightened.

"My lords," he began. "There is a matter of national importance on which I wish to address you this day."

His voice was calm and clear, and he didn't seem the least bit nervous. Melissa, sitting on the edge of her seat, restrained from biting her fingernails only by her gloves, was nervous enough for both of them. At last he was making his maiden speech, and she so wanted him to do well. Together they had worked over it, deciding first on his topic, and then how he would phrase what he had to say. Finally had come the hours of rehearsal. All the work had paid off. He stood straight and tall and confident, and though he held a sheaf of papers in his hand, rarely did he refer to it.

His topic was simple, and yet one dear to his heart: the plight of the common soldier in the army. For most of the time Wellington had been fighting, support for the war had been slight, and it had been the soldier who had suffered, Justin said. He went on to talk about such deprivations simply, clearly, and yet eloquently, telling of forced marches with boots that were in tatters, men reduced to foraging off winter-starved lands because needed food hadn't arrived, and the pitiful condition of field hospitals. Why, he himself had nearly lost a leg because of the ineptitude of the surgeons, and it was only because of his batman that he could stand before them whole, instead of relying on a crutch. He was one of the lucky ones; others were not so fortunate. As he went on to outline the hardships, most of the hubbub died away, and when he finished he was met, briefly, with silence. Then a chorus of "Huzzahs!" split the room. The maiden speech in the House of Lords of Justin, Earl of Chatleigh, was a rousing success.

Melissa met him in the vestibule, bubbling over with enthusiasm and pride. "You were wonderful!" she exclaimed, grabbing his arm, and he grinned down at her. "So eloquent, and you didn't even need your notes."

"No. Well, Aunt?" he said, looking past Melissa to Augusta.

"Hmph," Augusta said, but her eyes, too, shone with pride. "You'll do, boy. Or you would, if you'd stick with it."

"No." Justin's voice was firm. "This was my first, and last, speech.

249

"Thank God for that," someone drawled behind him.

Justin stiffened. "Didn't realize you were here, Edgewater," he said, turning.

"Wouldn't have missed this," Edgewater said, and held out his hand. "Congratulations. Fine speech."

"Thank you." Justin shook the proffered hand, watching him warily.

"I must say, I didn't think you had it in you, old boy." Edgewater set his curly brimmed beaver hat on his head and tilted it at the proper angle. "Glad to see you proved me wrong."

"Really," Justin said, dryly.

"Yes. But I'm also glad you're retiring from the field." For the first time since Melissa had met him, he smiled, a quite genuine smile with no trace of malice. "You'd be tough competition."

"Thank you, Edgewater," Justin said, surprised. "Coming from you, that means a lot."

"Thought it might." Edgewater inclined his head. "If you'll excuse me, Chatleigh, ladies," he said, and turned away. Justin stared after him, his gaze so fixed that Melissa had to shake his arm several times to bring him back to himself.

"Hm? What?" he said, looking down at her.

"I said, even Edgewater!" she responded, beaming.

"Yes." Justin looked after the man again. So it wasn't Edgewater; his congratulations had sounded sincere. *Damn!* he thought, clapping his hat on his head. Who, then, wanted him dead?

Several days before Easter, the bell in St. Mary's in the village began pealing wildly. The sound traveled faintly over the fields of Chatleigh Hall, and Justin, astride Diablo as he watched the first crops of the year

250

being planted, glanced up. "What the devil is that?" he wondered aloud.

Tilton, his agent, turned. "Don't know, my lord, but someone's coming."

Justin turned in the saddle, to see Sir Percival Dutton riding wildly down the road. "Chatleigh!" he boomed. "Have you heard the news?"

Some moments later Justin slammed into the Hall, the massive carved door banging behind him. Melissa, arranging a bouquet of daffodils and tulips on the refectory table, looked up. "Heavens, what is it?" she said, mildly. Justin growled something in reply and stomped off to his study, and she and Phelps exchanged startled looks. "Heavens," she said again, and went after her husband.

He was standing by the window when she went in, one hand in his pocket and the other, surprisingly, clutching a glass of brandy. "Justin?" His shoulders stiffened. "What is it?"

Justin drained the contents of his glass in one long swallow before answering. "News just came. Wellington's in Paris."

"What? But that's wonderful! The war is almost over."

"Yes."

Melissa glanced at his back, solid and uncompromising, and a pang of pity went through her. She suspected she knew what was bothering him. "And you couldn't be there," she said softly, laying her hand on his shoulder.

"Yes, damn it! I should be there, Melissa, it's where I belong!"

"I know." She rested her head against his arm, and he looked down at her in surprise. "It must be hard, after all you went through, not to be in at the victory."

"Damned hard," he agreed, still looking down at

her, really seeing her for the first time since he had heard the news. His wife, beside him, at last. If he reached out to touch her, to pull her close, would she let him? Or would she pull away, as she had so often these past weeks? Justin studied her upturned face, the eyes that held a faint sheen of blue from her muslin round gown, the small, freckle-spattered nose, the full lips he ached to fit with his. He had never wanted anyone so much. He was about to reach for her, make her his own, but then she moved, and the moment was past.

"They'll be needing diplomats," she said, toying with the inkwell and the silver letter opener on his desk.

"Yes, well?" he said, turning to watch her.

"That's something you could do."

"No." He shook his head. "I'm a soldier. And a farmer."

"Not a bad thing to be," she said, laying her hand on his arm again.

"No," he said. "Not bad at all." He gazed down at her, wanting to answer the unspoken invitation in her eyes, gather her closer and—

The door to the study burst open and Harry, home for the Easter holiday, came in. "Have you heard?" he demanded. "Wellington's in Paris!"

Justin's sigh was almost inaudible. "Yes, halfling," he said. "We've heard."

"It's capital, isn't it?"

"Yes. We should do something to celebrate this, Justin, don't you think?" Melissa said.

"Such as?"

"Oh, a dinner party, perhaps? We've been so quiet since we returned."

"Missing the season, are you?"

"No. But it would be nice to entertain again."

"Sure you're up to it?"

Melissa glanced up, surprised. "Of course I am. Why wouldn't I be?"

Justin shook his head. She had changed since they'd left town. The look of strain had left her eyes, and her color had returned. More importantly, she had relaxed, and though she still held him at arm's length, he thought she was thawing towards him. Whatever had bothered her had been left behind in the city. "No reason," he said. "Go ahead, plan what you think best."

"I will. And perhaps we could invite Aunt Augusta."

"Spare me," Justin groaned. "She still hasn't forgiven me for giving up politics."

"She'll come around. Well. If I'm to plan a dinner I'd best get started." She smiled, and Justin turned to watch her go, wanting her so much it hurt, regretting lost opportunities. What, he wondered, was he going to do about her?

What, Melissa wondered, frowning slightly as she walked towards the kitchen to consult with Mrs. Barnes, was she going to do about Justin? When they had left London, all she had thought about was getting away from her stepfather and the threat he posed. It had been a profound relief to return home and have Justin be safe. Not that she believed Sir Stephen had given up. She knew she would have to face him again someday, but for now, Justin was safe. That was all that mattered.

Or, it should have been. Instead, all her feelings for her husband had surged to the fore again, and lately it seemed she could think of little else. She couldn't seem to stop watching him: his easy grace when he walked, his smile, his strong, corded arms in shirt sleeves. She remembered, all too clearly, how they had felt about her, and she rather wanted to feel them again. She loved him, and she wanted to be his wife. It had nothing to do with the dark, dirty way her stepfather had

253

made her feel. This was clean and good, but what was distressing was that Justin didn't appear to feel the same way.

Melissa stopped for a moment, standing at a window looking out on the drive. It wasn't as if she hadn't given him any chances. Heaven knew she had tried, wearing her prettiest dresses and trying always to be present when he was in the house. In a way, it had worked. They were closer now than they had been since before the ball, talking to each other easily and naturally about the estate, or national events. It was a friendly, open relationship, but it was not that of husband and wife, which was what she wanted.

The question was, how to get it, without risking his rejection again. She would have to be more subtle this time. But what could she do if he wouldn't respond? She had tried, tentatively, to draw closer to him, and when she had laid her head against his arm just now she had thought he might react. And perhaps he would have, if Harry hadn't come in. That couldn't be helped, but she was not defeated yet. There was the future ahead of her, and many things she could try. Yes, she thought, nodding her head decisively as she turned and continued on her way to the kitchen. It was time to bring up the heavy guns.

Melissa finished fastening the chain around her neck, then stepped back to study her reflection. There, she was all ready to greet their dinner guests. From the chain hung a pear-shaped emerald. A gift from Augusta, it nestled in cleavage revealed by the décolletage of her ivory satin gown. The strategic placement of a few stitches had lowered the neckline even farther, and the satin glistened and slipped fluidly over her waist and hips to the floor. Melissa carefully draped a gold zephyr scarf about her shoulders before standing back to check her general appearance. As she had expected, the sheer, diaphanous scarf tantalized, shrouding the skin beneath, but not covering it. Heavy guns, indeed, she thought in satisfaction, drawing on her gloves. Justin's reaction would be interesting.

Justin was standing in the hall, ready to greet their guests, when she glided down the stairs. "Good evening, Justin," she called, her voice clear. He turned, and sputtered into the wine glass he had just raised to his lips. "Melissa!" he bellowed, slamming the glass down on the refectory table.

Her gaze was questioning as she glided towards him. stopping a scant few inches away. "Yes, what is it?"

Justin swallowed, hard. "You will go upstairs and change that gown. Now."

"Why, what is wrong with it?" Melissa looked down at her décolletage, and his eyes involuntarily followed.

"I will not have every man in the county ogling you."

"But that is what the shawl is for." She let it drift lightly across her skin, and he swallowed again.

"I don't care. You will obey me in this."

"Oh, pooh! You can be so stuffy, Justin." She reached up and trailed her fingers lightly across his cheek. "Besides, I suspect that some of our guests are arriving," she said, as the door knocker sounded. "Now look what you've done, you've mussed up your hair again!" She reached up to smooth locks he'd ruffled by raking them with his fingers, and the shawl fell away from her shoulders. He made a noise that sounded like a groan. "Did you say something? No? Ah, see, I was right. Sir Percival and Lady Catherine."

"Yes, I see," he said in a low voice. "I could strangle

you for this."

"Oh, pooh!" she said again, and went forward to greet their guests.

The figure slipped through the shadows leading from the terrace, carefully avoiding the light that streamed out through the French windows. Bent low in a crouch, the man ran across the sculpted lawns until he reached the shadows and the safety of the trees. "Some kind o' party, looks like," he said in a hoarse whisper, and his companion, Sir Stephen, nodded.

"And my daughter didn't invite me," he said mournfully. "How undutiful of her."

Jenkins snickered. "She'll learn. You'll own the place soon, guv."

"Yes." Sir Stephen looked towards the Hall with hungry eyes. The Chatleighs' removal from town had come as an unwelcome shock, upsetting his carefully laid plans and forcing him to hire new accomplices. The stable boy he had placed in the Chatleigh town house, for example, had had to go, but he had served his purpose, acting as spy and saboteur. Here in the country there were other things that could be tried, and enough people willing to work for a dishonest wage. On the whole, Sir Stephen was pleased with his new plan. Chatleigh and his bride would get their comeuppance for the way they had treated him, and he would finally get all that he deserved.

"What do you think, Jenkins?" he said, now. "Can we still carry the plan through?"

"Not tonight, guv." Jenkins shook his head regretfully. "Too many people. It'll never work."

"Damn. Tomorrow, then. You know your part?"

"Yes, guv, haven't forgotten. And we'll meet at the

ruined mill."

"Yes. But not too soon, mind." There was immense satisfaction in his voice. "My daughter and I have much to settle."

"Yes, guv."

Sir Stephen nodded and glanced towards the house again. Tomorrow. It would all come right for him, tomorrow.

Chapter Eighteen

The dinner party broke up late. Everyone was in a festive mood due to the recently arrived news of Napoléon's abdication, and there were music and charades after dinner. Justin fidgeted through it all, trying hard not to stare at his wife and not succeeding. Damn! Why did she have to look so beautiful, so enticing? he asked himself. She was driving him crazy, and, what was worse, she knew it. He had seen that in the little glances she tossed him throughout the evening. Inwardly, he groaned. When they were finally alone and he could get his hands on her, he would beat her for what she had put him through this night. When he got his hands on her . . . *God!* He raked a hand through his hair.

Melissa glanced at him and bit back a smile. There, it was working! He hadn't taken his eyes from her all evening. Tonight, she thought, almost singing the word to herself. Tonight, tonight, and when would all these people leave?

"A very nice evening," Augusta said sometime later, settling back in her chair in the drawing room. The last guests had finally departed, and the house was quiet. "Boy, pour me some claret."

Justin gritted his teeth, but crossed the room to do

as she asked. "Aren't you tired, Aunt?" he said, handing her a goblet.

"Not a bit of it. Life in the country is not at all what I feared." She held up her glass in a salute to Melissa. "A tolerable evening, child."

"Thank you, Aunt," Melissa glanced up at Justin. He prowled the room like a caged tiger, and she suspected she knew what was wrong with him. She, too, wished Augusta would go to bed so that they could be alone.

Augusta, however, was in a reminiscing mood, talking about Paris, which now would be opened to them again. She spoke of the gallant cavaliers she had known, the beautiful ladies; and Melissa, who would have been fascinated by such tales at any other time, could only listen patiently and try not to fidget. Eventually, however, Augusta wound down and discovered that she was tired.

"I'm for bed," she said, getting stiffly to her feet and reaching for her cane. "Walk with me, girl."

"But . . ." Melissa looked helplessly at Justin.

"Come. Help a helpless old lady." Augusta snapped her fingers, and Melissa gave in.

"Helpless is one thing you are not, ma'am," she said as she took the old lady's arm.

"Nonsense, I am old. Now be a good girl and come along."

"Yes, Aunt," Melissa walked beside her out of the room, throwing a look back at Justin.

It took some time to see Augusta settled; the maid Melissa had provided for her didn't do things just the way Augusta wished, and Melissa had to rectify most of the problems. At last, however, she was free, and she nearly ran down the stairs to the drawing room, pausing at her room only to discard the shawl. But when she reached it breathless and flushed, the drawing room was empty.

"Oh," she said, her shoulders slumping in disappointment, and Justin, sitting in a chair in the shadows, rose.

"Yes?" he said.

Melissa's hand flew to her heart. "Oh! You startled me."

"Sorry." He walked a few paces towards her and then stopped, frowning. "Damn."

"What is it?"

"That damned dress."

"Justin, there's nothing wrong with it."

"Everyone was staring at your br— chest."

Melissa bit back a smile. "It is all the crack in town, Justin."

"Nevertheless, I will not have my wife dressing like that."

"Why? Don't you like my br— chest?"

"Of course I—Melissa!" he spluttered, and his face turned a mottled red.

"You seemed to, at the Hart and Hind," she said, advancing farther into the room. He stood still, watching her. "What was it you said? Oh, yes. 'Ah, your breasts are so beautiful, m'dear, like two ripe fruits—' "

"Stop it!" He pressed a hand over her mouth.

She jerked free. "Actually, I believe you said 'apples,' rather than 'fruits.' Yes, that was it. Though I wouldn't call them apples, precisely." She frowned down at herself. "More like peaches. Ripe, full peaches, of course."

"Stop it!" he shouted again, and quieted her the only way he could, with his mouth on hers. Startled, she went still, but then her mouth opened under his, and her arms twined around his neck, and the kiss went on much longer than he had expected. When he finally released her, she looked up at him, her eyes shining.

"Do you like apples, Justin?" she said, her voice husky.

Justin had to clear his throat before he could answer. "Yes," he said finally, his voice as rough as hers. "I like apples very much." He gazed down at her décolletage and then raised his eyes, suddenly sparkling with mischief. "Like peaches, too."

Melissa gave a crow of laughter and threw herself into his arms. His lips were warm and firm on hers, but after a moment, he pushed her away. "But," he said firmly, "you will not dress like this again."

Melissa pouted. "Not even for you?"

"What?" Justin looked startled. "Well, maybe for me."

"All right."

Her smile was so sweet and so inviting that it nearly distracted him from his purpose. "But for no one else, is that clear? I don't care how fashionable it is, I will not have my wife exposing her wares to all the world like a common wh—"

"Don't say it!" Melissa's fingers swiftly covered his lips, and he regretted the pain that darkened her eyes.

"Ah my love, I haven't thought that of you for a very long time," he murmured, pressing his lips against her palm. Her hand tingled so much in response that she snatched it away. "Will you forgive me?"

"Yes," she said, breathlessly. His love. Was she really his love? "It was never a fair thing to say, Justin. Because, as it happens," she hesitated, her fingers toying with the lapels of his coat, and then went on, raising her eyes to his, "I am still untouched."

Justin's eyes lit up, and his arms tightened around her. "Well," he murmured, "that we can do something about." And with that, his mouth came down on hers.

They were both ready for this now, with no memories of the past or fears for the future to taint their need. Her hands clutched at his shoulders, his roved over her curves as the kiss lengthened and deepened. "I've always liked the taste of peaches," he whispered in her ear, before his lips trailed down her arched throat to her chest.

"Oh, Justin," she gasped, torn between laughter and the heat that was invading all her senses, making her knees grow weak, making her clutch at him. "Justin."

"Yes, princess." His fingertips followed the path his lips had taken, and she squirmed against him, on fire with the exquisite sensations he was evoking within her. Justin groaned low in his throat and bent to put an arm behind her knees, lifting her, and it was only as he cradled her high against his chest that a sound from outside broke through the haze of desire that surrounded them.

"Justin?" Melissa said, when he didn't move for a few moments.

"Shh."

"What is it?"

"Don't you hear it?"

"What?" Melissa cocked her head, listening, and then she heard it, too, the frantic pealing of a bell, echoing through the night's stillness. "What—"

"My God!" Justin suddenly relaxed his grip and, to her immense surprise, set her down. "My God, it's the fire bell!"

Melissa scurried after him as he strode out of the room. "But where—"

"Somewhere on the estate," he called over his shoulder as he ran for the stairs. "Phelps. Phelps!"

"Yes, my lord, I hear it," Phelps said as he came into the hall, pulling on his coat.

Justin ran down the stairs, and Melissa wasn't far

behind. "Any idea where it is?"

"No, my lord, but Jeffrey's gone to see."

"God! Of all nights. I'll have to go." He turned to Melissa, raking a hand through his hair.

"Yes, of course," Melissa said. "I'll just go change—"

"No, you'll be better off here."

"But—"

"I want you where you'll be safe." Heedless of Phelps, Justin bent and placed a brief, hard kiss on her lips. "Later," he promised, and headed for the door.

"Later," Melissa murmured, her fingers going to her lips. Then she became aware of Phelps's presence. "Phelps."

Phelps cleared his throat. "Yes, my lady?"

"Let me know when you find out where it is, please? I'll be in my sitting room."

"Yes, my lady."

Melissa climbed the stairs again, tiredly this time. All her hopes, all her plans, gone for naught, but it couldn't be helped. Still, there was always tomorrow. She tingled at the thought.

In his room at the hedge tavern, Sir Stephen suddenly jerked awake. At first he wasn't sure what had aroused him, but then he heard it, the distant, frantic pealing of a bell. *Damn!* He jumped from the bed and began scrambling into his clothes. The fire bell!

He ran into Jenkins in the hall, just buttoning his breeches. "Guv'nor—"

"Damn it all to hell, Jenkins, what happened?" he demanded, and Jenkins swallowed. Sir Stephen was not physically imposing, but Jenkins didn't care to cross him when he was angry.

"Don't know, guv but—"

"You sent the message canceling it, did you not?"

"Yeah, I sent the message. Might be this has nothing to do with it."

"Damn, two fires in two days, even my dolt of a son-in-law would begin to suspect — Do you know where the fire is?"

"Heard it's the Watling farm. The one farthest from the Hall."

"The one we settled on! Damn, Stokes mustn't have gotten the message. This blows all our plans to hell." Jenkins prudently held his tongue. "Or perhaps it doesn't. All right, this is what I want you to do." He laid a hand on Jenkins's shoulder. "I want you to go to Stokes," he began, and swiftly outlined the changes to the plan. Jenkins listened in silence, nodding occasionally. "Is that clear?"

"Yes, guv, clear enough."

"Good. Oh, and Jenkins." Sir Stephen turned from the door to his room. "You might want to start thinking of a way to dispose of Stokes and his wife."

"Guv?"

"No reason to share the money any more than we have to."

An evil grin split Jenkins's face. "Right, guv. I'll be thinking."

The ivory satin evening gown was crumpled and rucked up about Melissa's knees as she dozed in a chair. Then, as the first rays of the sun crept into the room, she awoke, blinking at the unexpected brilliance. Morning, and Justin had yet to come home. The fire, at a tenant's farm on the edge of the estate, must be very bad indeed, but, sorry though Melissa felt for the tenants, she was far more concerned about her husband. In the past month she had seen him become a conscientous landlord, and she had no doubt that he would pitch in and help however he could. Even now, he could be lying hurt, under a burning beam perhaps, or . . ."

No. She got up, stiffly, stamping one leg to wake it. It was foolish to think that way. Justin was fine. She would have to proceed in that belief. He was fine, and would soon return to her.

And would they then take up where they had left off? Melissa glanced at her reflection in the mirror and grimaced. Heavy guns, indeed. Well, it almost worked, she thought, fumbling for the laces that fastened her gown. Better to wear something sensible, in case she was needed.

A few moments later, dressed in riding habit and boots, she went downstairs, her heels clicking loudly in the early morning silence. Hearing there had been no news, she went into the breakfast room. She was just finishing her tea and toast when a footman knocked tentatively at the door. "Yes?" she said.

"Begging your pardon, my lady, but there's a woman asking for you."

"A woman?" Melissa laid her napkin on her plate and rose. "Who is it, Hawkins?"

"Can't say, my lady. Never seen her before in my life."

Melissa frowned. "Is she gentry?"

"No, my lady, hardly," he said, scornfully. "Nor would she say what she wants, except it's something about the fire."

"The fire! Yes, of course I'll see her." Melissa hurried from the room. The sound of voices raised in argument reached her as she came into the hall, and ahead of her she saw the porter remonstrating with a woman. Short and stout, she was clad in rough peasant garb, a dress of homespun and an apron that was none too clean. Her cap sat askew upon lank, rather greasy hair. No wonder the footman had turned up his nose, Melissa thought.

"You wished to see me?" she said aloud, and the woman turned.

"Oh, my lady, thank goodness!" she gasped. "He told me, talk to you and no one else."

"Who did?"

"His lordship. He's—"

"Is he hurt?"

"No, not so badly, my lady, but—"

"Then I'll come."

"No, my lady, he said he didn't want you to worry, you was to stay here—"

"Not if he's injured," Melissa said crisply, and she turned to the porter. "I may need the barouche, if it's bad, but I will let you know. And you had best send for Dr. Porter." She turned back to the woman. "How did you get here?"

"Walked, my lady," the woman said.

"Walked! Very well, we'll get you home. Where do you live?"

"In the village, ma' am. My name is Mrs. Stokes."

"Stokes. I'll remember that. Thank you for your help."

Mrs. Stokes bobbed a curtsy as Melissa went swiftly out the door, and her eyes narrowed for just a second. "Weren't nothing, my lady," she murmured. "Weren't nothing at all."

Melissa strode into the stables a few moments later. "Saddle Lady for me, Jeffrey," she said, crisply.

"But, my lady—" the groom protested.

"Quickly now, I am needed at the fire." Jeffrey hesitated. "I said, quickly! His lordship is hurt, and—"

"Yes, my lady! And if you'll just wait I'll saddle Pepper and come with you."

"There isn't time!"

"Beggin' your pardon, my lady, but his lordship said as how we're not to let you ride out alone. Ever," said the man who was leading Lady out from her stall. He was new to the Hall, and though he knew horses Melissa thought him a peculiar choice for an undergroom. He was older, for one thing, and obviously of the city.

"When? When did he say that?" she demanded.

"When you came back from town, my lady," Jeffrey said as he saddled Lady.

"I wonder why? Well, no matter. What is your name?"

The undergroom looked up. "Lawton, my lady."

"Lawton. Is she ready, Jeffrey?"

"Yes, my lady, but—"

"Give me a leg up."

"Won't take me a minute to saddle Pepper," Lawton said, and at that moment Harry rode into the stableyard, just returning from his morning ride.

"Never mind, I'll go with my brother," Melissa declared, and rode out of the stable.

Lawton mumbled something under his breath. "What did you say?" Jeffrey asked.

"Can't let her go alone," Lawton said, throwing a saddle onto Pepper. "Her brother won't be any protection."

"Protection against what?" Jeffrey asked.

"God knows," Lawton said, and rode out of the stable after the Countess and her brother.

"Where are we going?" Harry panted, hard pressed to keep up with Melissa as they rode through the narrow lanes that crossed the estate, toward the Watling farm and Justin.

"To the fire," she called back.

"Oh, capital!"

"Harry!"

"Well, it isn't every, day something so exciting happens."

"Justin may be hurt, Harry!"

"I say, didn't know that!" He sobered. "Bad?"

"I don't know."

Harry studied her intent face. "You love him, don't you?"

"Oh, Harry, what a time to talk about that!" she said, impatiently. "Just ride."

"Yes, ma'am," Harry responded, subsiding, and for a long time there was nothing but the sounds of hoofbeats and the horses' breathing. Harry managed to contain himself until the lane crossed the road. "What's that?" he called, pointing with his riding crop to a carriage pulled up along the edge. It was old and ramshackle, its black paint dull and peeling, the team of horses harnessed to it the only sign of life. "Should we stop and see if they need help?"

"We can't, Harry," she called back over her shoulder. "Justin may need us."

He began to protest, but just as they drew level with the carriage two men rode out from its shelter straight towards them. Harry watched them curiously, but Melissa let out a shriek and shot ahead, using her riding crop on Lady in a way he had never seen before. The taller of the two men set off after her, and suddenly Harry recognized him. "No!" he yelled, as Sir Stephen, ungainly rider though he was, steadily gained on her, but then the other man reared up before him, and Harry had his own problems.

Harry put up a good fight, bringing his riding crop down in a slashing blow on the man's arm, but his opponent was bigger and more experienced at this sort

268

of thing. The man's riding crop connected with Harry's shoulder just as Melissa screamed. Harry watched in horror as Sir Stephen pulled her off her horse onto his own. Then a fist connected solidly with his jaw, and the ground rushed up to meet him.

of gaily. The mass lights only connected with
electric them. Across figures a sudden a garland, It had
extended its branches. Its ceased and ashes of her
flame some his own. Then a lip operated gently with
a ... and beginning to glad to this taken that

Chapter Nineteen

"The fire was set, no doubt about it." Alfred's face
was grim as he picked up the charred remains of an
oil-soaked rag.

Justin frowned as he looked at the ruins of what had
been a prosperous farm. Though the fire was out, the
full extent of the tragedy was just beginning to strike
home. The shell of the farmhouse, made of local
stone, was still standing, but the thatched roof had
gone up in an instant, and the inside was gutted. The
barn, opposite the house and far enough away to have
ordinarily escaped the fire, had burned as well. The
Watlings had been lucky to escape with their lives.

"But·why?" Justin said. "Who would do such a thing?"

"Who wants you dead, sir?"

Justin stiffened. "Melissa," he said, suddenly.

"My lord?"

"She's back at the Hall."

"But Lawton is there, sir," Alfred protested as Justin
strode towards their horses. "You're the one should be
concerned."

"Perhaps." Justin unlooped Diablo's reins from the
branch of a tree, and glanced back at the wreckage of
the farm. "But I'll feel better back at the Hall."

270

* * *

Sir Stephen rode back to Stokes, standing over his fallen opponent. "Want I should take him, too?" Stokes said.

Sir Stephen looked coldly down at Harry's unconscious form. "No, I've other plans for him. We're after bigger game now."

"So I see." Stokes leered at Melissa's limp figure, lying across Sir Stephen's saddle. Bruises were already darkening at her temple and jaw. "Hope she wakes up soon, guv. No fun if she's out."

"Take your filthy eyes off her," Sir Stephen snapped, and Stokes involuntarily stepped back a pace.

"Now, guv, I didn't mean nothin'—"

"Damn!"

"Guv?"

"Company." Sir Stephen pointed down the lane, at the figure of a man riding hell-for-leather towards them. "Damn!" he exclaimed again, wheeling his horse. "Back to the carriage!"

"But what of the stripling, he's a witness—"

"Leave him! There's no time!" Both men raced across the field towards the carriage. Stokes threw himself up onto the box and Sir Stephen crammed the unconscious Melissa inside, reaching to pull the door closed just as the carriage, with a lurch, started off.

"Stop!" Lawton cried, as he came even with them, and fired off his pistol. "Stop, I say!" But the carriage careened down the road and was lost to sight around a bend.

Lawton flung himself off his mount and stumbled over to where Harry lay, much too still and quiet. So now they knew the Countess wasn't in on the plot, but what a way to find out. "Come on, lad," he said, slipping an arm under Harry's shoulders. "Wake up." He

271

shook him. "Wake up, lad."

"Um." Harry groaned and opened his eyes, a brilliant blue without the protection of his spectacles. For a moment he stared up at the runner, a perplexed frown creasing his forehead, and then he sat bolt upright. "Lissa! He's got Melissa!"

"Easy, lad." Lawton's hand on his shoulder restrained him. "Who has her?"

"Sir Stephen, damn his eyes," Harry said, sounding oddly adult as he scrambled to his feet.

"Sir Stephen?"

"Sir Stephen Barton, my stepfather, may he rot in hell. Where are my spectacles?"

Lawton spotted something reflecting the sun and went to pick it up. "Here, lad. Lucky they didn't break. Why would your stepfather want to abduct your sister?" he asked as Harry put the spectacles, bent askew, on.

"He's always wanted her. She thinks I don't know."

Lawton stood stock-still as Harry limped over to his horse. Of all the motives he and the Earl had discussed, they had never thought of this, that the Countess might be the reason for the attacks, if not to blame. It fair turned his stomach. There might be no connection, of course, but he doubted it. "How many of them were there, lad?"

"Just two that I saw, unless there were more in the carriage." Harry swung up into the saddle. "Well? Aren't we going after them?"

Game 'un, this lad. "Not yet. Best you ride back to the Hall and get help." Harry's mouth opened to protest, and Lawton quickly went on. "Your sister's in danger, lad, and we don't know what we're facing. Best to do it with a few men."

"You're not a groom at all, are you?"

"No, lad, I'm from Bow Street."

"A runner!"

"Yes, so if you'll just ride back to the Hall—"

"No, look!" Harry pointed with his crop. Riding across the fields towards them were Justin and Alfred. "Chatleigh!" he shouted, and took off at a gallop. With an oath Lawton threw himself onto his horse and went after him. God save him from amateurs, game or not.

Justin glanced up as he heard his name, and stared in surprise at the figure riding full tilt towards him. "What the devil . . . Harry?"

"Chatleigh! Thank God. He's got Melissa!" Harry yelled.

Justin spurred Diablo forward. "What are you talking about, Harry? Who has Melissa?"

"Sir Stephen! He grabbed her off her horse."

Justin frowned, looking at Lawton as he rode up. "Lawton, what the devil is going on?"

"It appears the Countess has been abducted—"

"The devil she has!"

"—by her stepfather; Last I saw, they were in a carriage, going down that road."

"Sir Stephen? What the devil?" Justin's face was blank, and then grim. "Damn! What are we waiting for?" he asked, and wheeled Diablo around.

The carriage jounced over a particularly rough stretch of road, jolting Melissa's head, and she moaned. "Ah, so you're back with us, are you?" a voice said, and she was abruptly conscious. Slowly she opened her eyes to see Sir Stephen, sitting on the seat opposite, watching her.

She sat up quickly, putting a hand to her head as it throbbed in response. She was in a carriage, she real-

273

ized, looking around for a way to escape. A gleam of malicious amusement lit Sir Stephen's eyes as she dove for the door. When it wouldn't budge she shook it, and then scurried across to the other side.

"Locked, my dear," Sir Stephen said, and held up a key, his smile evil and triumphant. "But, come, don' you wish to spend some time with your stepfather?"

"I'd rather die!" she spat out, and he shook his head "Oh, no, my dear. But perhaps you'll wish it, when I am done with you." Melissa went very still. "You and I have much to settle."

"No!" She launched herself at him, her nails raking down his face before he could react, but after a brief struggle he caught her wrists and pulled them down behind her back at an angle that made her bones crack. She glared up at him, struggling helplessly in his grasp, and his smile deepened. "See, my dear, fighting does no good—Damn you!" he exclaimed, as she spat. He thrust her roughly away from him. She landed awkwardly on the floor between the seats and scrambled as far away from him as possible, her eyes never leaving his face.

Sir Stephen took out a handkerchief and wiped his face. "You shall pay for that," he promised, "and I shall enjoy making you pay."

"You're sick!"

"Ah, am I?" His eyes moved leisurely over her, and she clutched at the bodice of her habit. "But I shall get what I want, Melissa. I told you once. I always get what I want."

Melissa shivered and huddled into a corner, not looking at him. In the close confines of the carriage she could not fight him, so it was best to save her strength. Perhaps when they stopped, she could escape. She would have to bide her time.

The drive seemed interminable, with her awareness of Sir Stephen's eyes on her, but at last, all too soon, the carriage came to a stop. "It appears we are here, my dear," Sir Stephen said, withdrawing the key. "I do hope you're not going to try anything foolish? I should hate to have to strike you again. Besides," the door swung open, "I believe Stokes has a gun. Out you go."

He reached for her arm, but she pulled away. Then, head held high, she descended from the carriage, to see that his accomplice did indeed have a gun, and that it was leveled at her. "Such brave men," she said, scornfully. "So afraid of one woman."

The other man grinned, exposing crooked, stained teeth. "Like my women wild, I do," he said, and his eyes raked insolently over her. She looked wildly about, seeking a means for escape, but then Sir Stephen was beside her, grasping her arm again.

"I wouldn't, my dear. Inside with you, now," he said, and dragged her towards a ramshackle old building set beside an algae-covered pond. Though it was midday the place was gloomy, with the willows overhead blocking out most of the sun. Melissa recognized it with a jolt. The old mill! They were still on Chatleigh land, then. *Oh, Justin,* she thought, and wondered if she would ever see him again.

Sir Stephen kicked the door open, and she stumbled inside, floorboards creaking beneath her. A shaft of sunlight coming through a crack in the roof made dust motes dance and revealed a large, high-ceilinged room, empty except for the abandoned gears of the mill wheel. She wrinkled her nose at the smell of dust and disuse.

"Her majesty don't like the accommodations, guv'nor," Stokes said, grinning again, and Sir Stephen turned.

"Leave her to me. Go back and get the others," he said.

"And leave you alone? I see." He leered. "Wouldn' mind some time with her myself."

"Go!" Sir Stephen ordered.

Stokes turned, grinning. "Yes, guv," he said, good naturedly. "Talk about it when I get back."

The door slammed shut behind him. Sir Stephen stared fixedly at it, his hand still gripping Melissa' arm. He hoped Jenkins had arranged a suitable reward for Stokes and his wife, even if the woman had done a good job of luring Melissa away from the Hall. And he wondered if the Jenkinses had any idea what he had in store for them. No matter that they had earned their share of the ransom Chatleigh would pay for his wife. The money was his! He would share it with no one.

"Well, my dear." He turned to Melissa. "I believe you and I have some things to discuss."

Melissa pulled free from his grasp and turned towards the door, but he blocked her way. "Come, why fight when it's inevitable?" he said, walking toward her, and she shrank back. *Justin!* she screamed, silently, but he was far away. There was no help for her now.

"Down this way?" Justin said, standing in the stirrups and pointing down the road.

"Yes, my lord," Lawton said, riding up to him as Justin took off at a gallop. "But, my lord, we should have help!"

"No time! Justin yelled back. "If that bastard has Melissa—The day I can't take Sir Stephen is the day I die."

Lawton caught up with him. "Had dealings with him, have you, sir?"

"Yes. He must want ransom."

Lawton threw him a startled glance, but held his tongue. So his lordship didn't know. Could be the lad was wrong, but he didn't think so. God help Sir Stephen when the Earl did find out.

He would kill him, Justin thought, his mind working coldly and clearly. When he got his hands on Sir Stephen, he would kill him. Damn the man! If he'd known Barton would try something like this, Justin would have given him anything he'd asked for. Instead, Melissa was suffering for it, Melissa, who was blameless, who had been so soft and sweet in his arms the past night, his wife, his love—

Diablo stumbled as Justin jerked at the reins, and then regained his pace. Good God in heaven, he loved her. Why had he not seen it before? Oh, he'd been blinded in the beginning by what he'd thought was her duplicity, but since then he had learned how wrong he had been. She was a sweet, generous, loving woman. And a desirable one. Even now, when his whole being was intent on rescuing her, he could remember all too clearly the nights when he had sought a bottle to console himself for not sharing her bed, the times when just the touch of her hand on his arm or the merest hint of her soft fragrance set his blood to boiling. And last night they had so nearly become one! He groaned at the thought. God help him, he loved her. She had brought meaning back to his life and eased the loneliness that had been inside him for too long. If he lost her, he didn't know what he would do. She had to be all right. She had to be.

There was the rumble of hoofbeats ahead. "What's that?" Alfred said, and at the same time a carriage

swept around a bend in the road. The riders had jus
enough time to crowd to the side to avoid being
knocked down as it sped by, rocking back and forth on
the rutted road.

"That's it!" Harry shouted, and set off in pursuit.

"Damn!" Justin swore, setting off after Harry and
the fast-disappearing carriage. He had no hope tha
Melissa was inside, but he could not let Harry face
danger alone.

Up ahead there were shouts and the sound of gun
shots. Justin dug his heels in Diablo's side, reaching
for his own pistol as the carriage slued to a stop, end
ing up sideways across the road. Another shot, and
Harry went down. Justin leveled his pistol. He wa
coming up fast on the carriage, he could see the
driver, he took aim—and there was an odd, pulling
sensation at his arm, making the shot go wild. The
man fell off the box, clutching his shoulder instead of
his heart, as Justin had intended. Then he got up and
began to run before falling, face-first, in the dust.

"Good shooting, sir!" Harry yelled as Justin rode
up.

"Good God, Harry, I thought you were dead!" Jus
tin exclaimed, swinging off his horse.

"Ducked to dodge the bullet. But, sir, you're hit!"

"What?" Justin glanced down, becoming aware fo
the first time of a stinging sensation in his arm. "Jus
winged me," he said, taking out a handkerchief and
pressing it to his arm.

"You were lucky, my lord," Lawton said, riding up

"Yes, but it made my shot go wide."

"Just as well." When Justin stared at him, he added
"How else could we find out where the Countess is?"

Justin wheeled around and stalked over to the man
still sprawled in the road. Grabbing his collar, h

auled him to his feet. "Now, I am only going to ask
ou this once," he said softly, pressing his pistol against
e man's nose. "Where is my wife?"

The man's eyes went wide with fear. "I don't know,
y lord. . . ." Justin cocked the pistol. "In the old
ill!" he babbled. "The old mill."

"Excellent. And who is with her?"

"S-Sir Stephen, my lord."

"And no one else?"

"N-no. Don't shoot!"

"It isn't even loaded," Justin said, and thrust him
way.

"But mine is, so don't you get any ideas," Lawton
aid, holding his pistol at the ready.

"Alfred!" Justin yelled. "Can you handle this ruf-
an?"

Alfred rode forward. "Course I can, my lord. What
o you want me to do?" he asked.

"Take him back to Chatleigh. There's an old barn,
sed for storing hay. Put him in there. Make sure he's
uarded. And take Harry with you."

Harry, dusting himself off, looked up. "No, sir," he
aid. "I'm coming."

"Good God, boy, I can't let you get into this," Justin
aid. "Melissa'd never forgive me if you got hurt." If he
ot her back safely . . .

"I don't care." Harry's chin thrust out in a manner
rongly reminiscent of Melissa. "He's got my sister."

"And a gun, most likely." Justin raked a hand
hrough his hair. "All right. But you'll stay behind us,
Iarry."

"Yes, sir!"

Justin turned. "Off with you now, Alfred."

"Yes, sir. Where will you be?"

"At the old mill," Justin said, swinging up into

279

the saddle.

"There's no way out," Sir Stephen said, and Melissa who had been eyeing the mill's door, shifted her eye back to him. "You might as well stop fighting it daughter."

"You're mad if you think you can get away wit! this!" she snapped.

"Ah, but that's just what I do think. You see daughter, you are my safe passage." He took a step to wards her, and she fell back. "Your husband will hav to do as I ask."

"Which is?"

"Why, pay ransom for you, of course. He won't dar to do anything else, as long as I have you. And then may send you back. Maybe." He chuckled. "I hav been waiting a long time for this."

"I'll never give in to you. Never!"

"But you will, my dear, you've no choice. I intend t have you, at last."

"No—"

"Come, Melissa, why fight it? Give in and enjoy it

"No, oh no," she moaned, and as he reached for he her eyes rolled back in her head and she slumped t the floor.

Sir Stephen stared down at her, taken aback "Damn," he said softly, and he prodded at her with hi toe. "Melissa." She moaned in response, and he swor again. Damn! This was all he needed, for her to faint He wanted her conscious, fully aware of what wa happening to her. Only then could he enjoy it. "Dam: it, wake up," he said, bending over her, and at tha moment Melissa's feet came up and caught him full i the chest.

Sir Stephen staggered back, tumbled over a loose board, and ended up in an undignified heap. Melissa didn't stay to see the effects of her action, but scrambled to her feet, running for the door. Behind her she heard her stepfather wheeze and cough, and that spurred her on. She had to get out, onto the road where perhaps she could find safety.

The bolt of the old door was rusty and stiff, but fear lent strength to her fingers and at last it gave. The door creaked open and she was out, taking great gulps of fresh air and running, running. She hadn't gotten very far when there were footsteps behind her, and she turned just as Sir Stephen crashed into her. "No!" she screamed, and pushed him. He lost his footing on the uneven ground and tumbled again, this time landing, with a splash, in the mill pond.

Good, she thought, hoping he drowned! A sharp pain lanced her ankle as she stumbled over a rock, but she couldn't stop, she dare not stop. *Oh, please,* she thought, her breath coming in sobbing gasps. *Oh, God, please!* And then arms, slimy and dripping wet, caught her about the waist and knocked her to the ground.

"Where is the old mill?" Lawton said, as they rode off.

"Down here, about a mile. Used to be a busy place," Justin explained, "but when the old miller died no one was hired to replace him. Must be a ruin by now."

"But it's serving Sir Stephen's purpose. Wonder how he knew of it?"

"God knows, but he was hanging around here before we went to London. I never thought," he said, and then fell silent.

"No, sir. Unless Jenkins told him about it."

"Jenkins!" Justin stared at him. "My God, you think Sir Stephen's the one behind all the incidents?"

"Who else, my lord?"

"But good God, why?"

"He wants Melissa," Harry said, and Justin stared at him, blankly.

"My God, of course, that's it. He wants her money."

"But—" Harry began, and then stopped at a look from Lawton.

"Well, he'll not get away with it," Justin went on. "It's just him there, so we should take him easily, Lawton."

"And I'll be there," Harry said.

"No, boy, you'll stay behind—" Justin broke off abruptly. Up ahead there was the sound of a woman screaming, and he tensed. "My God! Melissa!" he shouted. He spurred Diablo forward, and at that moment the horse's foreleg went into a pothole.

Only Justin's skill as a rider kept him from toppling over as the horse stumbled. "Damn!" he exclaimed, swinging to the ground. "Of all times for him to come up lame—go! I'll follow."

"Are you sure, sir?"

"Yes! And, Harry, don't get shot! Go!"

They took off, galloping hard, and Justin, leaving Diablo to fend for himself, ran after them. That had been Melissa he had heard screaming. He would kill him, he thought. Sir Stephen's days were numbered.

There was a bend in the road, and when they were around it, the old mill was ahead. A woman ran frantically towards them, hampered by the full skirts of her riding habit, and behind her came a tall, thin man, water dripping from him. "Melissa!" Justin yelled, just as Sir Stephen caught her about the waist

282

and brought her down.

Harry flung himself off his horse and stumbled across the grass. "Get your hands off my sister!" he shouted, pummeling Sir Stephen on the back. Sir Stephen jerked up in surprise, then drove his elbow back into him. Harry fell back, but then, sobbing for breath, launched himself forward. Sir Stephen twisted about, holding his fist ready to strike, until the sound of a pistol being cocked caught his attention. He looked up into the barrel of a gun, and froze.

"I wouldn't," Lawton said. "Easy, lad," he added, as Harry let one more blow fall. "Get up, sir. Slowly."

Sir Stephen rose to his feet, his arms upraised and his eyes never leaving the gun. Melissa glanced up and then crawled away, huddling on the ground, her arms clutched convulsively around herself.

"Lissa," Harry dropped to his knees next to her, placing an arm around her shoulders.

"H-Harry!" Her breath came in great sobbing gasps. "Oh, Harry."

"It's all right, Lissa, you're safe." Harry looked up, his eyes full of appeal, as Justin ran towards them.

"Oh, Harry, he said he . . . he said he was going to have me this time, and—"

"Hush, Lissa!" Harry looked up as Justin stopped dead beside them. Justin's eyes sought Harry's, looking for confirmation, hoping for denial, and their gazes, somber and serious, held for a long moment. "You're safe. Chatleigh's here."

"J-Justin? No, I don't want him near me, I don't want him to touch me."

"It's all right, Melissa." Justin crouched beside her and reached out his arm. Good God, he thought, blankly. My good God. "I've got her, Harry," he said, and again they exchanged looks over Melissa's head.

"She's safe with me."

"Yes, sir," Harry said, getting to his feet.

"Good work, halfling," Justin called after him, and he gathered his wife against his chest, rocking her back and forth. "Easy, Melissa, easy now, my dear love, my wife, you're safe now."

"But he said, he . . . and I knew he always wanted to . . . but I thought he would, this time—"

"Hush, princess, you're safe. He won't bother you again."

"My lord," Lawton called. "What do you want I should do with this one?"

Justin looked up, and for a moment his face was so twisted with rage that Sir Stephen took an involuntary step back. "Take him back to the Hall and put him with the other, until we can get them to a magistrate."

"Yes, my lord," Lawton said, approvingly; he, too, had been taken aback by the rage on the Earl's face. "The Countess, is she . . . ?"

"Hurt? I don't think so." He bent his head. "Did he hurt you, sweetheart?"

"N-no, but he—"

"I know. I know."

That made Melissa raise her head, and she saw in his eyes the knowledge that she had tried so hard to keep from him, that she had never wanted to see there. Oh, God, she thought, and she closed her eyes, wanting to shut out reality.

"I think she's all right, Lawton, but she'll have to be got back home. Damn, I can't take her up on Diablo."

"You can have my horse, sir, and I'll lead Diablo," Harry said, and Justin nodded approvingly.

"Good lad. And you can help Lawton keep an eye on our prisoner."

"Capital," Harry said, with grim, adult satisfaction

284

Justin watched him for a moment. Then looked back down at his wife, huddled and shivering in his arms. *Good God,* he thought again. "Melissa," he said, softly, and she stirred. "We're going home now."

Chapter Twenty

A few hours later Justin stood at his study window, looking out at the drive and seeing nothing. He hadn't slept since the night before last, and he was tired, deep in his body, deep in his soul, with a long day still ahead. Melissa was safe, thank God, sleeping upstairs under the effects of the draught Dr. Porter had administered, but what he would do about her he hadn't the slightest idea. The events of the past hours all crowded together in his mind, and he wanted nothing more than to give all up and run, back to the Army where life had been simpler and he'd known who he was. Now nothing was easy.

There was a light tap on the door. Justin turned as Lawton came in, his hand firmly grasping Sir Stephen's arm. Sir Stephen's hands were securely bound behind his back, and there were bruises on his face that hadn't been there earlier. Justin eyed him coldly.

"Here he is, sir," Lawton said. "Though what you wants with him—"

"Thank you, Lawton. Leave us."

286

Lawton stared at him, then nodded. "Very well, my lord. But I need him in good enough shape to travel to Bow Street."

"He will be. Unfortunately," Justin added. Lawton nodded and went out, closing the door behind him.

The silence lengthened. Justin lounged, apparently at ease, behind his desk, and Sir Stephen, as if fascinated, watched his fingers toy with a silver pen knife. Finally, he could stand the silence no longer. "This is an outrage!" he burst out, and Justin's eyebrows rose. "I demand my rights. Why should I be treated as a common criminal—"

"When you are one?" Justin said. "Or would you prefer to be treated as you treated Melissa?"

Sir Stephen's face turned an ugly, mottled red. "I wouldn't have harmed her! Damn it, man, she's my daughter."

Justin leaned swiftly over the desk, stabbing at the air with the pen knife, and the other man pulled back. "And do you deny you would have asked ransom for her?"

"Yes! My dear daughter, once she knew how much I needed money—"

"Oh, cut line," Justin said wearily, and he got up, perching on the corner of his desk, the pen knife still in his hand. "We both know what you had in mind for her."

"I don't know what you mean. If she's told you some nonsense—"

"And I, for one, would like to see you hang for it." Justin's eyes were cold as they raked over Sir Stephen. "However, you will likely only be transported to the Antipodes, you and your friends. You did hire Jenkins, did you not?"

"Yes, but . . . No more. I will not say another word." His mouth set in a straight line, and he leaned back, glaring up at Justin with hate-filled eyes.

"No matter. They've said enough. We know it was you planned everything, not them." Justin prowled over to the window. "Don't think you'll like Australia. And, by the way, I intend to petition for Harry's guardianship. Don't think I'll have any trouble getting it."

"Look, Chatleigh," Sir Stephen said. "We're both reasonable men."

"Not feeling particularly reasonable just now."

"Listen to me! I don't deserve this."

"Ha!"

"I'll die in prison, Chatleigh. We aristocrats are not made for such a life. We are too fine for it." Justin's eyebrow rose, and Sir Stephen straightened. "Very well, then. If you will not relent, I will tell the magistrates all about Melissa. Every single, little thing." Justin turned slowly and stared at him. "There, my lord, what say you to that?"

"You will regret it if you do," Justin said, softly.

"Oh, no, Chatleigh. Not as much as you. When news of it gets around town—"

Justin crossed the room in two quick strides and leaned over the other man, his hands gripping the arms of the chair. "Hear me on this, Barton. If you do such a thing, I will not forget. And I will find you," he said. "I will find you, wherever you are, and then I will kill you. Slowly. It won't be pleasant." He straightened. "Learned some things on the Peninsula."

Sir Stephen glared up at him, and then a sly look

appeared in his eyes. "She's not worth it," he said. "She's not even that good—"

Justin's fist flew out and caught the other man squarely on the nose. Sir Stephen jerked back, his arms involuntarily straining to protect his face, as the blood began to flow. "My nose!" he cried, his voice muffled. "You broke my nose."

"You're lucky that's all I broke," Justin said, crossing the room to tug on the bellpull.

"Why did you have to do that?"

"I'm done with him," Justin said as Lawton came in.

"So I see, sir," Lawton said, looking with raised eyebrows at Sir Stephen's ravaged countenance.

"A handkerchief, please let me have a handkerchief," Sir Stephen begged, and Justin's gaze was contemptuous.

"Get him out of my sight, Lawton."

"Yes, my lord. Come on, you." Lawton grasped Sir Stephen's arm, hauling him roughly to his feet. "It's Bow Street for you."

The door closed behind them, and Justin was at last alone, to deal with his unruly emotions. *God!* He raked a hand through his hair. For all his calm demeanor before Sir Stephen, inside he was agitated and upset. The day had been a nightmare. Now what would he do?

Tired though he was, he couldn't relax. Restless, he went to the book-room, planning to talk to Harry if he were there. Instead, to his surprise, he saw Augusta. She looked up from her book as he opened the door, and he took an involuntary step back. "Sorry. Didn't mean to disturb you."

"Justin," she called, in her most autocratic man-

289

ner, and his heart sank. The last thing he needed just now was to be scolded by her.

"Yes, Aunt," he said tiredly, and went in. "What is it?"

"What is going on around here? Harry told me some garbled story about Sir Stephen abducting Melissa."

"Yes."

"Oh, sit down, boy, you know I don't like it when you tower over me. Now. What is this all about?"

"Oh, God," Justin said, and put his head in his hands.

Augusta regarded him in surprise. She had often wondered if her nephew had any emotions, so little did he react to things. Now she knew. "What is it, boy?" she asked, her voice gruff as she touched his arm.

Justin thrust his hand into his hair. "A mess. An unholy mess, and for the life of me, I don't know how to straighten it out."

"Melissa is all right, isn't she?"

"Yes. But God, Aunt . . ." He swallowed, and raised his head. And then, because he had to talk to someone, he told her of the abduction, and the reason behind it.

"So," Augusta said when he was finished, her voice thoughtful, "that was it. I wondered."

Justin looked at her in surprise. "You wondered? You mean . . . you guessed?"

"Yes. Didn't you?"

"No! I knew she was afraid of him, but I never expected . . . this."

Augusta reached out and laid a hand on his arm. "Melissa is a fine girl, Justin. She'll get through this." Justin raised his head to stare at her, and she pulled back. "I wonder if that was what she was running from when you met her?"

"God, I don't know." He raked a hand through his hair again. "It's a mess."

"It doesn't have to be, Justin." Augusta's eyes held a softness that few had ever seen in them. "She loves you." Justin looked at her, sharply. "And unless I'm much mistaken, you love her. A much overrated commodity, love," she went on, her voice regaining its customary tartness. "People of our class don't really need it. But it does make marriage easier."

Justin rose and began to prowl about the room. "If that's what she wants."

Augusta frowned, and then her face softened. "It may take time, Justin, and patience. But the love is there."

"Yes." He let his breath out in a rush. "But what do I do in the meantime, to let her know I care? I've never loved anyone before."

Augusta bit back a smile at the plaintive note in his voice. "Comfort her when she needs it, and she will, Justin. Love her when she needs it. It will work out."

"But—"

"When the time comes, you'll know what to do."

Justin didn't answer for a moment. "Do you think so?"

"I know so. I have great faith in you, boy."

He stared at her, and then, to his own surprise, yawned so hugely that his jaw cracked. "Well. Think I'll get some sleep." He rose and went around the table. "Thank you, Aunt," he said, dropping a kiss on her cheek. Her face glowed with pleased color as he walked out.

The long spring twilight was fading when Justin walked into his wife's room. Her maid, sitting on a chair by the bed, started up, and he put a finger to his lips. "How is she?" he whispered.

"Sleeping, my lord," Liza answered, her eyes huge at being addressed by the Earl, "but she's restless. I think she's having bad dreams."

"Not surprising." Justin glanced towards the bed. "Have you eaten, girl?"

"No, my lord, but Mrs. Barnes will send up a tray."

Justin shook his head. "Never mind that. Go on and get your dinner now, and then get some rest."

"But Mrs. Barnes told me to stay with her, sir."

"I'll sit with her. Go on, now."

Liza gave him one more glance and then, curtsying, left the room. Justin stood with his hands on his hips until the door had closed behind her, and then turned, paying little attention to the fresh cream wallpaper and the cheerful chintz draperies. All his attention was focused on the girl lying still in the bed.

The bruises stood out dark on her face and the circles under her eyes were deep. Again rage against Sir Stephen welled up in him, but he forced it down. Sir Stephen had been dealt with. It was Melissa he had to face now, and he felt no more able to deal with her situation than he had earlier in the day. He still wasn't certain how he felt about what she had gone through, but, as he gazed down at her, he realized he shared Augusta's conviction. Melissa would come through this, and so would he.

Walking with amazing quietness for a man of his size, he crossed to his room, retrieving a book and a glass of wine. Then, taking the chair Liza had vacated, he settled down. It was likely to be a long night.

The arms reached for her, slimy and dripping wet, smelling dankly of mold, of long-dead things, and when she looked down, the hand that clutched at her was bony, it was a skeleton's. . . .

"No! No, no, no, no, no!"

"Melissa." Hands on her shoulders, lifting her, shaking her gently. "Melissa, sweetheart, wake up, it's just a dream."

"No," she moaned, and opened her eyes. The nightmare scene of the millpond dissolved. She was in her own room, lit only by the light of a single taper. A man was holding her; she could hear his steady heartbeat under her ear, feel his hands smoothing her hair and her shoulders. Not Sir Stephen, certainly. She raised her face, puzzled, and saw her husband.

"Justin?" she said, her voice quizzical.

"Yes, princess?"

"What are you doing here?"

"Sitting with you."

"But, Liza—"

"I sent your maid to bed. It's late."

"Oh." She looked away, squeezing her eyes tight. "You shouldn't touch me, Justin."

"Why shouldn't I?"

"I feel," she shuddered, and his arms tightened,

"so . . . dirty, so soiled—"

"No." He took her shoulders in a firm grasp, and she flinched. Instantly his grip gentled, his fingers massaging her arms. "You're not to blame for this, Melissa. Sir Stephen is the one who's wrong, not you."

"But something about me attracted him, it had to."

"Melissa." Again he grasped her shoulders, forcing her to face him. "Listen to me. You know he was wrong in how he treated your mother, don't you? And Harry?"

"Y-yes." Melissa wiped at her eyes.

"Then why can't you accept that he was wrong about you?"

"I . . . do you really think he was?" she asked, looking up at him, her eyes shining with a new and fragile hope.

"Yes, my darling, I do."

"My darling?"

"Hm?"

"Am I your darling?"

"Don't you know?" he said, and bent to kiss her, lightly, on the lips. She neither flinched nor pulled back, and after a moment, he kissed her again, longer this time, while the familiar desire rose within him. Damn, this wasn't the time, he thought, and reluctantly pulled away.

"No," she said, and caught at his arms. Her eyes were clear, and if she had any lingering doubts, they were well hidden. "He never touched me, you know. He wanted to, but he never did."

Relief surged through him, and he pulled her close again, his hand on her hair. *Thank God.* "I'm glad," he said, simply.

"I never wanted him to. But, you—No, don't go," she said, clutching at him again as he started to pull away. "Stay with me."

He looked down at her in surprise. He wanted her. Oh, how he wanted her. In her prim cotton nightgown she looked wholesome and sweet and tumbled; her beauty caught at his soul. But to use her like that, after what she had just gone through, wasn't right. "Best not tonight, Melissa."

She caught at his arm. "Yes. Tonight. Please."

The light in her eyes nearly took his breath away. "Melissa. Are you sure?"

"Of course I'm sure."

"But—"

"Justin," she said, quite clearly and with more than a touch of annoyance, "do I have to beg?"

He chuckled, in spite of himself. "No, princess, you don't." He reached out and touched her cheek, wonderingly. "I'll be gentle with you. I promise."

"I know you will. Now are you ever going to kiss me?"

"Yes, darling," he said, softly, and brought his lips to hers.

She had no chance to regret her decision as he gathered her close, his hands stroking her gently, everywhere. For just a moment, as he loomed above her in the bed, she panicked, but then he kissed her again, and the fear eased. This was Justin, her love, loving her. Everywhere he touched her, her skin glowed with fire, and soon all the bad memories were burned away. There was only now, only Justin, his lips caressing her throat, her ears, her breasts, his shoulders broad and reassuringly strong under her hands, his hands removing her night rail. And then, at last, there were no barriers between them, and his hard, callused fingertips were stroking her with an amazing gentleness that made her writhe and reach out for him. He was above her, then he was within her, and the moment of their joining, though slightly painful, was so beautiful that it brought tears to her eyes. "Oh, Justin," she whispered, clinging to him as they moved together. "Justin," and then the firestorm overwhelmed her, and she was born anew.

Afterwards she nestled in his arms, feeling safe and secure and at peace, for the first time in a very long time. "Mm," she said, rubbing her head against his shoulder, and he turned to kiss her forehead.

"No more nightmares, mind," he said, softly.

"No," she agreed, her voice sleepy. "No more nightmares."

"Good." Justin tightened his hold just a little, holding her more securely against him. He could not recall ever feeling so content in his life. Aunt Augusta had been right, he thought, as sleep overtook him. When the time came, he had known what to do.

Morning sunlight was streaming into the room when Melissa awoke for good. She felt pleasantly relaxed and lazy, and she stretched luxuriously, wincing a little as muscles that had been ill treated yesterday protested. But it didn't matter. For the first time in much too long, she felt cleansed, whole, safe. She was herself again, and she had Justin to thank for it.

She turned her head and smiled at the pillow where his head had rested until he had risen earlier that morning, whispering to her that he would let her sleep in peace. She was glad he had such tact, glad to be alone to think over the extraordinary events of the past evening. After yesterday, after what she had gone through with Sir Stephen, who would have thought . . . but he was Justin, and he had made her see, at long last, that she was not to blame for her stepfather's actions. Whatever doubt remained would, she suspected, soon leave. She had been renewed, purified in the fire of his lovemaking.

Again she stretched, as sinuous and sensuous as a cat, her eyes closed and a small smile curving her mouth. Who would ever have thought that Justin, her sometimes stolid, undemonstrative husband, would be so loving, so passionate? Especially after yesterday. She was very lucky, she thought, and suddenly she couldn't wait to see him again.

"My lady?" a voice whispered, and, startled, Melissa opened her eyes to see Liza bending over her. "I'm sorry, my lady, I didn't want to wake you, but his lordship's been asking for you."

"Has he?" Melissa flung off the covers and swung her legs over the side of the bed, suddenly too filled with energy to stay abed, though Liza protested. "No, I am fine, Liza. Hand me my dressing gown, please. Is it very late?"

"Around eleven, my lady. I'll bring the tea tray—"

"Heavens, don't bother! I'll wait for luncheon. Though I must admit, I'm hungry." Her brow wrinkled. "Did I have dinner yesterday? I don't remember. Well, no matter, I shall survive. Hurry, Liza I shall require a bath, and my prettiest dress. The peach muslin, I think. Heavens!" She abruptly sat down at the dressing table and stared at her reflection. "Oh, just look at my face!" she wailed.

"It's not so bad, my lady, only two bruises."

"But what Justin will say—"

"I don't think his lordship will much care, my lady, way he's acting."

Melissa's startled eyes met Liza's in the mirrors and then dropped, her cheeks turning rosy. "Oh, well, I suppose not."

"And we could try covering them with powder. I'm sure the Marchioness has something you could use."

"Perhaps she does. Please draw my bath now, Liza. There's not much time."

The hall was quiet when Melissa came downstairs, wearing a round gown of peach muslin, embroidered about the hem, with long sleeves and soft white lawn filling in the low neckline. She was a little shaky on her feet but determined to ignore it. Phelps, sitting by the door, jumped up when he saw her. "Good morning, Phelps," she called.

"My lady!" he exclaimed. "Are you feeling all right? After his lordship brought you in yesterday, we didn't know what to think."

Melissa's' memory of being carried into the Hall in her husband's strong arms was mercifully vague. Though she wouldn't mind being carried by him again. Her face turned pink. "Is his lordship in?"

"No, he's out on the estate somewhere. But I'll tell him you wish to see him when he comes in," he added quickly, at the crestfallen look on her face.

"Thank you, Phelps. I'll be in the morning room."

But, once in the morning room, she couldn't settle to anything, not the purse she was netting, or the letters she should write. Finally, she gave up and rose, walking to the window. And then, though there had been no sound, something made her turn, to see Justin in the doorway, watching her.

He searched her face, his eyes concerned and anxious, and she gazed back, unaccountably nervous. Was he sorry about last night, regretting all that had happened between them, she wondered, but then he took a step towards her. It freed her from her paralysis, and they went swiftly, wordlessly, into each other's arms.

He held her close for long moments, and then pulled a little away. "You're all right?" he asked, and she thought he sounded uncertain. "After last night—"

"After last night, I'm wonderful, Justin," she said, smiling up at him, and the tension left his face.

"Thank God. I didn't know, after all you'd gone through."

"That's past." She laid her fingers on his lips. "You helped me put it there."

His lips brushed her fingers and then he pulled away, taking her hand and leading her over to the sofa. "Thank God. But there are still some things we have to talk about—"

"Here you are. I wondered where you had got to," Augusta said, stumping into the room. Justin jumped up and crossed to the window, raking his fingers through his hair, and Augusta glanced at him, curiously. "It's good to see you up, child. and

299

looking so well, too. That is a pretty dress."

"Thank you, Justin picked it out," Melissa said absently, looking past Augusta to her husband. "If you'll excuse us, Aunt, Justin and I have some things to discuss. Justin?" She touched his arm. "There shouldn't be anyone in the breakfast room yet."

He gazed down at her for a moment, and then smiled. "Excuse us, Aunt," he said, and took his wife by the hand.

"Now this is more like it," he said, surveying the deserted breakfast room a few moments later, and pulled his wife into his arms. Her arms twined about his neck, and for a long moment neither said anything. "There, that's better." He pulled away, just a little bit. "Now, where were we?"

"You were saying we had things to talk about—"

"Oh, excuse me, my lord, my lady," someone said behind them. They turned, startled, to see a maid hastily place some dishes on the table and then scuttle out.

Justin raked a hand through his hair again. "Damn! We can't talk here."

Melissa bit back a smile. "There's the drawing room. I'm sure there'll be no one there."

"There had better not be," he said grimly, and took her hand again. They hadn't gotten ten feet when Harry ran towards them.

"Melissa, you're up! Capital!" he exclaimed, hurling himself at her. "Did Chatleigh tell you? He's to be my guardian!"

"Damnation!" Justin said, and stalked off down the corridor. "A man can't find peace in his own house!"

300

"What's the matter with him?" Harry asked, perplexed.

"Nothing, Harry, I'll explain later," Melissa called over her shoulder as she went after Justin, her lips twitching. "Justin! Wait!"

He waited for her at the end of the corridor. "I swear, Melissa, if you choose another room that's supposed to be empty . . ."

Laughter bubbled out of her before she could stop it. "I'm sorry! All right, you suggest someplace."

"My study," he said, and set off, her hand clasped firmly in his, so that she had no choice but to follow at a half-run. "And the next person who interrupts us will be sacked," he said to Phelps as they crossed the hall.

"Yes, my lord," Phelps said, astonished, and watched them as they disappeared down the corridor, her ladyship radiant with happiness. Phelps relaxed, a smile lighting his own face. Looked like things were finally working out around here.

The solid oak door slammed shut behind them. "No more interruptions," Justin said, pocketing the key.

"Oh, I'm sorry, Justin, but if you could see your face—"

"Damn it, Melissa, it's bad enough we keep getting interrupted, this house is big enough you'd think we'd have some privacy, but for you to laugh—"

"I'm sorry," she said, controlling her laughter with an effort. "What was it you wanted to say?"

"That I love you, damn it!" he shouted, and then looked amazed. Melissa went very still. "Damn, I

301

didn't mean to say it like that."

Melissa had started giggling again, helplessly this time, and after a moment, he joined in. They sank into the armchairs facing the fireplace, and he reached across to take her hand.

"I mean it, you know," he said, when they finally had themselves under control.

"I know you do," Melissa said, wiping her streaming eyes. "I mean it, too."

His hold on her hand tightened. "We'll have a good life, Melissa. I promise you that."

"I know we will." She looked down at their linked hands. How lucky she was, after the way they had met and married, and what had happened since. If it hadn't been for her, his life would never have been threatened. She would happily spend the rest of her life making it up to him. "What will happen to Sir Stephen?"

"He should be at Bow Street already. Probably he'll be transported to Australia."

A hard little knot, of tension, of fear, that Melissa hadn't even known was still inside her let go. "Thank God. These last weeks, I so feared he'd get to you."

Justin looked at her sharply. "You knew?"

"He told me, the night of our ball. He said," she drew in her breath, "he would kill you if I didn't do what he wanted."

"God!"

"I didn't know what to do! But I couldn't do what he asked, Justin. I just couldn't."

"Thank God," he said, fiercely. "If any harm had come to you, I don't know what I'd do." He raised her hand to his lips and kissed it. "I love you."

302

Melissa's eyes closed briefly. How long she had waited to hear those words; yet there was still one more thing to settle, one thing she had to know, no matter the consequences. "In spite of what my stepfather tried to do?"

He was out of his chair in an instant, kneeling before her and grasping her hands. "I don't want you blaming yourself for that, Melissa, ever again. I thought we'd settled it last night."

"We did." She fiddled with his neckcloth, unable to meet his eyes. "But I may need reminding for a while."

"Like this?" His lips brushed her cheekbone. "Or this?" Her brow.

"J-Justin—"

"Or this?" Her throat. "Or this?" Her ear, his tongue tracing the delicate curve.

She shivered. "Justin!" she exclaimed, her hands pressing against his chest to separate them before they were both lost.

"I'll remind you every day, if that's what you need," he murmured, not a whit deterred by her action, and at last, with a little laugh, she gave in, allowing him to pull her against him, feeling safe and secure and cherished at last.

"Yes," she gasped, as his mouth came down on hers. "Every day. Oh, Justin," she exclaimed, when his lips left hers to explore her throat, breathless with the emotions rioting through her, "I do love you."

Justin pulled back and stared down at her, momentarily speechless, and then a smile, like sunlight, broke over his face. "Good," he said, and crushed her to him.

A long time later, someone pounded on the door. "Chatleigh," Harry called. "Lissa. We're waiting luncheon."

"Go away," the Earl said, and kissed his wife again.

Dear Reader,

Zebra Books welcomes your comments about this book or any other Zebra Regency you have read recently. Please address your comments to:

Zebra Books, Dept. WM
475 Park Avenue South
New York, NY 10016

Thank you for your interest.

Sincerely,
The Editorial Department
Zebra Books